PRAISE FOR TRIO

"If we can imagine a Faulkner who began with the combative intellectual playfulness of Queneau or Jarry, or a *Sound and the Fury* that ends with everyone dissolved in Benjy's idiocy, we start to taste Pinget."

—John Updike, *New Yorker*

"It can and should be claimed for Pinget that he has produced a sequence of some twenty books over the past three decades, all of which observe the kind of stringent laws of discourse and development that we associate with the Beckett oeuvre. . . . But the comparison with Beckett should not be allowed to mask the fact that this is a wholly original and distinctive achievement."

—Stephen Bann, *London Review of Books*

"The style seems like a combination of Joyce's stream of consciousness with Burroughs's cut-and-paste technique."

—Martin A. David, *Los Angeles Times*

"Robert Pinget deserves more readers."

—John Sturrock, *New York Times*

ALSO BY ROBERT PINGET IN ENGLISH TRANSLATION

NOVELS

The Apocrypha*
Baga
Be Brave*
Between Fantione and Agapa*
The Enemy*
Fable*
The Inquisitory
The Libera Me Domine*
Mahu or the Material
Monsieur Levert
Monsieur Songe*
No Answer
Passacaglia*
Someone*
That Voice*
Théo or the New Era*
Traces of Ink*

PLAYS

Abel and Bela*
About Mortin
Architruc
A Bizarre Will*
Dead Letter
Clope
The Hypothesis
The Old Tune

* Indicates titles available from Red Dust, Inc.

TRIO

Robert Pinget

INTRODUCTION BY JOHN UPDIKE

TRANSLATION BY BARBARA WRIGHT

Dalkey Archive Press
Normal • London

Publisher's note: Originally published in the U.S. by Red Dust, Inc. as three separate volumes: *Between Fantoine and Agapa* (1982), *That Voice* (1982), and *Passacaglia* (1978). While each of the three books are here reproduced in their entirety, the text has been reset and repaginated to accommodate publication in one volume.

Pinget titles listed on the previous pages published by Red Dust can be purchased by e-mailing <RedDustJG@aol.com>.

Originally published in French as *Entre Fantoine et Agapa* by La Tour de Feu, 1951, *Cette Voix* by Les Éditions de Minuit, 1975, and *Passacaille* by Les Éditions de Minuit, 1969

First Dalkey Archive edition, 2005

Library of Congress Cataloging-in-Publication Data

Pinget, Robert, 1919-1997.
[Selections. English. 2005]
Trio / Robert Pinget ; translated by Barbara Wright.
p. cm.
Contents: Between Fantoine and Agapa — That voice — Passacaglia.
ISBN 1-56478-408-8 (pbk. : alk. paper)
I. Wright, Barbara, 1915- II. Title.

PQ2631.I638A288 2005
843'.914—dc22

2005049353

Partially funded by a grant from the Illinois Arts Council, a state agency.

Dalkey Archive Press is a nonprofit organization located at Milner Library (Illinois State University) and distributed in the UK by Turnaround Publisher Services Ltd. (London).

www.dalkeyarchive.com

Printed on permanent/durable acid-free paper and bound in the United States of America.

CONTENTS

Introduction

It is with some embarrassment that a critic recommends to readers a writer whom he scarcely understands, whose works are more than a little exasperating, and who furthermore writes with a high degree of colloquiality in a foreign language. Yet Robert Pinget, as glimpsed through translation and through the cloudy layers of his own obfuscations, does seem one of the more noble presences in world literature, a continuingly vital practitioner of what, a weary long half-century ago, was christened *le nouveau roman*. Pinget, unlike Alain Robbe-Grillet and Nathalie Sarraute, is not a household name on this side of the Atlantic, and his jacket flaps restate the same few facts. He was born in Geneva, Switzerland, in 1919. He studied law and became a barrister. He went to Paris in 1946, to the École des Beaux-Arts, then intending to become a painter. He had an exhibition in Paris in 1950; the same year, he taught drawing and French in England. He was a friend of Samuel Beckett. He died in 1997.

Pinget's first book, *Between Fantoine and Agapa*, was published in 1951, and ever since he has explored a fictional terrain of which the local city is Agapa and the rather interchangeable villages are Fantoine and Sirancy. One wonders where, on the road between Geneva and Paris, Pinget acquired such a rich and fond intimacy with French country life, and what holds so cosmopolitan and experimental a writer to a provincial landscape of such unvarying ingredients—a moldering château; a crowded gossipy village; a sinister forest and quarry. One book jacket volunteers that "Monsieur Pinget divides his time between Paris and a country home in Touraine"; Touraine, then, "garden of France" and natal ground of Descartes, Rabelais, and Balzac, is indicated as the territory of Pinget's imagination. Though there is occasional mention of jeans and television, his world seems frozen between the two world wars, with a veritably medieval rumor of absolute evil arising from its darker places.

•

Pressed to name his reasons for writing, Pinget once specified, "the author's passion for fictional creation, his obsession with the destinies of individuals, his being haunted by imagination and by the efforts required to fathom the only reality there is, his soul, and finally his limitless love of the French language." This profession appears strikingly orthodox; realistic and indeed conservative impulses are at work in Pinget's art. On the other hand he has advised an English translator, "Don't bother too much about logic: everything in *Passacaglia* is directed against it." And a comment of several pages appended to *The Libera Me Domine* enunciates a principled surrealism inimical to logic and intelligible plot: "It is not what can be said or meant that interests me, but the *way in which it is said*. . . . There may well be a new point of view, a modern kind of sensitivity, an unusual sort of composition, in my books, but I can't help it. . . . One thing is certain, though, and this is that I never know at the outset what I am going to say. For a long time I thought this a weakness, but there is no way of avoiding it, as it is my only strength, the strength that enables me to continue. . . . My confidence in the mechanism of the subconscious remains essentially unshakeable."

•

Passacaglia (a type of Italian or Spanish tune, originally played on the guitar while the musician was passing through the streets) was published in 1969. There has been a mysterious violent death—this time, a body found on a dunghill. Pinget's training as a barrister shows in his fondness for investigations and inquisitions, and his skepticism regarding their final results: "The story would seem to have begun a long time before this, but talk about prudence, talk about vigilance, it looks as if only two or three episodes have been revealed and that with some difficulty, the source of information being permanently deficient. . . ."

A man, called "the master," sits in a cold room of a shut-up country house ("the garden was dead, the courtyard grassy") looking at an old book, making notes in the margin; he has just torn the hands off the clock in the room. The body on the dunghill at first appears to be his ("the man sitting at this table a few hours earlier, found dead on the dunghill") but then it becomes that of an idiot the master adopted in the past who has mutilated himself with a chain saw (or fallen off a ladder or swallowed a sponge). The original flap copy has it that both are dead: "The 'Master' ruminates about the death of an idiot who lived with him for which he may or may not be responsible and about his own death. He is found dead over his notebooks." His jottings, indistinguishable from his thoughts, constitute the book's text, and give its ebbing hero a certain status of authorship; "like a street-corner musician, he had reconstituted a kind of passacaglia."

•

An endgame of a refreshed sort is being played here; though modern art has exhausted art's possibilities, the world goes on, idiotically. Unable to write stories, Pinget can still write about the popular will to make a story: "This is where people's imaginations take over and make them start questioning everything again." A kind of cave art, like Dubuffet's rough-textured daubs, arises from the voices of hearsay and gossip amid the final dilapidation of the mansions of nineteenth-century narrative. . . . Yet a certain incidental delight lives in many a well-struck phrase, and a real psychology and topology and sociology press toward us through the words. Unlike Beckett, he has not turned his back on the seethe of circumstance, or, like the mature Joyce, taken refuge in nostalgic reconstruction. For all his flouting of conventional expectations and all the sly comedy of his rambling village talebearers, Pinget strikes one as free of any basically distorting mannerism or aesthetic pose. His recourse remains to the real, without irony. In a France of smiling mandarins and chilly chic, he manifests the two essential passions of a maker: a love of his material and a belief in his method.

•

One might suppose *Between Fantoine and Agapa* to have a certain geographical focus and to lay claim to the imaginary territory of provincial France where the later fictions—preeminently, *The Inquisitory*, still Pinget's most impressive and cogent work—more or less take place. Alas one is fooled again, for the little book is a collection of disconnected pranks, or prose poems, which take place not so much between Fantoine and Agapa as between Pinget's ears. The first chapter, or sketch, or whatever, "Vishnu Takes His Revenge," deals with the curé of Fantoine who is bored. "He subscribes to theater-magazines. He dips into the fashionable authors. He gleans in learned vineyards. He passes for a scholar, but he's a rotter." His parishioners don't provide much amusement for him: "The inhabitants of Fantoine are hopeless. They drink. They work. They drink. Their children are epileptic, their wives pregnant." In the title story, "Between Fantoine and Agapa," a man, his wife, and their child prepare to picnic between these two fictional towns when a sign in a field proclaims, "Alopecia-impetrating [patchy-baldness-obtaining-by-entreaty] prohibited"; this makes them so frightened they skip lunch. Later that night, the child vomits jam and the wife's hair stands on end. "But not for long, because half an hour later she was as bald as a coot." But for these two tales, there is no mention of Fantoine or Agapa, and the subject matter gravitates toward the mythic and the facetiously geographic—episodes take place in Manhattan, Menseck, the Forest of Grance, and Florence, and characters include Don Quixote, a parrot called Methuselah, Aeschylus and his maidservant Aglaia, and the Persian King Artaxerxes. As he roams through these prankish fancies, the young Pinget reminds us of various comrades in surrealism: of Alfred Jarry and his frenzies of mechanical precision, of William Burroughs and his gleeful wars and plagues. Pinget also shows something of the antic sunniness of Raymond Queneau and of Beckett's clownish desolation. His playful dabbling with history and myth suggests a host of experimental modernists, from Borges to Barth, from the *Fabrications* of the late Michael Ayrton to the *Eclogues* of our contemporary Guy Davenport. Literary experiment and surrealism have certain natural channels into which to run, it would appear, not so unlike the well-worn grooves of realism; nonsense, being an inversion of sense, is condemned to share a certain structure with it, and a finitude of forms. Pinget, even in this early, rather frolicsome and eclectic work, does look forward to what is to become his mature tone. The last and longest piece in *Between Fantoine and Agapa* is titled "Journal," and though concerned with such absurdities as snowstorms of fingernail clippings and dwarfs sold at auction to be used as candelabra by religious communities, it foreshadows the sinister cruelty and gloom of the later work. An inbred, joyless, cannibalistic sexuality is a recurrent theme in Pinget, and occurs here. Pinget's preoccupation with the menace of the organic and with the Stygian stirrings of the dead emerges side by side with characteristic flashes of aesthetic theory: "In a work of art we do not try to conjure up beauty or truth. We only have recourse to them—as to subterfuge—in order to be able to go on breathing."

•

That Voice concerns . . . well what *does* it concern? The phrase "*manque un raccord*" ("a missing link") is used seventeen times in the French text, the translator claims on the jacket's back flap, and a phrase rendered as "impossible anamnesis" ("anamnesis"—"recalling to mind") returns a number of times also, as do "invincible fatigue," "traces of effacement," "psspss," "take a hair of the night that bit you," and "an invisible manitou." The author, in a special preface to the American edition, assures us that "the structure of the novel is precise, although not immediately apparent. The different themes are intermingled. One cuts into another point-blank, then the other resumes and cuts into the first, and so on until the end." The two themes named are "the theme of the cemetery" and "that of the gossip at the grocery." In the cemetery, evidently, at the intersection of alleys numbered 333 and 777, on All Saints' Day, near the tomb of the minor belletrist Alexandre Mortin, a young man called Théodore, coming to arrange and leave some chrysanthemums, meets a ghost, or walking dead man, who identifies himself as Dieudonné, or Dodo for short. Dodo, it slowly dawns, is Théo's uncle. Maybe Théo killed him, for his money. Alexandre Mortin has a brother, Alfred, who perhaps is also called the Master; he seems to be keeping little Théodore in his house by force, according to gossip down at the grocery store, where "that otiose, never-ending story" acquires ever more characters (the servant Magnin, Mademoiselle Passetant, Madame Buvard, Monsieur Alphonse, many of whom we have met before in other Pinget novels, or imagine we have) and effaces itself as it goes, like a slate being covered over and over with new versions, until with the best will in the world the reader starts to feel sandy-eyed and itches to turn on the eleven o'clock news, where things are said once or at worst twice.

In such a close-knit village, the dead are not allowed to die; they continue to hold their place in the fabric of gossip, of remembrance, their deaths incidental within the pervasive dissolution of life erasing itself as it goes . . . Pinget locates us in the gently moldering, nowhere solid hell of communal remembering, of mutual awareness, never exact, never obliterated.

•

To a crowd gathered at New York University in October of 1981, Pinget, reading his French text in a hard-to-hear monotone, explained (as translated by Barbara Wright), "My attachment to the technique of intermingling of themes and their variations is due to the admiration I have always felt for so-called baroque music." He is also attached to the concept of the collective unconscious:

> In my eyes, the share allotted to the irrational is one of the ways that may help me to arrive at a personal "truth," which is only to a very limited extent present in my awareness of it. This is a kind of open provocation to the unconscious. . . . We are all, indeed, more or less dependent on the collective

> unconscious, whose nature we can only glimpse by examining as best we can those manifestations of it which we perceive in ourselves.

Later in this address he spoke of his "declared intention, from the very first book, to extend the limits of the written word by replenishing it with the spoken word." Confusion, contradiction, "all the suggestions, refutations, prolongations and metamorphoses of fragments of speech" are intrinsic to this intention; his reader will have "the impression that the book is being composed, and decomposed, under his very eye." Not that the books were written for the eye; they are "to be listened to, rather than read."

•

In his address at New York University, Pinget announced, "I have great respect for the present-day critical methods." And, moreover, behind his work, with his persistent rumors of the old religion, lies a less orthodox religious impulse:

> The *homo religiosus*, linked to the essential—if we admit his presence in every one of us—rebels against the lacerations produced by the succession of days, and seeks refuge in the time which knows neither succession nor laceration, that of the Word.

This comes from a beautiful statement given to the Mainz Academy of Sciences and Literature on the subject of "literary baggage." "The sole 'baggage,'" Pinget says, "that helps us to conquer chronological time and to participate in the other, absolute time, is a bouquet of texts. . . . Light baggage buzzing with words, which, ever since the world has been the world—and there are many legends that vouch for it—has ensured our passage, without let or hindrance, over onto the other bank."

John Updike

TRIO

● BETWEEN FANTOINE AND AGAPA

Preface

This little book is the first I wrote in prose. I had written a number of poems in my youth and I was still very much under the influence of the surrealists, of attempts to approach the unconscious; in short, of experiments made on language in what might be called its nascent state, that's to say: independent of any rational order. A gratuitous game with the vocabulary—that was my passion. Logic seemed to me to be incapable of attaining the very special domain of literature, which in any case I still equate with that of poetry. And so it was a fascination with the possibilities, the absolute freedom of creation, an intense desire to abolish all the constraints of classical writing, that made me produce these exercises which neither the logician, nor the philosopher, nor the moralist, will find to his taste. That doesn't mean to say that the imaginative reader will not be able to find something in them to *his* taste. A reader in love with language, and with the multifarious echoes that his emotions absorb when he is attuned to words. Hence, for him, a profusion of contradictory meanings, and the feeling of being released from the prisons of rationalizing reason.

I would like to add that this gratuitous game is here coupled with a mystifying game which gives it an appearance of serious, or let's say secret, truth . . .

What more can I say? This: this little volume contains in embryo all the forms taken by my later work. That is why I am grateful to Joanna Gunderson for publishing it, and for having asked Barbara Wright to translate it. She could not have chosen anyone more expert, more subtle, more faithful to the text and to its spirit.

Robert Pinget

● BETWEEN FANTOINE AND AGAPA

Vishnu Takes His Revenge

The curé of Fantoine is an amateur. He hasn't much of a gift for God. He's bored. He subscribes to theater magazines. He dips into the fashionable authors. He gleans in learned vineyards. He passes for a scholar, but he's a rotter.

The Fantoine belfry dates from the ninth century. It is extremely stylish. It's a pity that it goes for walks at night. It can't read. It visits the church, the village, the environs. You get used to its moods.

The inhabitants of Fantoine are hopeless. They drink. They work. They drink. Their children are epileptic, their wives pregnant.

The Fantoine postman is a wag. When he goes to the café he orders a vermouth. The proprietor asks him: "Dry?" He answers: "No; wet." It's always the same. When he's finished it he goes out, saying: "Love and kisses, see you soon." An epistolary convention.

The Fantoine crocodiles are stuffed. The cows are made of whitewood. The haylofts mumble. At midday, they shout from one street to the next, they strangle the hens, they cut the calves' throats.

But the curé of Fantoine is bored. Luckily, someone from Agapa-la-Ville takes an interest in him and sends him a book on Cambodia. The curé buries himself in it. He's no longer bored. He teaches himself the Khmer language. He says: "Ban, La'a, Ke mien, Yuo, Kandiet, Pisa bay, Pisa Kraya." Likewise Khmer mythology. He says: "Vishnu, Lakshmana, Rama, Raksava Viradha, Sita, Hanuman." Likewise Khmer art. He says: "Angkor Wat, Bayon, Neak Pean, Naga, Nang Sbek, Ram-Vong, Ram Khbach, Sayam."

The Fantoine belfry no longer goes for walks at night. It listens to the curé divagating.

The inhabitants of Fantoine become interesting: they ape the royal dancing girls.

The forest of Fantoine becomes populated with yak demons, with Mrinh Kangveal spirits, with Banra trees. Paddy-fields cover the country. The Mekong river carries alluvial deposits.

The sacrilege is complete.

It was at this point that the curé of Fantoine made a mistake during the Consecration and said: "Hic est enim corpus Yak" . . .

A gigantic demon sprang out of the Host, dispatched the curé, and pulverized the church.

And Vishnu the Eternal deigned to smile.

Ubiquity

"One day, a certain person happened to be in a certain place—Manhattan, let's say." No, that won't do. We must say: "A horse dealer happened to be in Bucharest just at the moment when. . ." I'd prefer: "In Vaugirard, one rainy day, my wife . . ." No. The simplest is:

Once upon a time sometime, in Manhattan, a person who was a horse dealer in Bucharest just at the moment when Vaugirard was annexed to Paris, in the rain, my wife . . .

The result is that people don't understand. If they are determined to look for a meaning they'll more or less grasp that it's a question of one and the same person. Now such is not the case. It's a question of several persons who were each several persons, in different places at the same moment. It's impossible to say this synthetically and with precision. One can only suggest synchronism by enumerating and linking propositions together by adverbial phrases. But the effect would be spoiled. A story must make an immediate impression. Never mind, to hell with elegance, I'll tell it just the same.

One day in 1860, the date of the annexation of Vaugirard to Paris, at the very moment of the signature of the document, a lady who lived in Manhattan took the boat for Bucharest where she had been working as a horse dealer for two years, and waited for me near the Medici fountain.

At the same moment a Bucharest horse dealer, a real flesh and blood horse dealer who had lived in the town for two years and who was not to budge from it until his death, left Manhattan and waited for me in the rain in Paris.

At the same moment my future wife, who was waiting for me in the Luxembourg Gardens and was furious because I was late, sold a packhorse in Bucharest and left Manhattan.

So far, it's clear. I must now say that the person from Manhattan was going to Bucharest to visit the horse dealer. The horse dealer was waiting for her. My future wife, at the fountain, was waiting for herself between the two of them. When the person had arrived in Bucharest and gone into the horse dealer's premises—the latter was therefore visiting himself—the person kissed herself on the mouth, my wife did both (I was married by this time), and all three were in my bed.

I may add that my wife was the person from Manhattan, whom I met six months later and whom I had arranged to meet in the Luxembourg Gardens on the day of the annexation of Vaugirard. Given that while she was waiting for me she was thinking of her departure from Manhattan and of her Bucharest horse dealer, it follows on the other hand that she must have been present at the fountain six months later, for she was madly in love with me. Love does things like that, and many others, that's a platitude. As for the horse dealer, he knew beforehand that he'd be jealous six months later. Hatred has the same effect: so he was present at the Medici fountain right from the start. My wife and her lover, when they met in Bucharest and found themselves at the same time in my bed. . . . But I won't dwell on it, it's crystal-clear.

Baramine

Miss Goldwick-Baramine's guests were late. She wandered around her apartment, checking that every object was in its place—this was important to her, as you will see. She slid open the glass door in the hall, which gave onto the underground River Menseck; not long ago it was unknown, but she owned half its course. Menseck!

Miss Bara had been a great sportswoman in her youth, and she had a passion for speleology. From the sporting point of view at first, but later from that of science. The fashion for caves, in both the literary and plastic arts, was then unknown. It was the discoveries of the speleologists that created it. Miss Goldwick, with some of her friends, was the first to embark on the adventure of the grottoes. This was the result of a wager.

The "Fifth Club," of which she was a member, was inquiring into the childhood of its members, to pass the time at their evening meetings. When Miss Bara began her story one day, everyone's attention was riveted. Obviously, a tale that begins: "I was born on a dunghill in Krasnodar. My mother was probably a Georgian. My father, who was a descendant of Valerius Flaccus, had abandoned her in Pomerania . . ." is bound to arouse interest. Miss Baramine never tried to make an impression, no, never. She was simple and straightforward. Her confession, which she disclosed the way one peels an orange, gradually revealed a dramatic existence. At the age of fourteen, in a factory that made mousetraps, a Kalmuk workman had violated her on a steel plate. Sickened, she had run away. She had lived for more than eight years in quarries in the Urals, feeding on Jupiter's beard. This diet had caused her physiognomy and her whole person to become so mannish that she took a job as a railroad mechanic, and trafficked secretly in diamonds and magnesium. Next she became an innkeeper in Calabria, then a torturer in a prison, then the mother of two stillborn dogs, and finally the owner of a passport found in the sub-office of an embassy. At twenty-six, having come into an inheritance from one of the passport's relations, she settled in Menseck. This was when she was introduced to the club.

After this story, her friends wanted to put her to the test: she was to lead a roped party of four people and climb the north face of the Menseck peak. Miss Bara did so, with her comrades. Halfway up the rock face she called a halt. She had observed a deep crevice on their right. Her partners agreed to go down it. No one suspected the importance of this rift. Abseiling by stages, they arrived at the bottom. The rift was the exit of a series of linked galleries which the explorers took twenty days to traverse. On the twenty-first day they arrived at the underground river.

For ten years without a break they prospected this chasm and its side-branches. Through their abnegation they became the pioneers of modern speleology. The account of these ten years of research and work can today be found in every library.

Miss Goldwick-Baramine had a granite bungalow built on the river bank and, at the age of thirty-six, she settled there for good. She had found the habitat that suited her.

The spirit of mortification that she had inherited from her mother gradually surfaced in her: "I must expiate," she said, "I must expiate my turbulent youth." People recognized in this the exaltation characteristic of her race, for one could just as easily say that all she had done with her youth was to suffer it. But it was in vain that they found excuses for her. She persisted. As these years of retirement went by, her ideal became deformed. Having judged her former exploits absurd, and stigmatized their realism as horrible, (she said "howwible," barely pronouncing the two w's), she perched herself, if we may so put it, on the extreme point of an abstruse irreality. She paced over subliminal distances, inhaled cosmic vapors, sustained herself on pulped clay, in one-gram doses, and on the moisture oozing from the stalactites.

Nevertheless, her mannish nature suffered a convulsive movement. At the age of forty-five, Miss Bara finally became unhappy. She wrestled with her chimeras and her underground habits.

It was in this frame of mind that she was preparing to entertain her friends that day. They didn't come. She went out onto the bank. She reached a secret stairway and climbed up it.

Her friends were waiting for her in the sun, on a terrace in Saint-Cloud.

SUICIDA, -AE, M OR F

By following the abscissa from the point 1317, Mahu emerged onto a lawn where a cat was lying in wait for a wood pigeon. He sat down, interested by this stratagem. His chair was resting against a prunus tree; he moved it a little and observed that the lowest branch of the tree was in line with the coordinate axis. But he didn't want to think about it. The time was comfortable. The cat intrigued him.

After a moment he saw, sticking up through the grass, some fingers holding some wires. The wires converged towards the cat. They were manipulating it. Mahu was disappointed. These outdated images annoyed him: they were the negation of freedom. The scene had lost all interest. Mahu stood up and said to the other people who, like him, were watching: "It's full of fingers." The others counted on their hands. They understood, and turned their backs on the spectacle.

"Victory," thought Mahu. And he sat down again. The lowest branch was now in line with the axis of the abscissa. So he must have changed chairs, and now be mentally locating point 1317 in relation to the ordinate. A simple geometrical theorem comprises many corollaries.

Mahu was relaxing when someone touched him on the shoulder. He turned around and saw a group of statues. "It's not possible," he said to himself, "they weren't there just now; let's not be a fool." But the statues were coming closer. Mahu kicked a bronze Hercules. His foot cracked from the inner cuneiform to the astragalus. The Hercules murmured: "Well, well!" Furious, Mahu stood up and exhorted the sightseers to pass along there, please. His task was facilitated: he only had to point to the statues. They obeyed him, and were soon persuaded.

Mahu reacted further by deliberately deriving another corollary from his problem. "Given that the lowest branch starts at point 1317, determine its coordinates." That changed the picture. On the line Y" Y"', at one sixth of the distance from the new 1317 to the intersection of the axes, he marked a point which he very arbitrarily named S. Then, lowering the perpendicular, he put his chair down. He was not surprised to find himself thus raised to the level of the lowest branch, maybe because this branch was strictly parallel with the first level, but especially because no one is ever mathematically surprised. Seen from above, the lawn was in the form of a hexagon. This reassured him. He relaxed again.

This time, all the termini of the subway, as dishevelled and aggressive as the Furies, bit him on the thighs. Mahu howled, but out of vexation. After all, it is extremely annoying not to be able to get a bit of rest when you feel like it. But he didn't acknowledge defeat, he went back to his calculations, repositioned his chair, and so on until the park closed.

On his way home he went down the wrong street. Fatigue. The window of a bookshop brought him to a halt. Among the visible titles, he read the following: "Formula absolutionis ad usum suicidarum." Flabbergasted, he went in and bought the book. Its imprimatur was on the flyleaf.

All night long he annotated the text. The next day he'd got the formula off by heart. That evening, without even thinking, he recited it. The penknife with which he was about to cut a slice of bread plunged itself, of its own accord, between his two eyes.

Velleities

Amused, the lady in the "Tout-Cuit" (short orders, French fries, fast food), says to the yellow customer: "Huh, you look just like Don Quixote!" Whereupon the customer shows her his ring, which is in the form of a windmill: "You don't know how right you are." The lady laughs like mad: "And Sancho?" The customer points to another customer, a fat one. The lady laughs a little less heartily. The yellow man takes his bag of French fries and departs. Sancho orders a boiled beef. The lady serves him cautiously. And then a croquette. The lady hesitates. "A croquette," he repeats. Right, she adds a croquette. "A purée." Oh-oh, what a bore. The lady ventures: "Wouldn't you rather have a herring?" He says no. She scrapes a portion up the side of the saucepan. "And some cauliflower!" The lady beckons to a policeman. He grabs the pseudo-Panza, who drops his grub, and takes him off to the police station. The next customers give their orders without turning a hair. The lady can't see the dishes anymore. She just gropes. She serves blindly.

At half past one, the kitchen closes. The lady drags herself into the back room and vomits. "I've killed him. The season of rings. Cyanide. Didn't you announce a Mendelssohn concert? Poor beige soprano. It'd be just great if they all carried on that way . . .

On the sidewalk, in front of the door, a man dying of hunger is lying between the tar and the asphalt. Instanter, DANGER appears on the door. Underneath, can be read: *Attempted poisoning.* The false Don Quixote, who's finished his meal, passes the shop again and picks up the starving man. They go to a bistro where the starving man gulps down a sandwich. The yellow customer is as proud as anything. Which makes him quite forget that he's lost his ring. As it's Saturday, they play cards.

At the police station, the little fat man is released, with apologies. He decides to lose weight, so as not to look like Sancho anymore.

The beige soprano is practicing at her home. She gives a recital three weeks later but her career stops there. A question of cash, of her family, etc. The concert marks the close of the season of rings and the eatery is reopened to customers.

Rotten season of phony promises, of velleities! If only they did away with it once and for all it would put an end to people having to tremble at what, every ringed day, they saw on naive faces.

The Cucumbers

Once upon a time there was a young cucumber, but, well, he wasn't a bit likeable. He tanned himself. He turned orange-tawny. Always the first on the beach and the last to leave it. He would swell and swell, with half-closed eyes, with provocative peduncle. The cucumbresses were crazy about him. He had a special way of sidling up to you, of rubbing himself against . . . And what's more, such enormous veins. . . . So, well, he was the idol of the beach. Which made the beans dry up. And the viper's grass die by the kilo. Soon the only things left in the market of this little seaside town were cucumbers. Encouraged by their colleague's conquests, they proliferated. The police had to impose restrictive measures to control their growth. In spite of this decree, the cucumbers overran the district. They were to be seen everywhere. They climbed up balconies and smothered the nasturtiums; they filled the bathtubs; they rotted in linen baskets.

"My goodness," said Mademoiselle Solange to herself one day, "I'm going to have to change my lifestyle. I'm going to have to eat cucumbers in the morning, make Pernod out of cucumbers, scour my pots and pans with cucumber." And indeed, she did adapt herself. It's incredible how a beautiful vegetable can hold you at its mercy. Mademoiselle Solange became pregnant by a cucumber, and gave birth. The mayor, with his clerk as witness, drew up an official report of the birth. He couldn't believe his eyes: Mademoiselle Solange, on her bed of suffering, was all cucumber leaves, flowers and fruits.

At the school, it was a huge joke. Children understand everything. On their way out of school the little girls made the old ladies blush: they pulled up their skirts and exhibited cucumbers, they sucked them all day long.

As for the boys, we won't talk about them. They invented a new game: the hooded cucumber. Stuffed with explosives and equipped with a rubber cover, you chuck it at a passerby, where it explodes. If the hood holds out, you've won; if not, you've lost.

Monsieur le curé had to preach a sermon on cucumbers. It was a terrific scandal, even though he went no further than the etymological analysis of the word.

But do you think that the guilty party, the first one, on the beach, was at all put out? Far from it. They let him indulge in his filthy goings-on in the sun for the whole of the season. So he'll probably start all over again next year.

The Pumpkins

When the supreme neutron finally settled on the idea of Pumpkin, he couldn't believe it. It was beyond him. The pumpkins got by very nicely. The neutron vaticinated. The prophetic style certainly suited him. When you consider the number of practical jokes he perpetrated, you can only gawp. Mystifying, that was his forte. And the poor world made mysteries out of these mystifications. Where's the evidence? No one knows the origin of pumpkins. You can ask the greatest experts if you like—but the answer will invariably be: "It's a mystery."

But *I* can tell you how it happened: after the neutron's failure, the pumpkins took it upon themselves to grow of their own accord. They started to bulge, like bottoms. They existed. There you are.

But the best of it is that they supplanted the neutron. He'd become deflated, they were the bosses. If we don't grasp the implications of this phenomenon, we run the risk of understanding nothing about the cosmos. Anyone could have cultivated his own way of seeing, but pumpkins see in the round: they've imposed their own vision on the universe. From then on, everything was an excuse for roundness, sphericity, orbicity, ellipsoidicity—and gravitations in general.

Man in no way escaped the virus. Everything that touches him, from near or from far, cucurbitaces—I mean: belongs to the gourd family, like the pumpkin—starting with the spirals in shells, cow pats, and velodromes, and ending with his own body, which pullulates with oblate spheroids. But it's in his thoughts that man is really the most pumpkin-headed. He can't write "in the beginning" without being obsessed by "at the end." Look at philosophy, where the summum bonum is when you come full circle. You get there, roughly speaking, by sticking on a bit of hope, "in termino speculationis," and you've done the trick.

There's no doubt that an antibiotic is within reach. Someone catches an infectious disease such as pride, pomposity, etc., you give him some pumpkin, and he gets well.

I'm bombarded by ideas, but I still can't wait to finish this story: like the one about the cucumbers, it is indeed pretty third-rate. How do I know? Self-criticism. Soul-seaching. Vicious circle. Pumpkin.

I'll still mention this trivial incident, though: the other day, a schoolboy had a problem that stumped him, so I expounded my theory to him. He applied it to the solution of his problem. Believe it or not, his teacher was fooled and gave him top marks. Ever since, the old idiot himself has been nuts on my doctrine. He's become incapable of seeing a nicely-rounded behind in a tight-fitting summer dress without getting his hands on it.

The Parrot

Stuck out in the courtyard since time immemorial, Methuselah the parrot never saw a soul—except, sporadically, the concierge, a maid who got herself tumbled by a hawker, and a nun who had got lost on the service stairway. Until the day when a corrosive theme began to haunt him. With no experience of these phenomena, his ears throbbing and deafened with fever, Methuselah soon became no more than a decorative motif on his perch. Some people who had lost their way in the courtyard took him and exhibited him in the market square. This was where his calvary began.

Serious things should be approached obliquely. He was unaware of this. He judged, too hastily, that the only honest way was to meet them head on. The years passed in the horror of cross-purposes, of rejected passion, of vulgarity.

People got into the habit of coming to consult him as if he were a third-class prophetess. And, ever scrupulous, he prostituted himself in this service. People flocked around his perch, recipes were transmitted from mother to daughter in the new built-up area. In three hundred years Methuselah was decorated thirty times with all the orders of the magi, the sibyls, and the fortunetellers.

Nevertheless, the theme plagued him. A wild, heterogeneous orchestration, in which the leitmotif played the paradoxical role of bait, was improvised. It took the form of an internecine conflict which ravaged the city. For absolutely no reason. An illustrated magazine was conducting a survey into the origins of dialogue. Tendentiously, the author of the articles made out a case designed to prove that dialogue was a bastard form of monologue. He insisted on its degenerate character. A monologue, seen from its most abstract angle as "a reflection of oneself"—did that not contain, he asked, all the creative power of spontaneity? When you talk to yourself, your assertions and repartee have a freedom and vigor which any intrusion by a second party immediately eviscerates. The interior monologue, like the primitive forest whose vegetation later spreads over the entire globe, is a concentrate of various forms of expression—amongst which, in particular, is the dialogue—in its original, healthy form.

When they hear the word "healthy," which in theory implies "hygienic," the partisans of dialogue react violently. This stupid allusion, which has nothing to do with the premise, is enough to envenom the argument. The magic power of hygiene! The newspaper supporting the opposing political party retorted that no dialogue could be fully achieved without a confrontation between two people, as this would oblige the parties holding divergent opinions to become incisive and precise; that to speak of a unilateral dialogue was merely to play with words; that the inquiry was simply one more mystification to be held against the newspaper. The latter replied that if one needs an opponent in order to clarify one's thoughts it is improbable that the said thoughts will be original; and that in any case, in the hypotheses of the Dia party the persuasion factor actually acted as a catalyst, seeing that in the final analysis the fellow with the glib tongue completes his triumph by talking to himself.

In short, civil war. And one of atrocious cruelty. Once the steak-tracts had been launched, an epidemic of the bacteria of contradiction broke out. Every individual affected by the microbe considered that his arm and his head, his eye and his foot, his navel and his spleen, were irreconcilable. He destroyed himself by tearing out, burning, or vivisecting the contradictory organ.

Methuselah was physically preserved from the disease, but he contracted it spiritually because of his great porosity. Thus the painful theme became an integral part of the orchestral score, and Methuselah's identity was realized through the absurd, by the projection of his psyche beyond the confines of parrot identity.

When the carnage came to an end and Methuselah's body was discovered intact on its perch, a qualified psychoanalyst equipped with an oscillograph approached it. The currents recorded by the machine traced a graph which was deciphered a thousand years later. Translated, this is what it says:

"What-I-don't-understand-is-that-in-spite-of-my-confusion-and-the-absurdity-of-the-world-I-am-still-happy."

"Alopecia-impetrating prohibited." My wife and I came across this notice. This was on our last weekend. We'd taken the tandem, with the tarpaulin, the camping equipment, and the kid on top. We'd gone along the autostrada as usual, but instead of branching off to Fantoine we'd carried on in the direction of Agapa. After riding for a couple of hours we decided to stop. We stopped. We pushed the tandem into a little field to have a nice quiet picnic and we were just going to sit down in the hay when my wife saw the sign. I read it. I wondered whether I wasn't going haywire. What did it mean? Me and my wife, we aren't very educated. I work in an office. I met my wife and we got married. The kid came along right away.

There we were, wondering whether we could sit down or not. My wife said: "Better not. You never know." But the kid was hungry. So we did sit down, a bit farther on. We didn't eat it all. It's my opinion that we were scared slightly shitless. Then we set off again. We hadn't had anything to drink. We stopped at an inn. My wife was worried. Even though she isn't very educated, she does sometimes look things up in the dictionary. She asked the innkeeper for one, she gave us a funny look and brought us a Larousse.

Prohibited, we know what that means. For *impetrate*, it says: "To obtain from the competent authority." *Alopecia*: "Baldness occurring in patches on the scalp." That already made it more complicated. I'm a bit bald, but not completely. Did it have anything to do with me? My wife asked the innkeeper whether she knew of the prohibition. The innkeeper made a face as if she thought we were talking balderdash and we didn't dare insist. There was a bit of a rumpus at the inn. The grandmother had got drunk. The previous night she had urinated in the jam pot on her bedside table, thinking it was the other one. At teatime they'd given her the jam pot without noticing and she'd swallowed the lot.

So we left. The whole of the rest of the journey we were cudgeling our brains:

"Could it mean that people are prohibited from obtaining the right to be bald from the competent authority? Would it ever occur to anyone to ask for it? And why write it in the middle of a field?"

"Maybe on account of it makes people think?"
"It didn't stop us sitting down . . ."
"But we didn't have much of a lunch, did we?"
"You're joking, I stuffed my guts."
"Not true; we left half the roast."

My wife wanted to get me to say that we'd been upset. I didn't like that. We dropped the subject. The kid was snoozing on the luggage. That evening, we got to Agapa. We put up the tent in a field. We put the kid to bed and then went straight to sleep.

In the middle of the night the kid woke up and vomited jam. My wife was terrified, it made her hair stand on end. But not for long, because half an hour later she was as bald as a coot.

The Roadman

Blimbraz the roadman went home to lunch. He said to his missis: "I saw Marie go by. She was wearing her mother's hat. It didn't last long." His missis shrugged her shoulders and served the soup. "Do you really expect me to be interested in those tales about Marie?"

But these tales are worth some consideration.

A very long time ago, under the last Merovingian kings, the ones they called the fainéants, a noblewoman by the name of Albergonde gave birth to a daughter. Who was brought up in the country. When she was fifteen, the fainéant took a fancy to her. Albergonde was jealous and decided to take her revenge. She broke a dish which she ground into powder and mixed into a custard. The custard was served to Chilperica, who thought it would be the end of her. Hence the expression: "vengeance is a dish that should be eaten cold." Chilperica had her mother's throat cut. She too had a daughter, who was the mistress of the next fainéant.

The Carolingians passed on mothers and daughters to each other, then the Capetians, the Valois, the Bourbons and the Bonapartes. The Empress Eugénie herself was one of them. Before her marriage to Louis-Napoleon she had given birth to a daughter, the grandmother of the present-day Marie.

But all that is just a sidelight on history. The truth is that Marie has just hanged her mother. We realized this on account of the spinach not growing anymore. But we don't dare start an investigation. Why not? Because Marie is a redhead. "Every person of the fair sex who is congenitally redheaded enjoys the privilege of absolute immunity," says the law. The new law, that is. The old one merely accorded jamboreeing immunity. They forgot what that meant. They revised the text. In spite of strict capillary control, women started to become redheads. But with Marie there was never any doubt: she was a redhead from the day of her birth. And everyone knows her weakness for firemen. There's nothing to be done against her. So as not to attract people's hatred, these days she wears a hat. It was this hat that Blimbraz recognized. He repeated to his missis:

"Her mother's hat, you understand?"

"Since I tell you . . ."

"You're not interested, you're not interested? And what about our spinach? You think I'm going to eat turkey every day?"

"Turkey isn't so bad . . ."

"It makes your beard grow."

"So what?"

"So—that I always cut myself shaving."

"Have to change the cut of your jib!"

Blimbraz stood up. He clouted his missis round the earhole. They ate their soup. When they'd finished, the roadman looked out of the window. Marie was already waiting for him. He didn't mention this to his wife. He took his mattock from the coal bucket and departed. He went up to Marie and took her hat off: she was as black as ink.

"Are you crazy?"

"I can't bear it any longer. I had me hair dyed."

That evening, she was under arrest.

Polycarpe de Lanslebourg

From the street, you could see a big head silhouetted against the curtain. It was Polycarpe de Lanslebourg. He was putting the finishing touches to a paper bird, the nine hundred and forty-sixth of the day.

For a Lanslebourg, it's a delicate matter to find work. Ancestors who were Crusaders, a long line of patricians, intimates of princes, counsellors, flourished in the XXth century in Polycarpe. He had been looking for the ideal employment for a long time.

An advertisement had appeared in "The Blazon":

"Wtd. yng. m. anct. fam. 16 quart. home fab. ppr. birds of distinc. proj. avic. mus. sbrbs."

Polycarpe immediately offered his services. An old aristocrat living in the suburbs replied, making an appointment for him to call on her. Freshly gloved, he went. A little villa, surrounded by factories. No bell. He knocked. A tame leopard came and opened the door. "Whom should I announce?" He proffered his card and was shown into an attic. Hens of all breeds, wyandottes, leghorns, houdans, barbets and pheasants, rubbed shoulders with others that were stuffed, cast in plaster, or photographed.

"When I reveal the fact that the first brahma hen was imported by a Lanslebourg," he said to himself, "I shall make a sensation." He waited without moving, for fear of walking on eggs. The aristocrat entered. Abundantly feathered, flowered negligee, espadrilles. Polycarpe paid her his respects and trod on an egg. The lady had to suppress a manifestation of ill-humor, but the young man's excellent pedigree appeased her. She informed him of her intentions.

"In these days, my dear Monsieur, we no longer have the right to remain indifferent to the aspirations of the third estate. Our congenital charity must adapt itself to the troublous times in which we live. I have decided to create an avicultural museum in my house. Few such exist. The suburban folk will welcome my enterprise with enthusiasm. You see here a few specimens supplied by my leopard. Matters of greater moment closed my eyes to the somewhat larcenatory method he judged fit to employ to this end. The gallinaceans other than the living ones come from a family collection. The weathercock you see there is that of our own chapel, in the provinces.

"Your task will consist in helping me convert the premises. Before that you will have to make some ten thousand paper birds. It is essential that the walls of the museum be covered with them. Between one and two in the morning you can obtain a supply of wrapping paper at the Central Market, where it is disgracefully squandered. When you have completed this work we shall be able to transform my apartments and prepare a catalogue at our leisure. We shall get in touch with the authorities to organize a bus service. We must aim high, my dear Monsieur, we must aim high."

The lady breathed no word about retribution. Polycarpe suspected that she was appealing to his honor. "This lady is right: how can one reconcile work, charity and wages?" He was being called to a vocation. He accepted.

Hence, behind the curtain, he had just finished his eighth day. Only three more, and the ten thousand paper birds would be done. He stood up, drew the curtain and opened the window. The wind rushed in. The birds flew. He shut it again quickly. The birds had already taken over three quarters of the room. He hadn't stacked them properly. By the fifth day he couldn't even get to his bed. He slept under the table. And since yesterday the door had been blocked. But he still had enough paper to finish the job, and a few scraps of food to eat. Everything would be all right.

On the eleventh and last day, the lady and her leopard were outside his house. They knew. They didn't attempt to go up. Polycarpe couldn't let them in. They brought a ladder and climbed up to the window. Through it they saw Polycarpe de Lanslebourg, smothered in paper birds, beseeching Providence to come to his aid.

And they laughed, they laughed! . . .

The Swan Café

"God, what a load of crap," she said.

I don't at all like her way of expressing herself, which in any case is symptomatic of her lack of culture. How often have I told her: "It's better to confess your ignorance and try and educate yourself than to come out with a crude judgment," she still hasn't understood. I have striven in vain to cultivate her. I couldn't appeal to her intelligence:

she has none. But I did try to develop her sensitivity. My efforts were so totally wasted that I now see intelligence and sensitivity as synonymous. To hell with casuistry.

We were looking at a work of art by the sculptor Dâd Surprise. True, it was botched, and amorphous. Above all the intention, to my taste, was too obvious (it was precisely this intention that escaped my wife). And there were a few echoes that bothered me in this sculpture, but on the other hand there was a sure sense of the inexpressible that made me like it.

I didn't try to convince Ida. I merely said: "I adore that limp arm. It looks as if it's stroking an invisible bear."

Coincidence: I hadn't even finished my sentence when Dâd Surprise came into the gallery. He had probably come to talk to the director. He approached us and said to me: "I like your idea very much. You understand my art. It's made from very little, but there are so many cosmic geniuses about these days . . ." Was this naive artist aware of what he was doing, then? He interested me enormously, and he felt it: "Would you," he suggested, "like to come along to my place for a moment? I have several works in progress. Maybe we could talk about them?"

His studio was in the traditional style: glass roof, loggia, etc. We were expecting the master to confide in us. But instead of initiating us into his technique, he told us this:

"I'm almost certain that the cashier in the Swan café, at the Oublies crossroads, is accumulating other charges. To be quite sure, she would not only have to be watched for a whole day—which I have done—but someone would have to manage to get behind the counter. This is impossible for anyone but the barman. And the barman is the proprietor, and he never leaves his post. No waiter ever goes behind the counter.

"The cashier keeps an ever-watchful eye—a far too watchful eye—on everything that goes on. Every so often she makes an imperceptible, but unusual, movement: she stretches her arm out under the counter, as if to reach some object behind the cash drawer. A switch? A bell? I wouldn't have been worried had it not been for a few disturbing facts, not altogether unconnected with this movement, it seems to me, which put me on my guard. I will mention only the two latest ones:

"The other day I was sipping my little glass of rum when I saw the violet seller some way away, coming towards us. She was making her daily round. The cashier saw her too, and in the most casual way she bent down. Then I saw the violet seller fall all of a heap onto the pavement. There was talk of a heart attack.

"Only yesterday, a terrible accident occurred under our very eyes: a motorcyclist ran into an ambulance and was killed outright. Instinctively, I looked round at the cashier: she had just withdrawn her arm . . .

"What do you think?"

A paraphrase would have left me skeptical. But such concision—no.

From then on I was far better able to fathom the intentionally faltering art of the sculptor: he was afraid of coming into direct contact with the cashier.

27

The Chaise-Longue

"At Whitsun? Oh, it was a drag. We only had the Monday. I couldn't leave the shop on Sunday. We left in the morning for Sirancy-la-Louve, just to get a breath of fresh air. My husband has an old cousin there. The train was jam-packed. You know what the suburbs are like.

"When we got to Sirancy we still had to walk two kilometers to get to the cousin's. She'd given us up. The nurse explained to her that it was us all right, that we hadn't been able to get away the day before but that even so we'd come to see her for a short while. She didn't seem to recognize us. She touched our faces and necks, as she usually does, and then went back to sleep. The nurse told us to go and sit down on the terrace as if nothing had happened. That suited us fine. I was tired. I spent the whole afternoon in a chaise-longue drinking fruit juice. My husband fished for frogs in the pond.

"In the evening we had dinner with the nurse in the kitchen. We weren't in any hurry: a neighbor had offered to drive us back in his car. We still had an hour before we were due to leave. We chatted to the nurse. She told us that the cousin wouldn't be with us very much longer. I asked her whether the house was heavily mortgaged. She didn't know.

"At one moment the nurse asked us whether we'd brought the chairs in. I told her no. She asked us to be so kind as to do so. Her rheumatism was predicting rain. I went out with Louis to put the chairs away in the shed. It was impossible to move the chaise-longue. Louis gave me a hand. We both started tugging at it, trying to wrench it out of the ground. It had taken root.

"When the neighbor came to fetch us he examined the feet of the chair with his flashlight for a long time. I suggested sawing them off. He replied: 'What an idea! Let's just simply tell the nurse.' The nurse told us that this wasn't the first time. We took our leave. I was even tireder than I'd been in the morning, after tugging at that damned chair.

"I nearly fell asleep in the car, which is very bad manners when you're with strangers."

Monsieur Maurice

Instead of going down the rue Gou he stops at the Swan café and orders a Pernod. It's six o'clock. Hes just left the printing works. He puts his bread down on the little table. It isn't every day that a café table tugs at your sleeve. Mustn't jib.

In front of him, the fairground stalls. Multicolored pennants. From one plane tree to the next. The blues are the most attractive. In London they aren't so bright. Kilburn, Mr. Smith's printing works. The days were never-ending, even the least drab ones. Georgia? She thought I was faithful to her. Personally, I was counting the days.

The baker's boy goes by on his bike. An old boneshaker you see all over the district. The boy and Monsieur Maurice bumped their heads together just now, trying to pick up a five franc piece. The boy went off, rubbing his head. A customer with made-up eyes—nothing but her eyes—said to the printer: "It isn't Easter anymore! You're at it again!"

Monsieur Maurice's concierge sees a note on his door: "Dear Maurice, I'll expect you at six at the Oublies crossroads." She tells herself, Monsieur Maurice isn't back yet, he'll be late, it must be his friend Louis.

The printer, at his table, is thinking about his friends. You don't choose them. They impose themselves on you. You go on seeing them just to please them. "Waiter, the same again!" The pennants are blue. The boy goes past again with a hamper of oysters. Oysters? Why didn't I stay in Kilburn? And marry Georgia. She didn't like oysters. We'd have hung up blue pennants.

The concierge sees that Monsieur Maurice is still not back. She wonders whether she should go and tell Monsieur Louis. What's the point? He'll soon see he isn't coming.

The boy goes past again, whistling "God Save the King." Georgia is sitting on his crossbar. You can guess that she isn't wearing any panties. "Still that filthy habit," says Maurice to himself.

He leans back in his chair. A pennant caresses his forearm: it's the lady with the made-up eyes. She asks him: "Why are you sad?" Instead of answering: "Because I don't love anyone," he says: "Because the concierge's dog has got fat." She retorts: "Yes, but if they cut off his head and tail he'd make a nice little bench."

Hippocrates

"Rash? You call that rash? Good lord! Obviously, with your judgment, your wisdom, and the magnificent opinion you have of yourself . . ."

"My dear Dâd, don't get so excited. You know very well what I mean."

"Not at all. I acted consciously, weighing the pros and cons. I knew what I was doing. No one knows better than I . . ."

"My dear mountain-mover, once again, don't get so worked up. You're so impetuous. You're on the verge of cyclothymia, if not schizophrenia. I've been observing you for so long that you ought to have confidence in me . . . Be quiet. Yes, rash, I quite agree that people need to be shaken out of their lethargy from time to time, but advisedly. Otherwise, we miss the mark. Both heart and mind must be objective. That's the way we discriminate. How can you expect, with your temperament . . ."

"In other words, I'm incapable of acting advisedly?"

"That isn't what . . ."

"I'm a good-for-nothing, a man who should simply stay at home and work himself into the grave to produce, just like that, in the dark . . . ?"

"Let me speak. Your job is to express yourself, not to shout from the housetops. It's for other people to discover you. You can't assert yourself on two levels at the same time without risking catastrophe."

"That's the word I was waiting for! An obsession with catastrophe! What the hell do you think *I* care?"

"I'm talking about a catastrophe for your spirit, not for your entourage. If you acted like that you would inevitably dissipate your efforts, lose sight of yourself . . ."

"Lose sight of myself! I have no eyes for anyone but myself!"

"Precisely."

"Precisely what?"

"I mean . . ."

It was thus, between a gladiolus bush and an anonymous bust, that Dâd Surprise and the doctor were conversing.

It would take far too long to enter into all the details. and in any case, no one is interested in the psychology of artists.

I will simply say this, then: yesterday, a half-finished Venus, as tall as the studio, collapsed outside the premises of Dâd the sculptor. He had himself calculated the resistance of the wall and that of the material of the Aphrodite. With the help of three movers, he had tipped it up onto the wall, which caved in, and the statue was found in three pieces on the other side, having knocked out a horse, six people and a bus.

All this in Dâd's imagination.

The doctor knows about it—or knew about it. He quickly called the police. They didn't find anything, and the doctor nearly got himself locked up. He mentioned this to some acquaintances, who said: "Really? Not possible!" And he wrote an article for the Medical Review.

There wouldn't have been anything to it if the matter had rested there. But hasn't he just rented a warehouse to enable Dâd to work on an even taller block, all in one piece?

Dear doctor.

The Casket

Something that must be taken literally is language. We never think more than we express. People who never say anything are play-actors. I mistrust "eloquent silences." You think you're understood by someone who confines himself to adopting a thoughtful attitude after your remarks: ninety-nine times out of a hundred, if you do nevertheless get him to say something, you see that he hasn't understood a word.

Language also consists of interjections such as: ah! oh! ee! These are enough for me, for each one implies a whole world of astonishment, admiration, reproach, etc.

There are exceptions to this law, but no one takes any notice of minorities these days. They're quite right. Let those who can't speak, write. In books, the rule is reversed. When a fellow writes: "In the beginning was the word," you may be quite sure that he doesn't know what he's talking about.

The more hesitant and involved a text is, the more profound its author is likely to be. A style, in fact, is a technique.

This preamble has no meaning. It's my excuse for beginning this story as follows:

It would probably be difficult to describe—or rather to suggest—the impression made on us by the memory of the voice—or more exactly: of a certain tone of voice in certain forgotten circumstances—of a dead person. I should only get sidetracked if I tried to go into subjectivities, that would be fatal to the impersonal note I'm aiming at. I am so constituted that everything close to my heart irritates other people enormously. I think I know why. But enough of that . . .

I spent my childhood in soap boxes. My father was a filmmaker, my mother a glass blower at Murano. She had left me with my grandmother, who lived in a garret. This good old woman was a bit of a bat. I kept in a casket the membranes that joined her arms to her ribs: they're like parchment today. She passed for a witch, but her nocturnal forays had no other object than the search for a little extra sustenance. Our everyday fare at the time consisted of bits of plaster and raw rabbits.

We were very fond of each other, my grandmother and I. We raised the rabbits in the soap boxes. We couldn't light a fire in the garret. The advantage of living there was the solitude. The landlady was tactful and the tenants knew about us. Why didn't we ever go out? My grandmother was mistrustful: the goats grazing on the roof (a thatched roof, where grasses grew) might have got into our garret while we were out and turned the place upside down. In her youth, she told me, she had had a bit of trouble with the local goatherd. If he was still alive he would have no hesitation in harming us. She never told me about this adventure, but I guessed that it had been painful, or even tragic.

When I was twelve, my grandmother died. I cut off her membranes and put her corpse on the roof. The goats cleaned it up, and one rainy evening the skeleton rolled off into the pond.

I left the attic dressed in my Sunday best. I went and saw the land-lady, who lived on the ground floor. When she saw me, she said: "Aren't you like your grandmother!" "I think she's dead," I said. "Of course, of course, my child. I'll have you apprenticed to a skinner. You can specialize in zebra markings. Here's a letter of recommendation."

I had to look for a skinnery. Quite by chance, through a fellow traveller, I found one at Sirancy-la-Louve. I sent in my letter. The boss was quite willing to take me on. And as he was enthusiastic about the idea of the zebra markings, he was even kind to me. During my apprenticeship, he and I together perfected a camouflage technique. The skin of any mammal could be made into authentic zebra. We tried this out with several of our furrier clients.

My landlady's idea made the skinner's fortune. Naively, I allowed myself to be cheated. At the end of my apprenticeship I could have gone into partnership and demanded a share of the profits. My boss sacked me on a ridiculous pretext. I took to the road again without a single peseta.

In the Forest of Grance, where I thought of becoming a hermit, I set up with a woodcutter's daughter who was wild and beautiful. Our embraces left me in a bemused state which she took advantage of to get me to tell her a lot of things I would have preferred to conceal. The girl soon knew as much as I did about my deceased grandmother, and one day she declared that my armpits were becoming webbed. Very fortunately, I hadn't told her about the casket: she would have thought up some stratagem to get hold of it, and God knows what I'd have been caught up in then.

I left her in the September of the following year, full of resentment. I'd told her too much, the busybody. The result was that I never stopped thinking about my grandmama and the goatherd. We always talk best about what we don't know. I'd made a fable out of all my suppositions about the ancient liaison—it must have been a liaison—and given my tales a solidity and reality to which I was now a tributary.

And to pay my tribute to this tyrannical folly, I went back to the garret.

There was a new landlady. The tenants didn't recognize me. I almost had to come to blows before I was allowed to go up to the attic on my own.

The soap boxes hadn't been touched. The rabbits must have escaped through the skylight. The thatch on the roof had been replaced by bricks. My casket was there. I opened it. The parchment-like membranes didn't take up much room in it. I was perplexed. What should I decide? What new trade should I choose?

And then I went over to the door. At which point, just before I went out, I heard a murmur: "Be careful. The goatherd—is you."

He doesn't have a first name. When he goes past the fire station in the morning he stops and watches the firemen at their exercises. It's a bit like an operetta. He thinks that's why he stops, but really it's to get to the laundry just as it's opening. The laundress always says good morning to him. How can I let her know that my name is Paul? Then she'd say: "Good morning Monsieur Paul." We've known each other long enough, for goodness' sake!

After the laundry, the café. "A café au lait." And he adds: "As usual." What's the use? It's an obsession. That won't tell the waiter my first name. I'll have to think up some way. Maybe leave a letter addressed to me on the counter? The next day the waiter would say: "Monsieur Paul, you left a letter behind."

After the café au lait, the office. They don't interest me. They envy me my job. Poor idiots. You only tell them trivial things. "What's your salary?" "So much." "Who's your mistress?" "Annette."

"What's your ambition?" "Director." But: "my name's Paul"—you never say that. Annette? She calls me "darling." I hate that.

And he comes back from the office. He stops at the café. "Yes, Monsieur?" "The usual." "A Martini?" "No, for goodness' sake! half a pint."

And he passes the laundry again. "Good evening, Monsieur." Good evening, good evening, you old bag. My name's Paul! Paul like Paul! Paul, Paul! Do you hear? But she doesn't hear.

Back home, he finds a note: "Shall we go to the movies, pet?" What a drag.

Then he went on holiday. Abroad. They won't know my name. I'll introduce myself everywhere as "Paul." Then they'll have to.

After the customs formalities, he breathes again.

But wherever he went, it didn't do him any good to say: "I'm Paul," they simply called him "you." Among themselves, in their own language, they referred to him as "the foreigner," or "the nut." He stuck a notice on his stomach with "Paul" on it. They asked him what kind of business his firm went in for.

He didn't see a thing on his holiday. He lost a lot of weight.

On his return, his landlady takes him to court. On account of the door. She was claiming that he'd prejudiced her interests, before he went away, by not opening the door at certain times, and by opening it without being asked at other times. Some tradesmen had complained.

He explains his position to the magistrate. He says that he does his landlady a favor by opening the door occasionally, but that he isn't obliged to do so. The landlady claims that there's a gentlemen's agreement between them. "Monsieur knows very well that he has to open the door between eight and nine in the morning, and that in the evening it's my job."

The magistrate questions the witnesses: "Has Monsieur often opened the door to you between eight and nine in the morning?"

"Yes, often."

"Has Monsieur often opened the door to you between six and eight in the evening?"

"Yes, often."

The evidence is contradictory. The gentlemen's agreement can't be proved. After some deliberation, the magistrate pronounces against the landlady. He asks:

"Are you satisfied, Monsieur Paul?"

"Oh, your Honor! . . . Your Honor! . . . Oh yes, your Honor!"

Artaxerxes's Will

"The words of Artaxerxes, the servant of Ahura Mazda, King of Kings, sovereign of the empire of the shades."

The manuscript dates from the second half of the fourth century B.C. If it is apocryphal, the style is nevertheless of the period: I recognize the turn of phrase "sovereign of the shades," which was abandoned in later royal edicts. It was perhaps open to ambiguity. Originally, it meant that the king derived from the light all power over evil. In other words, that he was the supreme arbiter.

The text is on papyrus (which came from conquered Egypt), as opposed to the use of stone for decrees of this sort. It is almost incomprehensible, like everything of any importance. Nevertheless, this passage is worthy of note:

"To my sons, I bequeath the task of finding god (or the gods)."

From this may be deduced:

1) That it would appear to be a Will.

2) That Artaxerxes, in his last Will and Testament, violated the principle of the unity of succession. To delegate such a duty to several people implies that the sovereignty is to be shared.

3) That an idol had disappeared (?), or, more plausibly, that religious beliefs were on the wane.

4) That the Will was not respected, as Artaxerxes was succeeded by Darius II alone.

Which is mysterious.

I must confess that I have always been fascinated by everything to do with the civilization of the Medes and Persians. A haughty, passionate, monotonous art. A history of conquests in which cruelty and excess triumph . . .

The recent archaeological discoveries at Susa and the sudden infatuation of the sciences of the Orient with the era of the Achaemenids have enabled me to establish the following facts:

The Will in question cannot be earlier than 430 B.C., six years before the death of Artaxerxes, that is. An inscription unearthed in 194 . . . explicitly reminds us of the absence of any text relating to the succession before the thirtieth year of the reign. Furthermore, a second Will, dated 426 B.C. and known for a certainty to be apocryphal, in referring to the first, provides an interpretation of the clause: "To my sons." The document with which we are concerned was therefore the only known Will.

We know from some tablets discovered in the foundations of the palace of Persepolis that the King's sister, who had been converted to the Greek religion by a Phoenician, was denounced as a heretic. The sovereign had her eyes put out (bas-relief, British Museum). Would there be a clue here to the case of the missing idol? To come back to the more plausible hypothesis, it must be admitted that after the defeat at Marathon, the menacing force of Greece and the spiritual currents spreading from Athens over the whole of the Near East left people's minds in a state of utter confusion, hence the abandonment of the ancestral beliefs.

Artaxerxes's sons (with the exception of Darius II) perished, one after the other, while out lion hunting (see the ancient Syrian legends), hence after 430 B.C., since they are mentioned in the Will. From this it might be inferred that the court dignitaries were aware of the King's wish to divide the power. So the "lion hunting" would merely have been a fable to which they gave substance.

Why, then, did the King not recast his last Will and Testament? Was he prevented from doing so? And by what intrigues?

To this day, we do not know.

A Footnote to the *Oresteia*

Persuasion was held by the Greeks to the one of the supreme virtues, and I will concede that it is entitled to our deference. What is so admirable as its magic power? It is one of the faces of love, particularly when it mystifies. The Achaean warriors charged Ulysses-the-Crafty with the task of feeding all the baloney to the skeptical. He was immortalized as a hero, and as the typical lover, the man who triumphed over the sea (we would call it the unconscious, today), and who returned, ten years later, to a wife past her prime. Well yes, that's how it is.

In Eleusis (now just a large village), they still tell a story that confirms my views.

The poet Aeschylus, at the time he was composing the *Oresteia*, resided in Athens in the Thalassa district. The main duty of his maidservant, Aglaia, was to keep visitors at bay. The poet couldn't bear anyone to be around while he was working. One day, when he was furious because he couldn't finish a line in the *Agamemnon*, Aglaia comes into his study. Aeschylus fumes with anger. The maid flattens herself against the wall. She explains that three young men have called and that they want to speak to the master on a matter of the greatest urgency. He doesn't want to know. She stands her ground, and ties herself up in knots with contradictory excuses. "You're becoming a liar, Aglaia," says he. (The Greeks loved to play with words.) In the end she vamooses, but to get her revenge she advises the young men to start yelling under Aeschylus's window. Which they do. The poet appears. The air calms him down. He listens to the lads. They've come to ask him to attend the rehearsal of a play of their composition about which they would like his advice. Aeschylus asks them:

"How old are you?"

"Between seventeen and nineteen."

"Your play is worthless. We must suffer, to understand." And he draws the curtains.

Ten years later, at his summer residence, the same young men come to see him. He doesn't recognize them.

"What do you enjoy?"

"Women," says one. "Men," says another. "Adventure," says the third.

"We must suffer, to understand."

And he goes back into his hole.

Ten years later, the three make their way to the cemetery in Eleusis, Aeschylus's hometown, and bow their heads in homage before the urn containing his ashes.

"What are you doing?" the urn asks them.

"Making war."

"We must understand, to suffer," it murmurs.

Firenze Delle Nevi

"A town?"

"A magnificant town! It was destroyed by avalanches, and disappeared at the end of the Renaissance."

"On Mont-Blanc?"

"On the southern slopes of Mont-Blanc, 4,700 meters up. Founded around 1230, it was just a small alpine hamlet until the time of

Lorenzo de' Medici, who gave it its brief splendor. Florence, which he had endowed with the most beautiful monuments and made into the center of all the arts, was continually stirring up revolt. A clan of envious puritans was undermining the popularity of the prince. He decided to keep the Tuscan city in check, and, by a wager worthy of a great creator, entered into competition with himself.

"During his ascent of Mont-Blanc in 1488 with his friend and counsellor Luigi Campanello, nicknamed, 'Luigi the Capricious,' his companion, catching sight of the village isolated in the snow, cried out: 'Che bellissima Firenze potremmo costruire qui!' The idea was born. Within two years the wager had been won. We can imagine what a tour de force this constituted! Carrara marbles were transported through Tuscany, Liguria, and Piedmont. Thousands of masons, artisans, builders and architects headed north. An extraordinary treaty with the Duke of Savoy (February 12, 1489) fixed the toll traverse, arranged for the employment of Savoyard workers, and laid down the remuneration to be paid by the Medicis in exchange for their services.

"The chronicle of these events has been conserved in the Ambrosian library in Milan (C. 621. XI b.)

"In 1491, Botticelli completed the fresco in the Municipio, or Town Hall. This building, a replica of the Strozzi Palace, was adjacent to the dome on which Bramante had employed his genius. A square in front of it formed a belvedere above the abyss.

"On 7 June, there was a fair to celebrate the completion of the work. The most unlikely procession was to be seen in the streets: peasants from the districts of la Maurienne and Faucigny, from the Valais, and even from Lombardy, wild with admiration, mingled with the elegant gentry from the court.

"And the setting sun illuminated this prodigious spectacle: Florence resuscitated amidst the snows.

"What is to be said about the silence of the Information Service? Monopolized for centuries by a bunch of hirelings, it infiltrates everything. They make us believe the moon is made of green cheese. Open any encyclopedia and you'll see that H. B. de Saussure was, in 1787, one of the first to climb Mont-Blanc! It's intolerable.

"But the Savoyards haven't forgotten. It is the tradition, in certain families, to name the first son Laurent."

Journal

November 1

Ah, those fingernail races! They're one of the great attractions of these parts. The whole world and his wife uproots himself with his family, his house, his terrain, and comes and camps here for several months, for as long as the races last, in a specially reserved site. Whatever his financial situation, everyone finds the means to perform this rite. The unemployed are rare, for a sizeable labor force is needed for the harvest. The collectors go to work a year in advance. They visit every residence, whether official or not, with sacks which they fill with clippings, with broken nails, with nails that have been extracted—they can acquire an inexhaustible supply of the latter in garrets, on account of the tortures. They've stopped bothering about animals' claws ever since the day they ran wild and pounced on the spectators.

Once they've been collected, then, the nails are piled up in silos adjoining the racecourse. Usually there are only a few weeks to go before the start of the games. They are used for leveling the terrain and especially for stabilizing the atmosphere. This operation was delicate and even dangerous, only a few years ago. Today it is carried out with the aid of valves and giant compressors laid out along the track. The people who live in the neighborhood are warned when the stabilization is due to begin. They have to decamp within twelve hours. But there are always some hundred thousand laggards who get caught up in the currents and torn to shreds. This provides some extra nails.

The inaugural day arrives. People can sit wherever they like, entrance is free. It may be said that in theory people prefer to be at a certain altitude, that of the silos, for instance, or one or two thousand meters higher up. The very sight of this multicolored crowd rising up in tiers several kilometers into the sky is magnificent enough. What can be said about the entrance of the nails into the arena? There is nothing with which it can be compared—unless it be a snowstorm. At the signal, they rush off towards the East.

November 5

In high summer, mauve placards are stuck up all over the country to announce that the leaf-picking is about to start. All the natives are mobilized for a week. The territory is transformed into a veritable parade ground. The State health services are entirely responsible for the transport, board, and lodging of the workers. Given the density of the population, and that all private industries and businesses have to suspend their activities during this time, it is easy to imagine the extent of the task incumbent on the abovementioned authorities.

At first I didn't quite understand the reasons for this transfer of the inhabitants from one province to another on the opposite side of the territory for this chore. It's a question of productivity. I had the honor of being introduced to one of the members of the top organizing committee. He is a morose little man who has spent his life in perfecting the administrative mechanism of the "leaves week."

When they have arrived at their destination, the groups (about a million souls) are divided up into squads of a thousand in the province to be stripped. These squads, commonly known as "the dryasdusts," set to work immediately. This has been going on for so long that men, women, and children can climb trees like monkeys. Every native species of tree is a legal target.

Under this system, however, varieties tend to disappear in favor of one basic type of tree which is something between an apple tree and a horse chestnut. Hedges, copses, and the vegetation of the heathlands are similar targets. Every leaf must be picked without its peduncle; this requires great dexterity in the operators. The peduncles, which normally fall in the autumn, will be collected by private firms.

As the gathering proceeds, whole cartfuls of leaves are unloaded into the canals crisscrossing the country. They discharge their load into the rivers. At the mouths of these rivers this fearsome accumulation is controlled by a system of dredgers and cranes along the bank, thus raising a vegetal bastion which, when the seadrift reaches it, slowly decomposes until the spring.

The exploitation of this huge, putrescent wall is begun in March.

November 7

The whole of their private life is autopsied in their eyes, even when they are lost in thought. When you walk down the street you are surrounded by decorticated beings. They present a spectacle of monstrous psychological division. I met almost none for whom the present had any importance. They project everything into the future. A future constituted of present and past preoccupations. Encumbered by this impossibility, they trudge from distress to downfall.

They are dangerously haunted by eternity.

As for the children, I think they resemble our own. They dream of buns, balloons, and toy ducks. But they stagger under the weight of their anxieties, as heavy as planets.

December 2

The crowd didn't flinch at the sound of the leaves being torn off. It seemed as if it were being absorbed into an indiscernible, illocalizable object. This wasn't the first manifestation of the sort. The most celebrated one, so I was told, was that historically classified under the name of Good Friday. I made this comparison because a little girl by my side began to desiccate. First, her hair fell out like hay. Then her face, which had become fibrous, dropped down over her doll. With one hand the little girl hugged the fetish to her bosom, and with the other she tried to hold her head up. But her hands had become glued to her body, down to her pelvis. She took two more steps. Then her legs broke.

I had never before seen a mob immobilized. The place is usually so full of movement that you can only keep your eyes on an individual, or a couple, or at the very most a group. But at that moment one could only too easily take in the whole assembly. I had no need of proof, the spectacle was hypnotic. It was only when thinking about it later that I realized that the ease with which it could be seen confirmed its reality.

December 3

You ask your way, as a matter of habit, of a passerby. He doesn't answer. Right away, you are jerked out of your automatism. Because it's true, the way is there in front of you, almost on top of you.

The difficulty of fighting against your mania to understand is in proportion to your isolation. I am only now, thanks to a few friends, beginning to liberate myself to a certain extent.

One of my first experiences was buying my bread without leaving my house. It took me an hour of tension to be able to relax; an hour to delimit the feeling of bread and to confine my desire to my teeth, my palate, and my esophagus; an hour to evacuate the decision; an hour to abolish the time which had elapsed (I checked, later); and there we were, the bread was on my table, I was eating it.

All this was the result of an incalculable effort. *They* make no effort at all: they have never lost this astonishing faculty.

December 4

After the rains which saturate the furrows, the season of solidifying fogs arrives. These are dry vapors which emanate from fossils. They are extremely dense, and float around for several days at the level of the tall grasses, then later spread out at the average height of human lungs. The organic reaction of the natives is instantaneous: they grow, until emersion of the respiratory apparatus is achieved. This temporary change of stature gives rise to the traditional pleasantries. A dwarf will be nominated president of the "Lanky Club," a bigot who has finally reached the height of the font will scratch her initials on it, a girl nicknamed "the giraffe" will be given some stilts by her friends, etc.

Without this spontaneous hypertrophy, it would be impossible to survive. The fogs petrify everything on their level. With people, therefore, the region around the waist, which is then immersed, rapidly becomes like a slab of marble. This causes the momentary arrest of the lower functions, while the legs continue to move normally. I have been told that many natives with spiritualistic tendencies can't wait for the foggy period to come and put the brakes on certain of their appetites. The others, the creatures of habit, are obliged to lie or sit on the ground, below the fogs, that is, for as long as is necessary for the blocked organs to thaw, if I may so put it, when they want to use them. They have to do this three or four days in advance.

The small animals aren't disturbed. Nor are the large ones; pulmonarily, they are above the fatal level.

The foggy season, which returns about every ten years, lasts for six months of the Gregorian calendar.

December 18

When they are trying to escape from shame, they are the most pitiable creatures I have ever seen. Since the transparency of their souls is not merely constitutional but also an active function, a little like a walking windowpane which might go and shatter itself against an obstacle, no base action is the attribute of the person who commits it. It comes within the network of turpitudes that binds all these people together.

This kind of permanent link of omniconsciousness should, it would seem, exclude the feeling of the irremediable, which is egotistic, and substitute for it that of complicity, of collusion. But this is far from being the case; the sense of shame persists. I have seen poor wretches who were at odds with it perch up in the trees like owls and remain there sleepless for nights on end. The structure of sin and remorse, of their interpenetration and mutual influence, rose up, tangible and useless, in front of them, and up there on their perches they gave the impression of being false meeting points, artificial intersections.

For their notions of the absolute are deficient. They have but a vague knowledge of divine mysteries and allegorical redemptions, whose disproportion to their wealth of emotion is such that the slightest lapse from honesty plunges them into dejection.

Oh, those trees, with their weight of suffering flesh . . .

December 20

Superficially, one might take the meadows for doors, for the sides of swing doors. They open out lengthwise onto little fences, but close with difficulty if one ignores their inscriptions. The inscriptions serve as hinges. They are periodically replaced, blue letters alternating with red ones. This produces a pretty effect at the changeover, before all the inscriptions are unified.

Their agricultural work is backbreaking. They have to activate the doors at the same time as they tread down the excrescences that tend to form on the fences. I tried this, with the help of a peasant. But just as I was making an oblique movement over the unexposed part I let go my hold, the excrescence came and knocked on my foot, and the man only just had time to push me back out of the way. I had a narrow escape from what they call "rape" in those parts.

Such is the superficial aspect of the meadows. But beneath the surface, I know that they are tombs.

December 21

One may attach oneself to any ribbon. They sinuate through all the towns at the approach of a disease, either to conjure it or to provoke it. A gyratory movement is established, which sweeps the interested parties along in its train. The last to get moving are ejected laterally and form a buffer at the corner of the buildings. To tell the truth, no sooner has he joined the ribbon than each demonstrator degenerates in the web, where he becomes filified. In the workers' districts this superribboning is liable to cause disasters. Some time ago, the wave had become so compact at "Navigation" that it even dragged the buildings into its wake and rolled on as far as the Forest of Grance. No trace of either stones or inhabitants was found there. The web had devoured the lot.

Normally, the ribbons stop after six days. The disease either recedes or breaks out with violence, according to the rogations. It sometimes happens that the desired epidemic is considered to be insufficiently virulent. Then they hurriedly construct artificial ribbons. But their power is far less great, and the supplementary virus obtained never satisfies the need. This is what inspired the dictum: "evil be the virus of the evil ribbon."

March 15

One would like to be a Colorado beetle or a cockchafer so as to be able to gorge oneself on the sap of their plants. It is instantaneously intoxicating, but deteriorates on contact with our oral mucus. It has to be ingested through tubes. The pleasure is very mediocre. A study is in progress of the chemical composition of the mandibles of the cockchafer, in order to market a liquid gum based on its formula. Then one would merely need to paint one's throat beforehand in order to ingurgitate this beneficient sap.

March 16

Along the cutting edge of the lintels, along the sharp edge of the windowpanes, along the blade of a penknife, their sympathies advance backwards. How timid they are! The imperceptible drawl with which they weight a word makes their declarations of love falter. They cannot continue, they barricade themselves in. If you question them about their emotional troubles you will never forget their response. I felt the greatest respect for them, but I believe that this is precisely what makes them suffer. They would prefer to be ridiculed.

March 17

The parks are overrun by leguminous plants of the Papilionaceae family. They stifle every form of vegetation and proliferate in vast carinas. You get absorbed in the valvulations of the lianas, and then you find yourself surmounted by stamens. Mortises hollowed out in the trunks serve as a base for the props underpinning the upper floors where, in the botanical species, capillarimeters are located. A permanent check on the suction obviates any impoverishment of the soil. The unemployed can sign on at any branch of the Chlorophyl Center as assistants. They are invaluable to the children, who pester them with questions and use them as guides to the labyrinths. One of these government employees, whom I know well, piloted me around on a corolla. No one else was there. The marvelous tissue was melting in the sun and was as dangerous as a glacier. We made two crossings, equipped with the appropriate chisels, carving out our path, and bursting the blisters. What a joy to the eye! Every fold, in the shape of a cornet, opened out below onto the immense panorama of the garden! The capillarimeters seemed no bigger than acne pimples, the greenhouses looked like drops of water. The incurvation of the carinas, the assistant explained, promotes fructification. I had thought this was natural, and expressed my astonishment. He interrupted me with these words: "Nature dixit—genius fix it." Their habit of talking in proverbs is one of their defects.

The people who sleep in the parks are licensed by the government. In the twilight hours, when the strollers go home, they install themselves in the copses with their bird-organs on which they play the sempiternal Air of the Allobroges. Their crutches, which are their stock-in-trade when they go to mulct inns, crash down through the sewers and pervade the hotels.

March 18

Their artists work in isolation. They have no public. As they are recruited from common criminals, they are banned. Any kind of contact with them is a felony. Their penitentiaries are of a greater variety than ours and convicts may be placed in any artist's studio.

Far from being blunted, the sensitivities of this vermin increase in proportion to their guilt. When an interested observer, defying the risk of prosecution, goes to see them and admires one of their works, this feeling that the visitor is a kindred spirit is so unexpected that the criminals lose their heads. They whirl around, throw themselves on the work and trample it, lacerate it, pulverize it. Then they disappear into the walls, where for the rest of their lives they are racked by qualms of conscience at having deceived people.

March 19

If you lose a contour, or a segment, or one whole side of your body, the hachured surface is reduced by the same amount and your armpits are no longer included in it. You wander around with holes in you, carrying your charcoal-drawn silhouette in a satchel. Your cheek becomes emancipated. Your prominent jaw commutes between your neck and your glottis; the wings of your nose erupt in pharyngeal edemas; nauseating liquids ooze out down your apophyses. Your truncated sphincters flow back towards your nerve centers, your epigastrium becomes subdivided. The satchel finally drops, too, your hand becomes invaginated, and the sketch so carefully made the day before is stained with liquid manure. This is the result of a plasma deficiency. It frequently happens during country rambles. Several comrades have gone for a day's outing and come back unrecognizable.

March 20

This is the plectrum they use in orchestras. It is retractile in the hands of nonprofessionals, hence difficult to operate. But what harmonics it elicits! The instrumental solos, which are more in vogue, are confined to the higher registers. My eardrum can still only pick up the occasional snatch of a melody. Lack of flexibility. But regular listeners appreciate almost no other music. You can see it in their faces. They denote such spirituality, while the piece is being played, that their expression enables me to imagine the eloquence of the musical phrase. The slightest acoustical disturbance—a glove being pulled off, a lace coming undone—must certainly destroy the whole impression, for the soloist is requested to repeat the piece at the end of the concert. The encores are to a certain extent the failures. In the most select concert halls, listeners are obliged to wear special clothes made of soundproofed material.

The public flocks to the concerts where a singer of either sex is due to appear. Indeed, in their amazing concern for their art, they have cultivated a breathing technique which abolishes respiration. In this way the essential monotony of the melodic line is safeguarded. But at the end of the recital the virtuosi are irrevocably exhausted. They die in front of the ecstatic crowd. A ceremony bears them away from the stage to the cemetery. As the corpse goes by, every listener, one after the other, comes and breathes in from the martyred mouth what little oxygen has been introduced into it by the hiccups of the death agony.

March 29

There are numerous blanketers. This uninteresting trade is a popular profession here. During the very long apprenticeship the various aptitudes are demarcated. No one is ever sure of the result, for the appearance of a twelfth sense—or, according to some, a thirteenth—

takes place only after superintensive training. What then occurs, to the blanketer who has a genuine vocation, is a "blanket" phenomenon nicknamed "voltage" by clinicians. Strictly speaking, this is undefinable. It is a halo. The subject's nervous tension is transferred to it *en bloc.*

The ordeal which constitutes the investiture of the future artisan consists in confronting him with the prototype of a carding-brush—of no practical value—which unites all the essential parts, enlarged twentyfold, of all the material needed in this work. The candidate is bound hand and foot, and, using nothing but his voltage, he must be capable of making three blankets of varying thickness and weave. These test-samples are the property of the syndicate.

June 1

Marks, topographical signs, and standard measures of all sorts—whether monetary, spatial, or whatever—are symbols that are as antiquated as the embolismic concordance. It's ages since this whole arsenal of conventions was practically abandoned.

Indeed, disciplines such as for example geography or astrology now stimulate only those whose intelligence has become sclerosed, following the example of mathematics.

Nevertheless, there is still a danger threatening their teaching, and that is the superstitious survival of scientifico-historical notions which no longer correspond in any way to the evolution of their minds. Hence, in university lectures, frequent confusions and anachronisms. A distinguished professor recently risked the statement that the druids used to immolate the azimuths and centipedes of Reason. This is regrettable. But I am optimistic, in spite of these aberrations. For they do no harm to anyone except the academic young, who in any case are more and more losing their memory.

June 13

In the burying-ladies' huts, there is room for only one person. When you are going home at night, you are only too glad to stop at one of them. Their occupant is rarely there. Her task requires her presence elsewhere, among the bushes, or the ravines, which she examines at dusk. A strange task! So you go into the shed, where digging tools, hoes, and grappling-irons are piled up pell-mell. The cutting-up hemp has been rammed into a crate, it's merely the work of a moment to throw it onto the fire and thus thaw yourself out a little. This custom of cutting up corpses with hemp goes back a long way. By dint of unremitting friction on the joints, the burying-ladies finally manage to detach the flesh, which they stuff with bits of lint before tying them to the grappling-irons. Next, they pitch them down, simultaneously, into the bottom of the twelve or so surrounding wells. It is only the carcass and the viscera that are interred, and not by the burying-lady herself, but by her nearest neighbor. They travel leagues through the woods in order to meet each other, and sink waist-deep into the bogs.

The grubs that they fatten up in these marshes are as big as sausages when they come to eat them.

But their existence can only be called wretched. It consists in sleeping standing up in their shacks, suffering from cranial rheumatism—at the frontoparietal suture, which is very slack—from which they have no respite, fighting against the blisters that periodically erupt on their epidermis—and these may sometimes attain the dimensions of the shack and the strength of its framework—and living in fear and trembling night and day in case they've left a grappling-iron down a well . . .

They mate amongst themselves, without the slightest desire, and give birth to edible daughters who are a kind of saprophyte.

July 28

"You can take it or leave it": an injunction frequently used by hairdressers. Their clients make no bones about it. The poor women know their duty; they hang their heads. To prevent the spread of dandruff, they are scalped. Then their cranial periosteum is curled. The slum kids adore this calcined odor. During the operation they hang outside the windows in bunches. They get dispersed with insecticide. But since the hairdressers' salons are located under the ballast in the stations, and the upper parts of their heating pipes serve as buffers for the freight cars, the kids don't go far. They wait for the next client, perching on the gauges. And every time, it's the same to-ing and froing. The railroad employees have signed petitions. Waste of effort! The wives of the minister responsible are all clients.

July 29

When you make an inventory of your matches, one thing strikes you: how few there are. What! this derisory portion allotted to each national is the sole source of light in the country? Judging by the light they diffuse—and there is never any shortage of it either in the built-up areas or in the countryside—there must be some sort of magic at work.

They often maintain that God has too much pleasure. And from there to doing without daylight by having recourse to this makeshift expedient, there is but a step. Potential rebellion? Ill-disguised rancor? I'm merely making an observation. The natural light is suspended. Polyhedral receptacles, mounted on steel shafts, keep it prisoner. These pseudo-street lamps, whose architecture is of the greatest austerity, are the characteristic feature of the landscape. No more is needed to divert the thoughts of a layman from their habitual course and fill him with doubt. The match solution, which is only a last resort, even for the nationals—which they don't deny—nevertheless provides some opportunities for certainty. How many times have I not burned my last twig to convince myself of this! The moment it has burned out, others spring up between my fingers—irrefutable proof of the mystery.

Let anyone try to tell me, after that, that they don't believe in God! The pseudo-street lamps are the childish symbol of the temptation.

July 30

The redhibitory songs which the malcontents hum in the mornings tend to help them recover their desire, or return to a less precarious mental state. This matutinal drone expresses great candor. But we should be on the alert for rapid metamorphoses: these are due to the ferryboat "noyou." Contrary to appearances—the suavity of the refrain—the tremolo is not in order. Watchword: not to employ any reflexive verbs in the threnodies you hum. "Noyou" is the pleonastic reflexive pronoun which means: "we to ourselves"—"*nous nous à nous-même*," in their language. It has been stigmatized by popular imagery, which represents it in the form of a small modern replica of Charon's ferryboat.

July 31

Wobbly knees are immobilized on bail. The bail money is paid when children are born. It is collected by the register offices. Earth taken from molehills, with the addition of pulverized Molasse and water has proved to be an excellent "barbotine," or potter's clay. Provided that a supply depot can be found not far from the place where the sick person collapses—for he cannot be moved—they immediately immobilize his knees. They coat them with barbotine and leave it to dry. The patient stays on the ground, wherever he happens to be, until a decision has been taken by the coater on duty at the supply depot. The latter declares the fall to the register office himself. The bail money is then reimbursed to the parents, or, if they are dead, to the victim. It is irreclaimable in cases where they haven't managed to master the wobbling. It's a barbotine-insurance.

September 1

Their dwarfs are sold at auction a few days after their first bout of jaundice. They are much sought-after by religious communities who destine them for the vocation of candelabra. When they come of age, a paraliturgical service is celebrated for their benefit: this is reputed to endow them with petrifying grace, and it invests them in their sacred charge. A bogus priest places them on the altars while a mixed choir intones the "Nanum neutrum Deo." A poignant ceremony, on condition that grace descends. Unfortunately, I have seen some burlesque ones in which the dwarfs, not in the least petrified, bawled their heads off and had to be tied to the tabernacle. You could no longer hear the canticle, the deacons and sub-deacons broke out in a sweat, and the faithful lost their faith.

September 5

The relative importance of their acts bothers them. And when you think of the intentions some of us impute to what they do! *They* do not have this *amour-propre*: they counter you with an uncontrolled gesture, phrase, or absence. That they are not creators—in the sense in which this function demands a permanent watch on oneself—that I will grant, but what is serious is that their attitude leads us to doubt the validity of the work of art. "Even so," I used to say to myself when I was in their company, "if that is the truth, just one more second's obstinacy in my researches and I shall become a clown, a liar." I had to reflect at length before finally justifying my dissimilarity. As I am incapable of being a gentleman who walks, who smokes, who sees his friends, my natural reaction is to invent, in clay or on canvas or on paper, a walk, a taste for smoke, or a visit which makes my arteries throb.

And that is why I am now convinced that in a work of art we do not try to conjure up beauty or truth. We only have recourse to them—as to a subterfuge—in order to be able to go on breathing.

September 6

A person of medium height, by my side, stepped onto the automatic weighing machine. We're always interested in other people's weight. With apparent nonchalance, I watched the needle. It went all the way around the dial, once, twice, three times . . . What does that mean? One ton, two tons, three tons! I was at a loss. The person wasn't upset. And then I heard, coming from her ribcage: "Hallo, hold the line. I'm connecting you with Warsaw. Who's speaking? Shares, 320-4, debentures. . . , etc."

This woman was a telephone exchange.

September 8

Blizzards, while they do not occur every day, are nevertheless so frequent that they have had an influence on their habits and customs. And in particular on their diet—with the reservation that they only cook hailstones for very precise purposes.

If a little girl, or a boy, shows signs of irascibility or violence, they cultivate this tendency and elevate it to the dignity of a national virtue—by giving them a surfeit of explosives. Of these, hail is one which has the advantage of operating by delayed action.

The moment the blizzard has abated, cooks, nursemaids, and mothers are to be seen everywhere, rushing out of doors and filling tubs with hailstones.

They make them into puddings (by adding baking powder and other ingredients) which the child devours. There must be an idiosyncratic phenomenon here, a need inherent in these choleric temperaments, for I never heard tell of any child who made the slightest fuss about taking this tonic. Where are the dramas associated with cod liver oil!

They persevere with this treatment for three or four years. The child grows "in age and in anger." He becomes insufferable, but he must be treated with the greatest circumspection. At puberty, he becomes subject to trances: to demolish a street door, a party wall, a drainage system—this is mere child's play to him.

His virulence then decreases until his thirtieth year. But the diastase operates in depth. So it's far from rare for the storm to flare and the blizzard to blow up his gizzard.

● ● THAT VOICE

Preface to the American Edition

The structure of this novel is precise, although not immediately apparent. The different themes are intermingled. One cuts into another point-blank, then the other resumes and cuts into the first, and so on until the end. The first example of this procedure, at the beginning of the book, is the theme of the cemetery, cut into by that of the gossip at the grocery, then resumed shortly afterwards.

Apart from this peculiarity, as from the middle of the book the themes are taken up again in the inverse order of their appearance. The last themes of the first part, that is, become the first of the second part and are thus retold in reverse. A procedure resembling anamnesis.

Further, to give the impression of the interdependence of the different inspirations and the multiplicity of the sources of the voice heard by the ear, the French text was written with no other punctuation than a period at the end of each paragraph.

In order to make the book easier for the Anglo-Saxon public to read, I put the commas back. To my surprise, the text has lost nothing of its impact. On the contrary. But just a moment! This is very largely due to the art of Barbara Wright, whose profound knowledge of French enables her to render its slightest inflections into English. She recreates in her own language, which is of remarkable flexibility, richness and subtlety, the exact tone of this novel.

I thank her with all my heart for the work she has done with such care and enthusiasm, and I should like to take this opportunity to pay her the tribute she also deserves for her translations of three of my other novels. I also thank Joanna Gunderson for the warm, sustained interest she takes in my work.

It must be rare for a writer to be so fortunate.

Robert Pinget

Preface *

Nothing is more comic, from a certain point of view, than the tragic adventure of a brain becoming unhinged.

Someone is speaking, someone is lying, someone is playing at dying by degrees and at killing his family circle.

Who is the uncle? Who is the nephew? Who is the maid?

A voice, the same from beginning to end, despite the diversity of tones.

Anamnesis, whose literal meaning is the recalling to memory of things past is, in the language of psychoanalysis, a patient's remembrance of the early stages of his illness.

In the present case, the anamnesis is triple:

1) That of the narrator,
2) That of the chronicler (relative to the work achieved up to the present time),
3) Formal (relative to the structure of the book which, after the halfway mark, is recomposed or decomposed by reascending; in other words, the themes are resumed in the reverse order of their formulation.)

In the end the attempt proves too difficult, but this doesn't matter since the primary aim was to capture a voice.

Robert Pinget

*Original jacket material written for the French edition.

● ● THAT VOICE

That Voice.

Cutting in from time immemorial.

Or that letter addressed no one knows to whom, you keep coming across rough drafts of it.

Ask Théodore to sort papers.

His name whispered, he screams, he wakes up sweating in that bedroom where everything is starting all over again, that table, the dark, he went out and retraced his steps from the courtyard to the fields, following a narrow path.

A missing link.

The days slimy, the horror of memory.

A background noise, a murmur, a whisper, pledge or prayer or long speech, a nonsuit without appeal, the Parca jabbering.

Everything frozen in the cataclysm.

What voice, what faith.

A schoolboy's slate here, but above all its sponge.

Two or three words.

Traces of effacement.

Two or three words, you can't hear very well, the rest unpronounceable, nothing, zero name age place, zero.

To emerge from less than nothing below zero, actually impelled by you don't know what, that mercury suddenly become nostalgic, searching for let's say maternal warmth, vague whiff of a symbol but what does it matter, no one left to consider, two or three words amongst which this one, psspss.

A missing link.

Step over a wall or a foundation, a brick or concrete construction, the memory of something rough and cold to the touch, it could be stone, then step over other constructions more or less cold to the touch, now tread on gravel now on grass and stumble into some equally vague foliage, yes but to say tread on, step over, is to exaggerate, given his unstable equilibrium, very weak on his legs, more often flat on the ground than on his feet, crawling as much as walking, falling, standing up again, trial and error.

A doubt too about what he had come into contact with, his epidermis couldn't be in very good shape, in short all this in the dark, the dense shadows and the scents of the glebe, the earth, the humus, how to put it, to try to forget the word putrefaction, for indeed rather than remembering it it's a question of forgetting what for years . . .

An All Saints' Day as shitty as they come.

The display outside a country grocery, a crop of multicolored plastic corollas alternating with the chrysanthemums which are sad by nature, for a whole week no sooner has the grocer's wife rearranged her display on the sidewalk, dangerous corner, than her customers arrive to do their daily shopping, a salesman in artificial flowers is there trying to peddle his wares but he's left it too late, they're fully stocked for this year, he's told to wait, these ladies have to be served, that's this November day started, a chilly morning, its slight fog soon dispersed, the sun's shining but it's no longer the light you get in summer, have to make the best of it.

Well yes then, the cemetery practically overflowing with flowers in memory of our dear departed, your late mother, your late son-in-law, do you think they're in hell, I'm only joking, do you believe in that absurd old wives' tale, the resurrection, how could anyone, can you imagine coming back for all eternity after I'm dead, me with my great big ass, do you need corsets when you're a glorified body, and with which of my two husbands, that's a big problem, indissoluble marriage, one of them would have to be ditched, I wouldn't know which one to choose, you see, the first one made me so very happy . . .

From less than nothing, below zero in fact.

Ask Théodore to sort papers.

A missing link.

Not say another word, not make another gesture without repenting it, contrition has always been my weakness and was probably my downfall until the day when all activity ceased, and I mean all, until the day much much later, it isn't a question of years anymore but of God knows what, when in the darkness I once again felt the need to move around, when I couldn't help observing that I was moving around among the constructions in question, and that compact darkness today, that darkness, this new time that I still don't know and that by trial and error I'm going to have to shape, reshape, organize for my own purposes, a poignant thing in itself if it weren't for the still unconquered fatigue of an ordeal such as no one has ever before undergone, not me at any rate.

An All Saints' Day as shitty as they come.

Three children, my God how young I was, and the second one, my little Alfred, such a good boy, always looking after me, never bad-tempered, always cheerful, at my service, oh yes I can say that, how spoiled I was, if I had my time over again I can't think of anything I'd want to change, of course I believe in it, it's the first principle of the catechism, the essence of the Christian, the life everlasting, it solves, it conditions, it perfects, it's just life, and without it no point in being on earth, personally it's rather that it helps me to imagine Paradise, I can't make sense of those circles one on top of the other that artist painted, what was his name again, the chosen few on the clouds, I'd be afraid of losing my balance, or is heaven a different sort of sky, a solid one, not the one we see, but in that case why call the sky the heavens.

Just life.

There are numerous contradictions, what is there to prove the existence of God, I was at a loss to know how to answer that woman, my daughter-in-law has a friend who believes neither in God nor in the devil, she says that suicide is quite normal, and anasthasia too, that's when you let useless old people die when they're suffering a lot, in one sense yes, but Thou shalt not kill, what d'you make of that, that's just it though, she says it isn't killing but where's the dividing line, it's like with abortion, at what moment does the soul enter the organism because it's only the soul that's important, you say someone's a body without a soul when he's lost his way, when he's unhappy, take old Magnin for example, ever since his wife put horns on him, that's the first expression that comes to mind, which only goes to show that woman is man's soul, say what you like that's my opinion and there's no doubt that every deceived husband and every bachelor agrees with me, wasn't she going a bit far though, so used to being in the right, her husband never contradicts her, he's a good sort, well let's say a bit of a wet rag, unless he's lost interest, it seems that for quite some time, have you heard, the Cruchet girl, quite so, but people are such scandalmongers, even so it would be rather droll, no one could call him a body without a soul, he'd have two.

Two souls, why not a dozen.

Numerous contradictions.

The entry of the soul into the organism.

Vagrant wind.

On my left, alley number three hundred and thirty-three, a few meters farther on side-alley number seven hundred and seventy-seven crosses it, symbolic numbers if ever there were any but I feel I have a right not to complain about that, let's say not to make any pretensions to a somewhat dubious lucidity.

So, to go back to the story of my exit, I had to dodge into alley number three hundred and thirty-three and zigzag along it up to its intersection with the side-alley in order not to lose sight of the numbers written on the metal plates at right angles to each other, and this in spite of the darkness, which comes to the same thing as saying that I stumbled at this spot, that I fell flat on my face, and that the numbers were just a few centimeters away from my nose and I could read them in what may have been a fleeting moonbeam, or more plausibly the phosphorescence coming from a nearby tomb, unless my eye had become luminous like a cat's, I'll leave the question open.

It was Madame Thiéroux's or Piéroux's turn, the ladies were lining up on the sidewalk, it was such a lovely day that she was tempted to buy some frozen shrimps, are they at least edible, and chicory already, doesn't time fly, those are the last grapes of the season, haven't they gone up, but as sweet as honey, apropos of which she bought a pot while a lady from the town who was a bit lame made her way through the line to choose some chrysanthemums for her dead, she comes back every year on All Saints' Day, she was born here, she must have left when she was very young but she'll have herself buried here with her family, very comfortably off to judge by appearances, car driven by her husband, which of her two husbands, he opened the trunk for the flowers and when it was their turn they bought four pots, I'm all for people loving their deceased but even so, could it have been ostentation, she didn't jib at the price, whereas the next one, Madame Dubard or Buvard, had a lot of trouble making up her mind, she counted the flowers in each pot to get value for her money, this question of different circumstances in the same little hamlet is rather shocking, everyone ought to have more or less the same possibilities, there are considerable discrepancies in people's resources, I'm not talking about the lady from the town but about the rest of us who stayed in the region, what do *you* think.

Zero region, zero sou, zero centime.

The other replied, you wouldn't have become a communist would you, what a way to talk, you such a religious woman, but it seems that the new Church is carrying on quite a flirtation with the Left, it's becoming politicized, don't talk to me about it it's enough to disgust you with religion, didn't God say the poor always ye have with you, well then you see, their modern theories are heretical, she wanted some candy too, some sweetmeats, but not just anything, something like licorice or bubble gum or whatever, you understand, that you get the most of for the least money, because she has hordes of grandchildren who show up on Sundays and holidays, she says they'll be the death of me I can't wait to see the back of them but she mopes about the whole week waiting for them, hasn't she got fat by the way, it's elephantiasis, have you seen her legs, she has to bandage them and walk as much as she can so they don't explode, which means that she's the only person you can see on the sidewalk, and after all it isn't as wide as all that, she can barely efface herself . . .

Traces of effacement.

. . . for the tourists, those disgusting swellings, poor thing, if I was the mayor I . . . how can you forbid a citizeness to go out, what an idea, what's the matter with you this morning you aren't your usual self, I know what it is, you didn't sleep again, I've discovered, just imagine, a miraculous herb tea it's called psspss, whispers its name in her ear, unless it was something to do with some intimate ailment, a vaginal discharge, salpingitis, how should I know, suddenly they start whispering interminable obscenities to each other taking not the slightest bit of notice of anyone else, the other woman carried on with her account of the death of her husband, all the gory details, his phlegm, his wind, his soul trying to find its way out, his death throes, his convulsive movements . . . choosing carrots, taking her time, well yes my dear, these indestructible females, their carcasses are built to enable them to perpetuate the race of maladies, annoyances, calumnies, obscenities, liturgies, posologies, necrologies, ah, it's Mademoiselle Passetant, what a pretty dress, how's your poor father.

But the children too, sneaking up to the chewing gum, the grocer's wife gets mad then sees an adorable little cherub in a stroller outside, is that little darling yours, be careful, dangerous corner, they drive like idiots on Sundays, half drunk, the entire brood in the Peugeot going to visit their cousin, their grandma, their auntie, their uncle, shit, to think we still haven't got any farther than that in this day and age but you have to admit that they adore their families, spending your whole life putting up with your cousins, visits, Sundays, the same conversation from one end to the other, from one edge to the other, from one mouth to the other, their gab-holes going hell for leather, don't let me go on, thanks, once I get started, well, that's life, I was only thinking this morning while I was putting my socks on, no one has ever known whether happiness was any good to people, shh, someone's coming, it was the tippler, concealing an empty bottle under her coat, the grocer's wife took the bottle and handed her another, you can pay me next time, some people still call her Chenu's or Chevu's floozie just to make it quite clear, that antediluvian affair, women are such bitches, I'm not malicious but really, sometimes I wish they would find themselves in the shit like that poor woman, by the way Adèle too is back for All Saints' Day, she's never lacked nerve, though mind you, today at her age, but there's no denying that no one ever slept around in this place the way she did, all the men she's had, that she used to follow to Paris, and then come back, and so on for years and years, she finally got married, yes, you wouldn't think it, that poor old girl, but I tell you there's still something in her look, haven't you noticed the way she eyes men, there, that one, look, psspss, funny isn't it, well it amuses *me*.

Vague whiff of a symbol but what does it matter.

Two or three words.

The soul looking for a way out.

A missing link.

These vagrant souls in their dozens or hundreds, you can't hear very well.

The housewives on the sidewalk, their gab-holes going hell for leather.

Talking about my late wife, him talking about his, I realized right away that she would be a good housewife, do you know how to judge a woman you've got your eye on, give her some cheese to eat, if she leaves the rind she's a spendthrift, if she eats it she's a skinflint, but if she scrapes it she'll make a good wife, yes, these things and their consequences, sorry to come back to them, they're enough to drive you mad, to kill you, repeat, I am dead.

To emerge from less than nothing.

Traces of effacement.

Then my route along side-alley number seven hundred and seventy-seven, no less difficult, no less slow, with its zigzags and occasional obstacles, which were only monuments, swards, piles of dug-up earth, bushes, pots of flowers either botanic, plastic or ceramic, which were only the monuments of mould and muck that misfortune accumulates in a feeble head at a turning point as they call it of life, with age and the regression of desire battered by the tempest of the great forgotten myths, evil suddenly regains all its force and leaves you defenseless in the jaws of the ogress, humanity triumphant, the Mother Ubu of nightmare.

Papers.

Take a hair of the night that bit you.

A great deal of distance, a great deal of height.

The gravediggers had come to make a clean sweep, to clear all the bones out of the old tombs, the out-of-date concessions, they spat on their hands, dug, and found the remains of skulls and tibias, poor children collected them in shoe boxes, cleaned them up in the stream and went and sold them for a couple of sous to medical students in the town.

They discovered a rabbit's bone in a sepulcher.

Surging back, the old myths, cockchafers of despair.

I knew your mother well, she said, but she had got the wrong generation, all the calculations had to be made again, the lateral branch, the child of the child of the child of, second, third, fourth, n^{th}, the whole repeated, harped on, drawn out, joggled from one age to the other and then forgotten, to leave room for . . .

Nightmare papers.

In that limp, nauseating darkness, it seemed to me that a decision had been taken, but by whom, that I should elect as my domicile an abandoned vault, its grille open and its paving still more or less stable, I installed my backside on the little greenish altar and I said, this is where I'm going to recover my wits, there was a slate on the ground, maybe left there by a gardener, a slate and a bit of chalk so I could make notes, but what is it like, this new time that I've mentioned, apart from being cut off, fragmentary and furtive, that has this very night come to replace former time like a big, fully-blown flower instead of the expected daisies, and which may be premonitory of eternity, what is it like.

Installed in my vault with my slate within reach, it's mild and humid, I only go out at night.

Do you believe in that absurd old wives' tale.

. . . then forgotten, to leave room for the outside world, let's call it a window open onto the world, as they say, but the illusion was in keeping, an imaginary landscape imposed itself and contracted from one speech to the next, no more open, no less secret than this room sealed off from every gaze, it was here that it started and restarted, never begun, never finished, listen, yes, the story, was it that of a father or of a son, listen, long speech in which the words of a father and those of a son alternated, those of the son being muddled up, intercepted, or intermingled here, even before this place was discovered, this place from the beginning of the murmur, an illocalizable whisper, voices from all around at first, and then here, without appeal, those who had chosen it remain in it unscathed, the voices went on speaking here, a few words exchanged among themselves, all this time the same, the unique web of their lives, the jabbering Parca span dismal or cheerful days according to whether a word here or there was said or not, the vocabulary or grammar of the being, at such and such a page a time to love, at another page a time to yield up your place, one word rather than another would make them last for all eternity.

This room sealed off from every gaze.

The life to come, it conditions, it contorts, it confuses, it's just life.

While the other was going back up to his room and once again immersing himself in old papers, old newspapers, old dossiers, and making notes, the obituary columns in the place of honor, the list of the deceased is getting longer.

The local paper followed on with a great many hypotheses, amongst them that of the death of the gentleman as a result of choking on the bone in question, that relating to the practices of sorcery and to the superstitions of the time which apparently attributed a certain power to the rabbit bone, that relating to the attachment the dead man had felt toward the rodent buried with him, after the example of pagan customs, that relating to a tame rabbit that tunneled its way into the said tomb where it apparently died of exhaustion or myxomatosis.

While the other goes on his way, carrying, dangling from a string, a parcel containing his bones, as he walks he reads a leaflet advertising copper or copiers, you can't read very well, comes to a dried-up well, sits down on its rim and unpacks his bones which he starts sucking to stave off the thirst that is torturing him.

Wait in this vault for the manifestations of a new life, not despise the little consolations of the former one, you never know, to reject them would be totally out of place since in fact reminiscences are making demands on me.

A probable observer, weary of probabilities, perched up in a tree, sees things I cannot discern from my refuge, things are happening outside my range of vision, the slate records them through some phenomenon which is beyond my scope.

The slate, always come back to that.

The voice on the slate which is becoming effaced.

The jabbering Parca.

That's how I know that some sort of action is taking place in the cemetery, controlled, like a ballet or a drama, by an invisible manitou, characters are moving around, I can hear orders being given, hear, that's saying a lot, orders, too, murmurs sensed like vibrations under the skin which coincide with this or that movement of the bodies, or should I say shadowy figures, in this darkness spreading like a patch of oil, the eye gradually becomes accustomed to it.

A gray slug crawls along the stone and disappears down a hole.

Its underground journey.

Irruption of slugs-hyenas making their way down to the depths of the tombs, at dawn they come back up to the surface, sated and slobbering, then go off to the lettuces in a nearby kitchen garden.

Illocalizable.

Or go over to the well, listen to the sound rising from its depths, a murmur, a whisper, go up, lean over, hands gripping the rim, an equally indistinct murmur would seem to be coming from the well, from the surrounding meadow and from the elm wood, but only audible at a point determined by the intersection of a straight line starting at the wood and going off in the direction of the hamlet, and of another starting at the corner of a farm building and leading to the forest, intersection, the well . . .

Lost, the key of the, the key of, lost, something at this place, you remember, an accident, you remember, repeating more distinctly the key, an effort toward an effort, tension, it's necessary, it was, it was there for a long time, listen, here, a long time ago, a certain thing, or, no, it was a pledge, or a prayer, or a speech, yes, a long speech, you remember, forgetfulness or loss, or what, judgement lost, judgement, a story about what, listen, lean over, no, it doesn't speak, the well doesn't speak, but this precise place, this very intersection, stay here, never give up, never leave this place, beyond it there is nothing, it was here that it started and restarted, never begun, never finished.

Repeat, I am dead.

Take a hair of the night that bit you.

This room sealed off from every gaze.

It sometimes happens that the observer sees nothing, but the slate goes on recording.

The altar-bench that is freezing my backside, on my left a cast-iron vase and a little iron candlestick, on my right an antimony crucifix and the mildewy remains of a holy image.

These slugs after all are the kind that are at home in cellars and underground passages, try not to think of them anymore or even to see them as edible creatures.

On the slate, all the time, the afterlife, eternity, light, entries crossed out and then effaced, but they come back.

The relief of no longer being the sole master of one's text.

The absurd amusement of establishing the definitive destination of the present lucubrations, the little mandarin games must make me laugh somewhere now, from now on my simple obsessions will be written for the benefit of simple souls.

Say everything again, for fear of having said nothing.

Went back up to his room and reimmersed himself in his work, what, actually, an essay, memoir, or diary full of reflections and unpleasant memories.

The soul, that vagrant wind.

Or another room, there have been several, whether hazy or crystallized, in the last room certain elements, even though inassimilable, recompose of their own accord a different place which stimulates dreams, during the time it takes to transcribe a phrase.

Calm reestablished, take stock of the unbearable situations within which he had to struggle, whereas he had hoped they would be his salvation.

A character in the drama is monologuing indefatigably, I try vainly to listen, he must be with the actors not far from the side-alley in the space where the family tombs form a little island of suffering.

The ceiling of the vault which must formerly have been made of stones in the shape of an arch must have been damaged, seeing that it has been replaced by large flat bricks joined to the cement without any mortar.

This imposition, invincible fatigue.

Ask oneself in what wretched, nauseating depths the germs of duty survive, the duty of pursuing the inventory of what is offered to the senses and springs from memory, to call that imagination would be to insult poetry.

My exit into the darkness of night, but which night, not that permanent night whose name may not be pronounced, a remote reference to nocturnal states for the histrion looking for the vague melancholy of the soul, profound, indiscernible darkness of the being and of love, in that case I should have made a theatrical exit, a false exit, I must put up with it, call on whatever signs may make it acceptable, even so there is an opening onto something, one can't deceive oneself with impunity, for the imposition was there at the outset, make punishment the basis of one's only chance of salvation.

As for those illocalizable people or rustling sounds, voices from all around, from before, from tonight, from after, a pointless distinction, I am their effacement, their spokesman, effacement, write the word again, unaware of what it means for the other people whom my solitude revels in.

That voice on the slate which is becoming effaced.

The former paths reascend up to the same points, the difficulty of keeping silent, the recollection of special moments when everything seemed possible without the aid of any other presence, but the myth is taking hold again, words no longer suffice to disconcert logic, the mouths that pronounce them find a face again, you fall back into primitive fable-making, this story for incorrigible babes in arms.

Other images ad libitum found in the master's papers, the abandoned cemetery is now no more than a jungle in which you clear your way with a machete, a thick, bushy curtain of dense lianas, inextricable, populated by snakes and predators.

They penetrate into the jungle and lose their way, darkness overtakes them, they camp where they are, they organize a meal, a flayed animal is roasting on a spit, some of these unfortunates cry vengeance, raising their fists, they can hear the muted sound of a military march scrambled by radio atmospherics and by the buzzing of enormous mosquitoes.

The mosquito hunt, then the meal around the fire, all of them pulling bits off the roast, arguments arise, but they had children with them whom they had left to amuse themselves among the flowers, suddenly shrieks from a mother who sees her child being carried off by a predator, more abductions follow, and more shrieks.

A missing link.

Calm again gradually, the mothers bathed in tears, you can see them with their mouths full asking for more roast lamb.

Songs of praise offstage from the sated vultures on the treetops.

Desert of stones under a torrid sun.

Then the whole cemetery is perched on a mountaintop, precariously balanced, gusts of wind tip it over to right and left, and then hurl it headlong down into the abyss.

Traces of effacement.

Go over to the well and listen.

A cold early morning in October, very bored in my tomb, sleep having deserted me for hours and my rosary between my fingers no longer commanding my attention, all of a sudden another decision has been taken to get myself out, right away I'm through the grille, I hesitate before starting down the side-alley again, pains in my knees, legs like jelly, I sit down on a nearby sepulcher on which when it gets light I make out, engraved in noble letters, the name of the deceased, Alexandre Mortin.

A brief thought for the unknown man, feeble reflections on the vanity of belle-lettrist inscriptions and the like, I was going to take up my rosary again out of indolence when at the intersection, quite a way from the side-alley and from alley number nine hundred and ninety-nine, I think I can spot someone, I only have to wait, and not in vain, the character takes shape, it's a young man carrying a pot of chrysanthemums, unexpected luck, the day of the dead is approaching, this boy has come to put flowers on a grave before the November rush.

He had the pale complexion of an aristocrat racked by remorse, a characteristic that isn't so common, my horror of the vulgar was thereby spared, luck had smiled on me, it could have been anyone coming up with chrysanthemums, I said to him young man, let's not beat about the bush, sit down there and open your heart to me, as you would have to the dead person whose grave you have come to put flowers on, it's so easy in the early morning, and in these circumstances I am full of all the indulgence, pity and softening that could be desired.

He plonks it down on the stone in all simplicity, his commemorative flowers too, but remains embarrassed and silent, no doubt so as to seem to want to say a great deal more, a subterfuge that is less rare than his aristocratic appearance, I come out with some vague words about the nip in the air, the matutinal hour, how was it that the cemetery had already opened its gates, he replied that the caretaker had died during the night, which had caused some confusion among the administration, and as he had come very early to wait for the opening he had taken advantage of this momentary disorder, he has not the slightest difficulty in getting up early because sleep has deserted him.

A miraculous herb tea, it's called psspss.

This story for incorrigible babes in arms.

Span dismal or cheerful days.

Me talking about my late wife, him about his, old history all that, good or bad times in days gone by are pleasant companions when you're old, a new contradiction, don't let's be sorry for ourselves but apropos of cemeteries where's your family vault, wasn't it beyond the fountain, so long since I set foot there, the time will come soon enough, as for his poor wife he'd met her, can you imagine, in the cemetery, or am I mixing things up, rather macabre isn't it, he'd been fascinated by her as she was putting flowers on her parents' tomb, an air of sincere piety, modestly dressed, and the little five-franc pot of chrysanthemums, that was quite adequate in those days, do you approve of useless expenditure, I realized right away that she would be a good housewife, do you know how to judge a woman you've . . .

Repeat, I am dead, I shan't keep silent anywhere no matter what happens, but isn't it cold.

The time it takes to transcribe a phrase.

Silence that you're afraid won't be . . .

Take stock of the unbearable situations.

The burial took place in the province he came from, the announcement said died after a long illness bravely borne, he rests by the side of . . .

A missing link.

The adjacent tomb was apparently that of a nephew, never any flowers on it, the family lives in the Antipodes.

What does he do all day.

And his godson, isn't it something like what they call illegal confinement, his mother complains that she never has her child to herself but you know how it is, the old man dazzles her with the idea of his inheritance and she accepts the conditions of his blackmail, neither more nor less, for in fact Théodore never leaves his uncle's side, the old man is so attached to the spoiled brat, he's his godson, as godfather the master had suggested calling him Théodore, at first his sister didn't want to give him that rather daft Christian name, but as it means gift of God she finally accepted it, being very religious.

Outside the kitchen door, out of breath, not having troubled to say good morning, where's the master, said Louis, the maid was shocked at his impertinent manner and turned around, look here, what's the matter, come in and shut the door, it was already open said Louis, the kid hadn't shut it said the maid, she was stirring a sauce, these drafts, my rheumatism, what brings you here, the master isn't down yet, I never disturb him before noon, I'll wait then said the other, it's not far off noon, no, the alarm clock says ten to but it's fast, it's a quarter to, she said, go and wait in the salon there's some magazines there but don't smoke your filthy pipe, tasting her sauce, adding a little salt, where did I put the pepper, pass it to me, there, on the shelf, no, there, by the tea-caddy, he picks up the pepper and hands it to her then goes into the salon which is practically adjacent, a little hall first where the stairs go up to the second floor, then side by side the dining room and the salon.

I was just finishing my toilet when I heard Louis questioning the maid, she told him to wait, the kid hadn't shut the door, he's gone off with the magazines, she said, but you can do without them for a few minutes, fifteen at the most, he'd taken them into his own domain, the barn where he's fixed himself up a cosy corner between the cart and the place where they keep the tools, he must have heard Louis arrive in his car but his little radio which he keeps on all the time will certainly have drowned all the conversation.

Or, recalling years later that he couldn't have been present when Louis had told the maid the news because he would have acted immediately, must have heard it a long time after, when it was too late.

But after twelve when the maid hadn't heard the master come down she went into the salon where Louis had dropped off, he spends his nights at the warehouse during the grape harvest, there's always something to be done, he's paid for it, she woke him up by yelling on your feet, in there, imitating in her stentorian voice that of a regimental sergeant-major, he jumped, then from the second floor came the old man's voice demanding what is it, what's the matter with you.

Voices from all around.

This imposition, invincible fatigue.

The slate, always come back to that.

They burst out laughing, she went back to her kitchen calling out nothing, nothing, come down, you're wanted, he came down a few minutes later, grumbling, went into the salon where Louis greeted him, asking him to shut the door, she would have liked to hear their conversation.

October, abundant grape harvests, superb skies, sunsets purple and pink, blue, green, mauve, ashen, opaline, mornings misty if not foggy, the sun breaks through around midday, sometimes a sudden shower but the season was splendid, still almost summer, no yellow leaves on the trees, and the temperature, they barely had to light the stove one day out of two but nothing lasts, it would soon be winter, they had laid in their supply of fuel, the price of wood is prohibitive but the master must have his log fire, an expense I don't approve of when you see all the misery there is in the world, that's not the way *I* was brought up.

Or tell the grocer's wife that some of the personnel at the winery are sick, they haven't been selling retail for the last month, and apropos of the flu, asking for news of several of her relations that she claims she never has time to see in order to steer the conversation around to her own health, her rheumatism, the drafts, and end up with the apotheosis, the bit of news that will go the rounds of the district.

Bedridden for years, helpless, fabulously wealthy, the old man had been cheated out of millions by an unscrupulous nephew, forged signature, no one any the wiser, he decamped with the loot, how could they bring proceedings against him, everyone thinks the uncle is deranged and anyway what about the family, his sister, no he wouldn't do it, you could never be too careful, whoever would have suspected the nephew of being a crook, always so correct, black tie, and a churchgoer, ah, how right they are when they say . . .

Or that no one had ever got to the bottom of it, there were so many papers on his table, old dossiers, old newspapers, the narration, as it's called, of the facts in question appears to have gone unnoticed, and you can say that again, or been lost, discarded with the rubbish, his wastebasket always full, I almost had to empty it twice a day.

Because he confused what he was saying, and when I say saying, his gibberish, with what was happening to him, not much but enough for, well, his conversation with Louis for instance, I won't insist on that given the circumstances.

Taking not the slightest bit of notice of anyone else, the women might have been alone in the world, psspss, those obscenities from mouth to ear, there's always something more to say, just try and imagine the scene but anyway it's classic, the old man, his night-light by his side, he isn't asleep, three in the morning, he hears a noise, but why make you waste your time with this antediluvian story, what interest is it, I ask you.

And personally, his habit of never finishing his phrases, it drives me crazy, just because he's losing his marbles is no reason why everyone else should suffer, but I'm boring you again.

Cutting in from time immemorial.

We'll get there in the end with a little method.

His eyes mist over, don't let's be in too much of a hurry, he was wearing the latest fashion in trousers, a little American-style denim jacket with patches over the elbows, that's the ultimate in casual elegance with the young people of today, and a hand-knitted, thick woolen scarf.

As he didn't open his trap anymore I try to get him to confide in me, have you killed someone, he nods yes, that's nothing, I say, it happens to everyone, nature, ups and downs, was it by poison, or firearms, or strangulation, or drowning, he was absentmindedly pulling the petals off a chrysanthemum, my question embarrassed him, well, let's talk about something else then, and turning toward the inscription on the grave, then you knew that Mortin, he jumps, turns around too, stands up, beating heart, and says, he is the person I have come to honor, how comes it, what . . .

He stands there dazed, then gives me a sideways took, don't worry young man, pull yourself together, nothing here that isn't natural, my presence must have distracted you, then, pointing to my sepulcher, look at my dwelling place instead, a vagabond with no history, no duplicity, tell me about yourself, that will calm you.

With a little method.

I knew Alexandre well, he said, a generous friend, unhappy, persecution complex, failed author, he'd chosen me as his confidant, I learned everything about him, the poor wretch totters, I hold him by the leg, sit down again, which he does and continues his confession, which, the farther it advances the less it holds my attention, in short, held himself responsible, having one day abandoned his benefactor, for the death of the latter, a bit later he starts sobbing, I try to console him, displays of emotion, a few entries deleted, then effaced.

Or that nonsuit without appeal.

Why make you waste your time.

My name is Théodore, he said next, arranging the chrysanthemums as best he could on the marble, and mine is Dieudonné, I said, call me Dodo, if there's anything I can do for you . . .

There were forget-me-nots around the edge of the grave, which made me say to the forlorn young man, nothing is sweeter than memories, don't you think, you don't have anyone anymore, this is what I suggest, over there, at the intersection of the side-alley and the alley where you appeared to me, you see that abandoned vault just like mine, make it your refuge and we'll correspond through our hearts, our thoughts, well, whatever you like, and he was already making his way toward the place indicated with a little rawhide suitcase in which he had put his things.

His things, yes, that suitcase, when was it that I dared ask him what it contained, one evening no doubt when we were sitting in front of his niche, but as it had just been raining the grass was wet, he pulls out of his suitcase a cloth which he spreads out underneath us, and what else of interest have you in that suitcase, I ask, it isn't just curiosity . . .

My things, he replies, nothing much, in the way of clothes I have a couple of pairs of socks left and I don't know what else, the important thing is my papers, he shows them to me arranged in little piles, I ask him are they classified in alphabetic order, chronological order, what are they about, it's fascinating, I was afraid he was going to turn out to be an obsessive collector of God knows what, no though, it was just his things, their order was only apparent, here, he said, this cutting for example relates part of the speech made at the inauguration of the Suez canal, and this one is the announcement of the engagement of one of my grandmother's uncles, and this photo a little two-month-old Newfoundland puppy, and those are my school essays, and so on.

We were surrounded by the papers, it might have begun to rain again, let's put them back in the suitcase, I said, we shall get the benefit of them gradually with the passing days, they'll keep us company, and since you seem to be gifted, then I tell him about the slate which had been hidden until then, maybe we could try to write some essays together on the subjects contained in your box of treasures, an absurd idea which would only complicate things by multiplying the number of the irresponsible.

He put away his cuttings, they were held together by bits of string, rubber bands, clothespins, paid no attention to me for a long moment, then put his suitcase back in his niche saying forget what's worrying you Monsieur Dodo, it can't be really serious, looking at you one envies your diaphanous state, everything can be seen on your face, it won't do you any good to cross out, delete, efface, consider me a little like your slate, I will only remember what you want me to of your words.

I had thought I saw innocence in his eyes, was it perfidy.

Traces of effacement.

The time it takes to transcribe a phrase.

Entries crossed out and then effaced.

Was it the story of a father or of a son, words of the one or of the other.

Surging back, the old myths, cockchafers of despair.

As for the kid, he was still listening to his radio in the barn, the maid had to call him to lunch once, twice, finally she went to fetch him, come on Théo, your uncle's already at table, and wash your hands quickly, the kid turned off his radio and first ran to the washhouse and rinsed his fingers then still running went and joined his uncle in the dining room, they ate in silence, the master just managed to ask his nephew what he was doing with his Thursday holiday, a vague reply from Théodore who was struggling to peel a pear, his uncle took it out of his hands and peeled it for him, then the boy went out and the old man drank his coffee by himself, the maid came back to clear the table, he was dozing in his armchair, she made an awkward movement as she was picking up the coffee tray, the cup fell to the floor and smashed, the master jumped and called her a clumsy creature, you can't pretend it was the cat.

He went out into the garden and made his way over to the well, what a noise coming from the bottom, that illocalizable murmur, never give up, words confused here, the web of their days.

While she went back to the kitchen where her niece who had lunched with her was waiting for her, and told her how her father had met her mother in the cemetery, your mother was putting flowers on her parents' grave like every first of November, she was trying to meditate but a man not far away was looking at her, captivated, he went up to her and asked her the first thing he could think of, where was the vault of this or that family, she replied by pointing in its direction, but the pot of chrysanthemums she had just put down was blown over by the wind and he set it straight, a conversation started up about the dead, you can imagine the sort of thing, is that any place to do your courting, you must admit, all the same he carried on with it, they walked home together and they got engaged two months later, if I'd been your mother I'd have been afraid of the evil eye, cemetery lovers, just imagine, but they were very happy as you know.

She went on chatting, after she'd washed the dishes, complaining about her master who was losing his marbles, gets confused in what he says, and when I say says, on account of staying alone all day in his study, his papers, he needs something to take his mind off them, God knows what goes on in his head instead of, I don't know, getting some fresh air, going out with the child a bit.

For instance a walk to the cemetery, why not.

But Théo has no such expectations, he likes it with his Uncle Dodo, as he calls him.

Your box of treasures.

Because the maid, who has always played the innocent, probably knows much more than she lets on about the occupations and projects of her master, it seems she ferrets through his papers, his letters, his dossiers, she knows enough to realize that a word let fall by the old man here or there, though it has no connection with the present moment, has one with his work, his reading, his researches, but what people are saying, is it true, is it all so important, the maid is a woman like all the rest, a bit of curiosity is better than none at all, it shows what an interest she takes in her master, he should be grateful to her.

On her way back she stopped at the cemetery, she meditated at her late husband's grave, set to rights the pot of chrysanthemums blown over by the wind, the grave is next to that of her daughter and son-in-law and their youngest and her mother and father, the whole tribe.

Old formulas, old papers, old filth, old chimeras, everything is disintegrating.

And there's something abnormal about that kid, a disguised adult curiosity, always prying, always by himself reading, how can you expect him to be his age, did we read like that, you remember, it was the devil's own job to get us to stick our noses in a book, he's got into bad ways, and anyway the maid tells anyone prepared to listen to her that he has ridiculous ideas, his imagination is in a ferment, he believes he's living the adventures in his novels, he's going to make life difficult for them.

A body without a soul.

His imagination is in a ferment.

Then went back up to his room and started work again, a kind of essay, memoir, or God knows what.

Entries deleted then effaced.

All the June flowers, cornflower, poppy, pheasant's eye, betony, cow-wheat, love-in-a-mist, white campion, centaury, hemp-nettle, coronilla, bugle, St. John's wort, Venus's navelwort, sweet clover, hemlock, honeysuckle, speedwell, broom, water iris, yellow rattle, self-heal, meadow sage, butter-and-eggs, marjoram, delphinium, a fearful avalanche, the voice begins to falter, who will take account of this passionate innocence, the innocence that causes the resurgence of the old myths, cockchafers of despair.

The lilies of the big sleep.

Oasis of the night.

The meeting in the cemetery, that suitcase full of treasures.

Guffaws.

A pause.

All regrets stifled, task accepted, to recompose as a defense against anguish, no matter where it may come from, that unforgotten dream, then finally leave it far behind, an old ceiling cluttered with birds and flowers in the taste of a bygone age, and progress toward the inaccessible without landmarks, without erasures, without notes of any kind, unattainable but present, which must be believed in for fear of never dying.

Make the journey again from one grave to the next, alley number three hundred and thirty-three, side-alley number seven hundred and seventy-seven, find Théodore, chilled to the bone, take him in your arms, warm him up, once again say some kind words to him, his papers, his treasures, say yes to him again, once again make the journey, that calvary, no other way out.

Fiery hues of the chrysanthemums, last blaze before the winter months.

White morning frost, little November sun.

Doesn't time fly, I'd left my topcoat in my hole, Théodore put his over my shoulders, we have, you may remember, many things to look at together, and opened his suitcase again.

Without landmarks, without erasures.

Multiplying the number of the irresponsible.

We shall get the benefit of them gradually with the passing days.

As for the old invalid, he hears a noise in the kitchen, he says who's there, no answer, he begins to worry, can't get up, peace reigned once more when suddenly the man bursts into the room, takes a key from the bedside table and empties the safe of all its gold, then effaces all trace of his visit, puts the key back where it belongs and goes off to make merry in the Antipodes.

Or actually murdered, throat cut with a kitchen knife, they discover him three days later, terrible stink, disorder, everything upside down, the murderer, it's clear, was looking for the key to the safe which is now wide open, the bedside table had been knocked over, he must have had to tug hard to open the drawer which had disgorged its contents into the chamber pot where toothpicks and matches are floating.

What are you saying, his nephew, such a distinguished gentleman.

Tittle-tattle, a different version each time.

The jabbering Parca.

The list of the deceased is getting longer, and the news items, preferably scabrous, like that business of the murder ten years ago which is the spitting image of the one last week, and when I say last, you remember, that old man found dead at the bottom of his bed, his nose in his chamber pot, a butcher's knife planted in his back, the murderer was a so-called nephew who escaped to the Antipodes with the loot, but the maid, who knew plenty about her master's goings-on, when she was tidying up the papers in the study, in spite of having been told not to, is supposed to have seen, apart from the newspapers, some dossiers, like all men of law have, a whole heap of horrible photos of people who'd been strangled or hanged or had their throats cut, enough to give you the willies, the old man really must have been losing his marbles to be interested in that stuff at his age, as if there weren't enough misfortunes and wars in the world, when he doesn't want for anything, him so well served, so well housed.

Was it by poison, or firearms, or strangulation, or drowning, he was absentmindedly pulling the petals off a chrysanthemum.

Low sky, slight drizzle, night was falling, the cemetery is two kilometers away, he was wearing a raincoat, walking fairly slowly so as not to arouse anyone's suspicions as he passed in front of Magnin's, then in front of Thiéroux's, and Dubard's, and Chenu's, might have been going to see his uncle in spite of the late hour, alibi, Madame Dubard saw him, she was at her window, distinctly, just about to close the shutters, was the old man ill.

For to come back to the conversation the master had with Louis, it could only have been about that old man's murder, since the master had claimed he hadn't been there when Louis was talking about it to the maid, unless he had been feinting and actually had heard it but, annoyed by what he was learning had feigned ignorance, yes, with a bit of cross-checking we'll get there, the kid had heard the maid talking about it either to Louis or to her niece so during lunch he comes out with his remark about uncles who have millions, which upsets the old man but doesn't surprise him in the least, he peeled a pear for his godson and said go and eat it in the garden.

Certainly everyone was preoccupied by this business, and with good reason, you say a distant relation, he only saw him once a year, stinking in his hole and as stingy as they come, all his life he had complained about the indifference of his family and friends, expressing surprise that they didn't visit him, that they didn't spoil him, didn't come billing and cooing around him, the old crackpot with all his millions, no one ever saw the color of them, you must admit that puts people off, some of his relations hated him, you know what adults' conversations are like, to harbor grudges against someone for years and years, not surprising that the children take a leaf out of their book and when the day comes avenge the family at one stroke.

What a lot of dead people around us.

The other one saying no you've got it all wrong, that business goes back to the time when Théo was a child, it could only have been another nephew, the mother didn't only have one son, as for the papers discovered in his papers, there's not the shadow of a doubt that they were concerned with murders of old men, or that according to his maid he used to study old dossiers dealing with penal matters that a nephew passed on to him, with plans of apartments, witnesses' statements, interrogations of the accused, borrowed from the office of the Clerk of the Court where his father is a judge, hence the master's brother-in-law, she knew him well, or knew them well, you lost the thread in all that din.

A lady who knew a lady who had seen the fellow in question with her own eyes at three in the morning, or was it Madame Buvard, she was young at the time, was coming home from a dance with her intended, the man had branched off at the corner near the mailbox and started running in the direction of the crossroads, you mean the cemetery, she thought right away that it was fishy, her fiancé went to see in the apartment block, the automatic light was still on, he went up to the fifth floor and that's where he saw . . .

An invisible manitou.

The landing door was ajar, he went down again and said we'd better go and tell the police, there's an old man living on the fifth floor, he's sure to have been burgled, at this hour the night watchman was asleep, we woke him up, he asked us our names and addresses and professions, he almost didn't let us go, my fiancé said it's a fat lot of use being public-spirited with these dimwits, if they come and question you you aren't to say anything if I'm not there.

They did come, Jean-Pierre was still at work, I said I was expecting him, there were two of them, after ten minutes he arrived, we told them everything all over again, they asked us could you recognize the murderer, but at that distance, impossible, even so they summoned us to appear before the judge, my God, when those chaps arrived there was only one thing I was afraid of, that I'd get into trouble on account of my age, I was only seventeen and I was living with Jean-Pierre, I'd given his address at the police station, my parents said they'd tell the police but the gendarmes didn't say anything to me.

She hadn't finished her story, the other lady was in a hurry as she had to go shopping in town, the whole business gave us a shock, he was ninety-five years old, as fit as a fiddle, he still used to go out on Thursdays with his great-great-nephew, such a distinguished young man, no, he wasn't liked, but some people still went to visit him, hoping for a present, he never gave anyone anything, when they read the will they'd all been had, it had been deposited with the notary for forty years and they found an almost identical affair in the papers, with a photo of the murdered man flat on his stomach on his bedside mat, his shirt tucked up so you could see his backside, and the picture of the murderer both full face and in profile, it must be said they all look alike in that blinding light, same boorish, imbecile air, unless all men look like that after a while, same as all wives and all fiancées though with slight differences in their dress, look at those fusty old postcards, would you be able to tell one fashionable woman from another, they all have the same old-fashioned air that our wives will have in the family album, and the cover-girls in the archives of illustrated magazines, and in any case cover-girls aren't exactly distinguished by their tits, don't you think it's disgusting.

Went back up to his room and reimmersed himself in his notes and papers.

Menacing distress.

Say everything again, for fear of having said nothing.

Dossiers dealing with penal matters, with plans of apartments, witnesses' statements, interrogations of the accused.

At such and such a page he turns right, opposite the mailbox, it's the main street, first there's the café, shut at this hour, the street light illuminates the jukebox and the clock which says three o'clock, then the doorway of a second block which he goes into, he uses his cigarette lighter and starts going up, he's wearing espadrilles, when he's arrived at the fifth floor he takes a key out of his pocket and inserts it into the lock, the door opens silently, he goes into the apartment, his lighter is burning his fingers, he puts it out, he waits a few seconds, then slips into the corridor, he gets to the far end of the apartment, he listens, he gently turns the handle of a door, it opens.

Who's there.

I heard something, beating heart, I switch the light on.

There's a pink light in the bedroom, a little lamp alight on the bedside table, he sees the old man asleep, he's pale, his breathing makes a little noise, the air he breathes out makes his cheeks swell a little, he goes over to the bed, there's an armchair, and there's a little table with a jug of herb tea and a cup on it, the dressing gown on the armchair was trailing on the ground, he caught his foot in it, lost his balance and knocked the table over.

Who's there.

The old man gives a little cry, the other man jumps on him and gags him with a scarf, then ties him up in his bed.

His name whispered, he screams, he wakes up sweating in that bedroom where everything is starting all over again.

He brings a big kitchen knife out of his pocket then goes over to the door, he can hear a noise in the corridor.

You can't pretend it was the cat.

He went out into the courtyard, Théo was passing, taking the magazines, the maid shouted you're wanted in the salon.

He woke up with a start, he heard a noise in the corridor, that murmur, he put on his dressing gown, the room was bathed in a pink light, he saw Théodore ransacking the safe, he called out who's there, the other turned around and threatened him with his knife, then the old man collapsed onto the rug.

Action controlled by an invisible manitou.

Asking himself in the nocturnal splendor, December the mirror of the constellations, what's the use of this absurd reading, but questions are out of place now, he picked up the dossier again, not being able to sleep.

Take a hair of the night that bit you.

Finally, the last hypothesis, he goes into the apartment and says in a loud voice, it's me, uncle, and makes his way to the far end of the corridor, he knocks on the bedroom door, enters and greets the bedridden man, how are you feeling, the invalid replies lousy, will you make me some herb tea, the maid didn't have time before she went out, the nephew goes and does the necessary in the kitchen then comes back into the bedroom, pours out the tea and says I'm in difficulties, lend me some money, the old man refuses and that precipitates the drama.

They immediately suspect the maid, they look for her, they find her at her niece's.

He closed the dossier, retraced his steps from the courtyard to the well, from the well to the crossroads, and to the cemetery where he was lost to sight.

Madame Dubard or Buvard was positive that she had seen him go by at that time.

We'll get there in the end with a little method.

Cut.

With stealthy steps he starts along the path to the south, which comes out at the residence after a long detour through the wood, two kilometers at the very least, the pond is on this side, an enormous stretch of water that you can barely make out behind the reeds, the path to the north follows it on the other side at first, then spans it with an ancient bridge, then arrives at the cemetery after less than a kilometer.

The wood lying to the south is very damp, horsetails and ferns, poplars, oaks on the drier terrain on the west side, but the path doesn't go into the wood, it continues on its wide curve across the fungous terrain, it's a good meter higher than this ground, being constructed like a dyke.

Every fifty meters, approximately, there is a kind of boundary stone both to right and to left, which is either the remains of some decorative element or the support for a fence that no longer exists, whether it was a chain fence or a rigid one, the outer edge of the path consists of slippery stones.

Finally you reach a place where you have access to the terrace by way of a second stone bridge which is shorter than the other and made from two arches dating at first sight from the reign of Henri Quatre, but no doubt built on the remains of gothic pillars whose base you can see emerging in the form of a prow.

The residence stands on a rocky platform which on this side, the west that is, has been turned into a balustrade terrace about twenty meters by sixty, and which is prolonged on either side of the edifice by two narrow strips of raised ground of recent construction which gives access to the east, and so far unrestored, side of the terrace, it formerly rose in three tiers of which only the foundations remain, all the decorative work, staircases and fountains having been destroyed during the war, beyond it the marshes begin, terrain that was cultivated in the old days, the river hasn't been canalized and is always flooding, this is what gives its romantic appearance to the landscape on this side of the forest which obstructs the horizon.

Reached the cemetery and remained hidden behind its surrounding wall until nightfall.

While the master, descending the terrace steps, took the north path and then shortly after, having made sure that no one could see him, started along a track that crosses the heathland and ends up at the family vault.

The bad weather had come, the countryside was flooded by the never-ending rain, the mud made all the paths impassable, he shut himself up in his library and only left it at mealtimes.

At such and such a page the maid was in her kitchen, explaining to her niece.

Or that they had by no means found the maid at her niece's, it was a fable to which some people gave credence, you can see why, but well and truly in her bedroom sleeping like a log, she hadn't heard a thing as her bedroom was up in the attic on the servants' floor, which implied that the trouble had been discovered that same night, immediately after the thief made his escape, as the old man had managed to free himself from his gag and alert the whole apartment building.

Another bedroom, there were several.

Or maybe he had simply telephoned his neighbors.

Or maybe these neighbors, coming home at a late hour, had seen his door open, had gone into the apartment . . .

But Madame Dubard claimed that all this was only a fable to which some people gave credence, with her own eyes she had seen the old man turning his bedroom upside down, knocking chairs over, pulling out drawers and emptying them on the floor, in short she wondered whether he wasn't losing his marbles, then had been told by her niece that in the days when he didn't live on his own he'd suffered a cyclothermic crisis as they call it, because she lives in the block opposite, her window looks almost straight into the old boy's bedroom, he never draws his curtains either night or day, his nephew will bear me out.

Because Théodore did indeed live with him in the old days, almost what they call illegal confinement through blackmailing the mother who didn't have a bean, the old man dazzled her with the idea of his inheritance in exchange for the child coming to live with him and the child just had to put up with it, because how can you pretend he had any affection for his uncle, he'd have had to be round the bend, he stayed four or five years after which his mother, discovering that her brother had been taking her for a ride, there was nothing left of his former wealth, took her son back and he never again set foot in his godfather's place.

As for the residence, which had become very dilapidated, it was only the main, Louis Treize part of it that was still habitable, with its graceless facade, its over-tall windows and its slate roof, two wings or recesses on either side were supposed to be undergoing repairs, the one on the right had a collection of reliefs from a medieval monastery in the cellars, storerooms and subterranean corridors that had been dug in the rock and which still exist under the building.

On the north side the little strip of raised ground is linked by a wooden footbridge to a little island where . . .

His beautiful eyes were closing, his head was dropping, what an idea to give a child such insipid stuff to read, the old man rang for the maid who took Théo off and put him to bed.

Dossiers with plans of houses and gardens.

Or that letter addressed no one knows to whom, you keep coming across rough drafts of it.

He was following the track along the water, it was well-tended at the time, that's to say the farmer had been given the job of cutting down the invading reeds and putting stones into the holes hollowed out by the winter weather.

Numerous moorhens and teals are frolicking on the pond.

To the left of the track, after the wood, a few maize fields, then the terrain becomes poorer and the heathland begins, and extends over something like ten kilometers.

He reaches the footbridge, seems to hesitate, looks at his watch and then continues in the direction of . . .

It's three in the morning, there had been a dinner the day before, cars had been seen arriving from eight o'clock on, they took the north path, you know the one, they crossed the big bridge, the only one suitable for motor vehicles, and parked on the terrace where a young manservant, at least we thought it was a manservant, helped them in their maneuvers, it was still light but night fell soon afterwards.

He was following the track along the water one morning, water lilies were in flower on the pond, the hum of a tractor could be heard in the distance, the maize was already high, when he stopped and took a letter out of his pocket, read it and then quickly put it back in his jacket because someone was coming from the opposite direction, it was the farmer, you can't get out of the chore of talking to him about the weather and the harvests, but the farmer had a suspicious air and replied evasively.

A cock and bull story about the master's inheritance, there was no heir, I shall have to take my family and clear out, he replied that there was nothing to be alarmed about, there's nothing more unreliable than rumors, patience, above all, patience.

And that some other people who were killing time in the bistro had also mentioned it after Magnin, or thingummy, what was his name again, had caught sight of the fellow crossing the road, he was sitting in front of the little window, precisely.

When you go into the café you have the counter on your left, an old, very big one made of wood, marble, and zinc, there's room for eight people to stand at it, it doesn't go right up to the corner but stops about one and a half meters away, which reserves a quiet little corner where two or three old men sit, among them the famous Magnin, in front of their Pernod or their dry white wine, under the Byrrh calendar which depicts a lady wearing a big nineteen-thirty hat, there's a houseplant at that end of the counter, it has always got in the way of the waiters.

From this corner of the café you have a perfect view of what goes on in the street.

Right opposite, on the other side of the street, there's a hardware dealer, his store painted blue, on the left a baker's shop, on the right the laundry, the day of the burglary someone remembered having seen a fellow going by at about three o'clock, wearing a raincoat and looking very odd, the habitués had had a lot of theories about that, people said the old man had died of shock but there had been nothing wrong with his heart, according to Louis the waiter.

He apparently didn't go back to the café after his visit to the master, it was his day off, but went for a stroll over by the ponds.

Saying that the Mortin brothers were well-known around these parts, they're respectable folk, the mother was a Levert from Rottard, the sons grew up in a good family atmosphere but they haven't done so well in life, they must have been bone idle, education very often has that effect, the youngest, Alexandre that is, he called himself a poet, he was quite a nice lad when he was twenty, had some elegies and rondeaux published in the Thursday number of the *Fantoniard,* but he was already less fresh at thirty and at forty he irritated the readers, he couldn't make a living from his poetry as you can well imagine, it was his parents who coughed up, and when they were no longer of this world Alexandre was on his uppers, picking up little items of what they call literary work here and there, he had no ambition, no character, no shame, it's heartrending to see a man in that walk of life end up like that, if all the bourgeois set a similar example, he can think himself lucky now he's fifty to have a retired brother who feeds him and pays for his laundry, good old Alfred, now there's one who's worth his weight in gold, he's the one who's most like their uncle, he was never away from his doorstep when he was a child.

Was mixing up the generations.

A missing link.

Got himself bamboozled by his ex, she ran away with a Spanish juggler who'd been doing a turn at the Swan café which goes in for a cabaret on Saturday evenings, a sad story but funny when you come to think of it, Alfred was dancing with a girl cousin while his wife was getting herself screwed in the crapper, she'd gone to have a pee in the ladies and Antonio cornered her there, he was as randy as a rabbit, he'd spotted her in the audience after his number, she was pretty at the time, it was fuck at first sight as Alexandre used to say, and pff the next day she was packing her bags with her seducer plus the jewelry she'd wormed out of that dopey Alfred over ten years, when he got back to his table he waited a while, thinking his wife must have had an upset but finally he went to see at the double U's only she'd gone, he asked everyone if they'd seen her, and when people began to laugh he understood, it wasn't the first time but it was the last.

What does he do all day.

The master was to be seen in the afternoons from three o'clock until half past three on the big terrace, winter and summer alike, taking what they call a constitutional, several times around the flower beds, seemingly engrossed in his thoughts.

And, the niece added, what they're saying, is it true, is that the master is keeping little Théodore there by force, his mama would like to have him with her, but . . .

Or that she had heard tell, how stupid can you get, that they put some sort of drug in Théo's glass in the evenings at dinner and the child immediately fell asleep, they had to carry him up to bed, to which the aunt, bursting out laughing, replied, they, who's they, I'm the one that puts him to bed, the dear little fellow, he's dropping with sleep every evening, you must be mad to believe people's tittle-tattle, what drug, I ask you, do you take the master for a monster or what, he adores Théo.

Adores, adores, that's precisely what they were saying.

Scabrous facts, for preference.

Just like the story of you know who, that they used to tell not so very long ago, what, what story, that old swine, no other word, I'm not talking about the master, who used to hang around waiting for the children to come out of the catechism class, you remember, but what's the connection, I ask you, what sort of mentality is that, ah, talk about the innocence of country people, all they ever think of is evil, I refuse to let you talk to me about that, do you hear.

People are such scandalmongers.

In short, she was working herself up into such a state, poor thing, that you might almost have doubted her sincerity.

And those fellows in the café are no better than the rest, you know what men are like, when it comes to certain types of morals they see red, people say that that tells you a lot about them but what was it he added, oh yes, that the man who was supposed to have been at the window and seen the malefactor running away, why not imagine that he knew him and didn't say a word, what did anyone care about that old crackpot, let the police do their own dirty work, he isn't the first person in our street to be murdered in four or five hundred years, just imagine, one of the oldest in the town, you might almost say that the population too have learned the hard way and don't get into a panic at the sight of one person more or less who's had his throat cut.

So now it was a question of someone who'd had this throat cut.

The other end of the counter curves around too but there's a passage between it and the wall for the barman and the owner's wife who takes care of the cash desk, here too is the trapdoor for the goods elevator that takes the supplies down to the cellar, it gets in everyone's way on delivery days, which gives rise to the odd spat.

A delivery day, precisely, anyone could have sneaked into the back of the bistro where the door to the crappers is and then gone out into the courtyard and from there up into the next-door block, why expect him to have used the big staircase of a bourgeois block with doorman and everything in the middle of the afternoon, simpler to use the service stairs, no.

Poor Alexandre, after his brother's death he inherited the family house which he immediately wanted to live in, I can still see him moving house with a little moving van overflowing with his books and his old papers, the maid had tacked on her own bits and pieces plus the kitchen utensils plus the dog's kennel, the whole lot jiggling and joggling along the little road, they were both sitting in front next to Louis who was driving, little Théo joined them that same evening, accompanied by his mother who was shivering in the dining room, drafts everywhere, the rain was coming through the roof, Magnin had fixed them an oil-burning stove in the little salon for the winter, it cut a sorry figure there, the paneling and tapestries may well be in a terrible state but at least all that still has class.

And then that old halfwit today dragging himself from one salon to the next, calculating the cost of the repairs, you know he hasn't got a bean, but he still talks about maintaining his rank vis-à-vis the neighboring landowners, it's enough to make you die laughing, and in any case he moved a long time before his brother's death, what's that you're saying about him moving, Monsieur Alfred died ten years later, I can still see the funeral, but she was mixing it up with that of Alexandre, my God it's only human, does it matter, and to mix up one move with another . . .

Human, that's the word I was looking for.

To mix one funeral up with another, that's what's staring us all in the face, no offense meant.

A missing link.

Listening to them I felt I was regressing to before the flood, which is the time they still live in.

At such and such a page a time to love, at another page a time to yield up your place.

The poor man took one dossier for another, what didn't he put me through with his checking the index cards, his classifications, his re-sorting, I used to spend weeks on end at it, it tired me out.

Whereas, according to Théo, the old man, after the maid's intervention, took a perverse pleasure in shuffling his index cards like playing cards, and muddling up his papers, not because he had lost his marbles though, still according to Théo, who in the years following his godfather's death had had a facsimile volume of Mortin's notes printed for their friends, which revealed the extraordinary lucidity of the old man.

A candle was burning at the deceased's bedside while the nephew opened the drawers as quickly as possible, looking for the key to the safe where he thought he would find the will, but he only discovered a dud key as if by this joke from beyond the grave . . .

Cut.

Burned in his fireplace, now autumn had come, the duplicates of some reports that were as long as they were insipid, whose originals he recopied during the winter, and then burned the copies again the following autumn.

And also, my goodness, that diary which he took up again a hundred times in the course of his existence, in which he recorded the various states of his soul caused by the coming of night, or that kind of event, some people claim that it was by his brother, they spent long evenings together writing something like the history of their family, I used to hear them asking each other about the date of birth of some of them and the date of death of others, they came of very good stock, being descended from country noblemen through the Quisards of Ballaison, I can remember the Christian name of one of their women ancestors, Josèphte-Françoise-Jéromine, isn't that charming.

But as for the diary, it's Monsieur Alexandre's, I'd go to the stake for that, he was forever pestering me to get me to recollect who he'd met on such and such a day, what he'd done another day, and even what he'd had to eat at his sister's or at the neighbors', or a word, that's right, that I'd heard at the grocer's, he wanted to know who'd said it and why and how, yes, he was always pestering me but I let him, because that man was only happy when he was mulling over his memories, which by the way he often mixed up with other people's memories, there's no denying that, as if everything that came from the past belonged to him as of right, I've never known anyone like him, as I was saying to my niece.

Either as she was saying to her niece, or as her niece was saying to her.

Because contrary to what people make out, it wasn't he who was responsible for Théo being badly brought up it was the mother, who spoiled him rotten, and it wasn't just that it was the uncle who paid and not her, all right I know he was rich but didn't he give the whole family the benefit of it.

Coming back to the horrible episode in the cemetery, Mortin's body found dead one November evening on the stone of their family vault, a butcher's knife planted in his back, when I think of it, it was half past five, something like that, night was falling, the cemetery was shutting its gates, Mademoiselle Passetant was hurrying toward the exit after putting flowers on her parents' grave as she does every year when she noticed a form lying stretched out on a stone, she screamed and didn't dare approach it, she ran to the caretaker who went back with her, he immediately said, as she was pointing out the grave in question from a distance, it was taller than its neighbors, but that's the Mortins' sepulcher, he went over to it on his own for Étiennette was feeling faint, her nerves are bad, she sat down on . . .

She had no idea where she had sat down, oh just for a brief moment, before she rushed over to the gate and got into her parked car, while the caretaker who had a torch recognized Monsieur Alexandre and then went back to his house to telephone the police, it wasn't a butcher's knife planted between his shoulder blades but a flick-knife.

His wallet stuffed full of banknotes, as testified by the bank where Mortin had been that afternoon, and his gold watch, and his signet ring, a sapphire as big as that set in platinum, and his cufflinks, moonstones if you please.

But he was got up like a whore, your Mortin.

In short, it had all disappeared, and what's more, an amusing, if you can call it that, detail, so had his new shoes.

Cut.

But that the caretaker had never seen the corpse, for the reason that he had died that afternoon at the counter, macabre detail, of the bank where he had been to collect his disability pension, Étiennette had found his widow and sons at his house in the state you can imagine, it seems that this man had been a paragon as a father and husband, it was one of his sons who had come and identified Mortin's body, which made a lot of dead people at once, counting the funerals that day, but you can't choose.

Stabbed him in the back while the old man was stooping to straighten up a pot of chrysanthemums, an All Saints' Day as shitty as they come, the man must have hidden behind a monument waiting for night to fall and then, no one any the wiser, gone over the wall opposite the entrance to the cemetery.

Different version each time.

To get nearer to the truth or lose all trace of it, you couldn't hear very well.

The man by the window sees a man cross the street, pass in front of the mailbox, go into the apartment block et cetera, another stands another round, another will stand another, and so on until evening when they all go their separate ways, that's when it isn't nice not to have someone to be going home to but to find yourself alone, wondering what you're doing, a question which leads to another, then another, like the rounds in the bistro earlier, you lose sight of the murderer or the burglar in another version, like the watcher in the café, he too was wondering, then another then another, and so on until when.

At such and such a page the maid visiting her niece.

At such and such a page the corpse on the bedside mat.

At such and such a page he closes the dossier.

At such and such a page she took the child off and the master wakes up out of his nightmare.

At such and such a page saw himself again with Théo in the cemetery sitting in front of the suitcase and undoing one of the piles of newspaper cuttings, looking for subjects for essays.

The slate, always come back to that.

A missing link.

Because personally, his illness, you can imagine how well I knew it, every morning the same old story, after the description of his dreams and nightmares he used to review the worries of the previous day, foresee those of the day, fear those of the following day, and the dead people in the newspaper, the list of the deceased is getting longer.

Corpses, cemeteries, a taste of putrefaction even in the rice I used to cook for him.

Say everything again, yes, for fear of . . .

On the slate they find regression of desire.

Painful anamnesis.

The days slimy, the horror of memory.

The underground passages are being hollowed out, exchanges now take place only in the opaque shadows.

Despair apparently essential for the desired mutation.

All regrets stifled.

His hands tied from now on to the words it is retracing.

As for Alexandre, as I was saying, he lived with his brother in their family house for many years, how many, my goodness, she didn't know anymore, you don't keep count of what happens to other people.

Or that she remembered what the maid had told her at the time, about the continual difficulties between the two brothers who each had his own idea about the education of their nephews, because at one moment Alfred was especially interested in Léo and Alexandre in Théodore, was it after their mother's death or before, people said she had no maternal feeling but I'd be more inclined to think that it was because she was on her uppers, absolutely impossible for her to feed that horde of children, as she said to the grocer's wife.

The contradictions you find everywhere once you stop to think.

It must have been a Sunday, then, and the ladies were talking religion, sacrament, Mass, miracle, hospital, pharmacy, salpingitis, psspss, at the grocer's, awaiting their turn, carrots haven't done too well this year but on the other hand the salsify, what, do you still cook that muck, I gave it up twenty years ago, anyway they say it causes cancer.

Because personally, his illness, his brother died of the same thing, it was congenital, the whole family had had a few spells in the asylum, the mother was as mad as a hatter and the grandmother was the same, in short it had carried Alfred off, an acute fit, but she couldn't remember whether it was Théo or Léo who had inherited the family house.

The same one who the previous Sunday had bought the frozen shrimps, and mussels today, they've always liked seafood, saying poor Marie, I do hope she doesn't catch her death of cold, she isn't as strong as she looks, because the grocer's wife had gone off the day before to her mother-in-law's funeral a hundred kilometers away in an unheated car, and churches, you know what they're like, the daughter-in-law was waiting on the ladies, the young one I mean, that was why things weren't going very quickly, she isn't very bright.

And the other lady it must have been, just a minute, no, I don't remember, she said, but don't you realize there isn't a word of truth in what she says, what, after all this time are you still her dupe, her dupe, what do you mean by that, I mean that she lies to you and you're a great ninny to have let your head be stuffed full of such ideas for so long, at your age, can you imagine.

A fat lot of good it did her to ferret through the papers, she . . .

Or, going back to all the subjects the old man kept trotting out to anyone who would listen to him, that of his death for example, or of his brother's death.

Or else, someone point-blank, at least this is my interpretation, someone there like a pebble in a pond who would go on relating that otiose, never-ending story in which the only thing discussed would be putting an end to it, finishing it, cutting it short.

And wherever he happened to be he would never hear people talk of anything but that, was it his own end or someone else's, or everyone's at the same time, you see the kind of thing.

Or rather the fruit of silence all of a sudden, the voices fall silent, the world collapses.

Which could be observed by going back to the letters, the notes, the evidence in question.

Impossible to end, impossible not to end, impossible to continue, to stop, to start again.

To be something other than this accumulation of drifting nothings.

What conjuring tricks you had to get up to in order to make anything understood there.

All that crossed out, deleted, effaced.

The repetition of facts from one age to the next, only a few years' interval and everything starts again, the voices are no longer the same but the words are, and hence the events as they unfold, from the dullest to the most dramatic, from the sweetest to the most bitter, so that a carefully worked-out chronicle . . .

Take another dossier and, here, read it, there, at that page.

The child started reading again.

The witness questioned states that he had only known the old man during the period when he was living alone, after the death of his brother that is, he is unaware of the existence of the brother, which seems surprising in such a close-knit society, everyone knowing everyone else's business, but as for Théodore, he says he remembers perfectly having made his acquaintance at the . . .

. . . who told him about meeting the young man in the cemetery one All Saints' Day, he was going to put some flowers on the grave of . . .

At the what, the grave of whom.

The names have been effaced.

Go on.

. . . and that he told him at the end of his life something he had never had a chance to tell anyone, that is, his reactions toward what he himself would have called problems, but which our times had solved, both within the domain of instincts . . .

Articulate properly, sit up straight.

. . . main of instincts and their implications in the moral order, and within that of metaphysics and its impact on the balance of the mind, he nevertheless remained perplexed when he observed that the light of reason did nothing to dispel the shadows of . . .

The child had fallen asleep, and the maid . . .

The old man picked up the document and in a sudden inspiration decided to sort out his old papers.

Then suddenly nothing left on the slate, nothing left in the dossiers, the registers, not a single line, blank sheets.

No trace anywhere of the torment, what should it be called, distress, or fever, or pain.

Was it grief.

Something importunate.

Nothing left.

Vanished.

It happened just before dinner, he was already at table, annoyed that his nephew had canceled his visit, old people dread solitude and the habits they adopt to ward it off are sacred, as they say, in short, he's hardly sat down when pff, he takes a header into his plate, Marie was just coming in with the soup, they laid him down on the sofa right away, who's they, she and Monsieur Alfred, and the telephone always on the blink, when the doctor arrived he was coming round, he asked for Théodore.

Or whether she was confusing it with the second heart attack, it seems to me that the first one was only a slight malaise, the third one on the other hand was fatal but we haven't got there yet, and a packet of washing powder, she added, it's like with my sister, what a fright she gave us even though we were expecting it, she'd got so frail, the old people's home hadn't done her any good, when they can stay in their own homes they last longer, that's unless they get themselves stabbed like that old man, what was his name again, last year, you remember, all by himself with his head in his chamber pot.

In his plate, in his chamber pot, something was wrong somewhere, but just think, at his age and in the state he was in, still writing reports, not surprising that it was all as clear as mud.

A new washing powder, it's been advertised so much on the television that you're tempted to try it, it's only human, a sou is a sou, there's no such thing as small economies, oh, you remind me of my mother.

She went back into her kitchen where she cried her eyes out thinking of it, it was All Saints' Day, it's understandable.

She wasn't so very fond of apples, personally, stewed fruit, except for those red ones there used to be, you remember, châtaignes, they were the best cookers, you just boil them up for a few minutes and there you are, you can't find them anywhere these days, there's nothing but golden delicious in the whole market, there was a terrific crowd, that music in the streets, that's new, have you seen the little woollies on the stall outside the Magasins-Prix, they're letting them go for twenty francs, I finally found some shoes that fit me, I can't wear heels anymore, the shape they make them these days my muscles would never stand up to it, can you imagine, my toes have seized up, massage, nothing's any good, it'll be my cross, you have to have at least one, what was I saying, the poor woman, yes, did you know that she'd left her daughter on the Friday to go and stay with her son and on the Saturday morning her daughter-in-law takes her up her coffee, she was already cold, that pretty little room Magnin had fixed for her in the attic, I heard it yesterday from Madame Moine, and I'll take this lettuce too.

Fresh flowers, clients, salesman, a chilly morning, here we were in November again.

For a dinner of that importance, all the local bigwigs, but there was no longer all the fuss there used to be in the old days, less expense and less of the real upper crust, the heroic days are far off, abracadabra.

Cut.

They arrived in full dress, one evening, through the forest, in open carriages harnessed with larger than lifesize horses, you couldn't hear them on the gravel, the occupants got out and climbed the steps up to the main entrance where the master was waiting for them under the vault wearing a carnival mask, they paraded past him for hours and then dispersed into the salons, and he said I recognized you, you can't bamboozle me, for in fact those fine gentlemen had concealed their faces too, out of consideration for their host, they were no longer really there, they were simply the medium for the old man's obsessions, his papers, his nightmares.

What a lot of dead people around us.

The maid got out of a carriage coming from her niece's, she went up the steps, he was waiting for her under the vault in full evening dress, she inquires after the deceased and goes into the bedroom with its black crêpe hangings, the fine gentlemen stand in a circle around her, the room was filled with a pink light, she brought some more suitable candles, and he was looking through his papers to find those concerning the deceased but there was a page missing on which the hour, the date, the place, the circumstances were written.

No one ever knew what he died of, according to Léo it was a heart attack, his third, found with his head in his plate, according to Théo in his chamber pot, according to Monsieur Alexandre with a knife between his shoulder blades, but at the time he was questioned he was already losing his wits.

Poor Monsieur Alfred, we were very fond of him, always effacing himself, in the shadow of his brother, he had an exaggerated admiration for him, when you think how spiteful Alexandre was, all the work for that review, what was it called again, that was interested in their family and the history of the place it had lived in for generations, all the work, yes, had been done by Alfred but signed by his brother, a glib talker who frequented this one and that, boasted of his efforts, complained about his . . .

Alfred who spent his whole life on his researches between Fantoine and Agapa, town halls and presbyteries, for their registers, but also all the stories going around about this one and that as far as Sirancy where they still had some family, pages and pages of notes, sketches, plans, which Alexandre used to consult unmethodically to give people the impression that he knew all about it but which he made a shambles of, this didn't make Alfred's work any easier, he never complained, you can understand why after his death the other couldn't find his way around in them, and that the chronicle, that was the word I was looking for, came to an abrupt end.

After that it was the period of Alexandre's delirium, he used to go the rounds of the cemeteries, you can imagine the sort of thing, you might well wonder who would ever write its history, it looked as if there would be no one but that cook who was losing her marbles at the time she was being questioned, ever since then any sort of evocation being devoted to . . .

That package of jumbled-up pages looking as if they'd been hit by a hurricane, what patient hand would restore it to order.

A missing link.

An invisible manitou.

Or else the nephew, which of the two, goodness how they bored us with that mythological figure, Uncle Alexandre, the old crackpot, there was nothing to be proud of.

To relive one of Mortin's days in that house, not that one, the other one, to go into all the details, salon, dining room, corridor, hall, yes really it was enough to make you lose your marbles.

Enough to make you believe that the deceased had only ever existed in the mind of a dangerous maniac.

To make it go down to posterity as Alfred's creation, but what of the memory of the survivors, then, those who were still around to be questioned, they remembered Alexandre as someone exceptional, inoffensive yes, sickly yes, furtive yes, but nevertheless there in their midst from this date to that, as his epitaph testified.

As if the dead man by that joke from beyond the grave were using the only power that remained to him to reproduce endlessly the image of his failures.

Two or three words, you can't hear very well, at your slightest movement piles of documents collapse, cuttings fall out, muddle up the words, waste of time, lack of method.

And the grandmothers, the grandfathers, the great-great ones, not forgetting the lateral branches, the children of, the children of, the whole tribe in the drawers, the wardrobes, the closets, he'd lost his specs, or was it a retouched photo of an uncle by marriage, what was his name again, I must have it in a notebook, a beautiful frame with a colored border in artificial tortoiseshell with wavy silver lines.

Or those visits to Aunt Marie for the New Year, her fritters were marvelous and she made her own tonic wine from essence of quinquina, a charming stout lady, a bit reddish, wore a wig, a little girl's voice, perfect diction, what memories she had, never left her kitchen, she lived in an annex of the ancestral house, their coat of arms in the armorial of our province, very corpulent, yes, wasn't there perhaps a smell of, note the refinement of the decor, of that little brownish-red dish, you can't find those anymore, wallflowers maybe, the garden will be full of them in a month.

He went on looking in the notebook for the name of the grandmother's brother, or of the sister of the one who . . . while they were looking at the details of the angular yellowish face, deep-set, very pale grayish-blue eyes, as if they were inwardly fixed on a disappearing landscape, problematical paradise, aquiline nose, very little hair, he's always in his dressing gown.

While they were changing something in the order of the, would it be pages or passages, you can't hear very well, last moments, a question of killing what remains of them, personally his habit of never finishing his phrases gets me in such a state.

As for the nephews, how many times did I tell him you spoil them too much, you'll turn them into delinquents, as if not spoiling them could change the fundamental rottenness of their nature, the little hoodlums.

She added, where have I put my glasses, I can't see a thing, what you could do to make yourself useful, here, the dust on all these little frames, I'm getting tired, they went downstairs, the aunt and the niece I mean, into the hall, the old woman was dragging her steps, I must go and see to the onions, she said, they adore that, a nice tart, and then you do the dishes, put an apron on, where did you find that little blouse, it's charming, those flowers with a big M embroidered over the left titty, she's called Marie as well, in short all the household worries, a fine November morning, no, doesn't time fly, the end of February, they'd already celebrated Candlemas, go over it all again from the beginning, from before the beginning, the central event, phenomenal upheaval, concierge's terminology but we'll get there in the end with a little method.

To reflect other people's hidden truth, as if our own mannerisms and obsessions could only create people who don't resemble us.

To give an idea of the vagueness that seemed to him to emanate from the spectacle.

The old man, cut to the quick, what vagueness, do I exist or don't I, shit, what more do you want, certificates, sworn statements, aren't there enough people around me, maybe there's not enough furniture, not enough junk.

Mythological figure of Uncle Alexandre.

Problem concerning Uncle Alfred, something wrong there.

Those people who run around from one folder to the next in the dossiers.

As for the house, he apparently never even lived in one until a few days before his death.

Remarks which certainly seemed somewhat long-winded to us, but who would have suspected that he was already not quite right in the head, such a clean, nice little old man, so levelheaded, so punctual, that work he had been doing so methodically for half a century, surely that was a reference, poor Monsieur Alphonse, I can still see him coming back from the library at a quarter past noon, with his bum-freezer frayed at the elbows, his leather briefcase under his arm, with the other one he used to raise his hat politely to his numerous acquaintances, at that hour everyone was going home to lunch, and with what amiability he accepted a drink in the café, always sitting in the corner near the window on the left as you went in, with the men he still used to call his pals, they used to tease him, they got him to drink one too many and he became so merry it broke your heart, telling about his youth, the pranks he used to get up to as a student, the Saturday evening dances, the war, the ration coupons, all this in an adorable confusion, his little pince-nez on a little ribbon failing off his nose, he would smooth his little moustache and repeat the story of the sick little elephant and the little mouse, what was it again, that story.

It seems that his maid used to give him a good hiding when he came home tipsy.

His maid, do you mean the first or the second.

He never had more than one until a few days before his death, poor fellow, and I'll take that piece of pumpkin as well.

Careful, you're on the wrong page.

No, it's the same one, what's pumpkin.

Go on.

He was lapsing into second childhood, memories assail you, two or three moments' inattention, bang, it's soon done, ah, he wouldn't have been the one to oppose the idea of evoking one of his days, not he, poor little angel, at six o'clock it was the first feed, his mama could barely open her eyes, exhausted as she was by all her housework, never in bed before midnight, you know what it's like when you're breast-feeding, the sound sleep you fall into just at the moment when the kid starts whining, quick she pulls him out of his crib so that the father, for Christ's sake, shitting hell, come on my love, bares her breast, shoves the nipple in his mug, how often have I fallen asleep with the brat on top of me, after that it's the father's turn, half the time he misses the pot he's supposed to be pissing into, even so couldn't you go as far as the WC in the morning, he managed to find some pretext for his filthy language, a sock under the bed, or a button coming off his pants, he's got a belly now, does yours . . .

And that he should have gone like that when he was in perfect health, everything was like clockwork, his liver, his stomach, his intestines, no one ever knew what of, according to his maid it was a sudden bad chill, according to the doctor it was some filthy thing he'd had for years, it didn't stop him doing his work every day, I used to see him on his way to the cemetery, his greasy little hat on top of his head, for that business of the concessions, a government employee I believe in the department of the deceased, what's it called, was he going to check on where the graves were, their upkeep, what space was available, the person who could have told us was the caretaker, he died last week.

And Monsieur Théodore, what could he have told us on this subject, he only knew him very late in life, already on his way out, practically gaga, it was an act of charity he was doing him, sorting out his papers, you can't imagine the disorder and lack of interest of it all, he used to collect any old printed stuff, he was incapable of throwing away even an advertising leaflet, Théo really went through the mill, to put all that junk away in suitcases in little piles, little bundles held together with string or rubber bands, et cetera, the old man never went out without taking a bag or a leather briefcase full of those papers, he went from bistro to bistro getting plastered, people took him for a down-and-out salesman, it happened more often than it should that he got thrown out by the waiter when he'd had a skinful and he used to sit for hours on a bench in the park, or else, when it was cold, take refuge in the post office and snooze against the radiator before he got his wits back and went home where he didn't even have anything to . . .

What are you saying, I tell you you're on the wrong page.

The little head dropped forward, the beautiful little eyes closed, and the maid . . .

Then they went over the text again together and saw that it was right after all, it was just that the child had skipped one or two lines, really, for one or two lines, no need to make a drama out of it.

And it was the same with restoring the decor, he found it impossible, it's all very well telling yourself that such and such an object was there, such and such another there, or even having a detailed photo of the place, restoration doesn't depend on the material elements you have at your disposal but on something very different, and anyway, restoration, what does that mean, and who does it interest, one imposture more or less, the uncle wasn't going to come back to life to order.

That voice on the slate which is becoming effaced.

As for the remarks about the family, the greedy, guzzling, insatiable family, no text, no paper, but the sound of things said, re-said, forbidden to be said from one generation to the next, which are swarming in the accursed head of the scapegoat of the herd.

Slaughter the animal before contagion sets in.

Or tie the heretic to the stake.

The procession of masks paraded through the corridor, then went out through the garden and got back into the carriages which drove off noiselessly, leaving the master alone under the vault, she heard his sobs, nothing impresses Monsieur Léo, she said, when Monsieur Albert took to his bed he didn't even call the doctor, it was left to me to telephone but it was too late, the harm had been done, we never really knew what it was all about, and the other said even so, listen, couldn't you make an effort, who was that Albert again, didn't we have enough with Alphonse, and Alfred, and Alexandre.

Cut.

They'd got to the evocation of the gala dinner which was supposed to recall the former splendors, but how could they suggest them with the facts at their disposal and in that framework of a sadness that almost kills you, we mustn't ask the impossible of them.

And then the great figures became blurred, became symbolic, no matter what you did the hour was past, the heart was no longer in it.

When my niece came to tell me that, I said at once let's wait a bit before we break the news, Monsieur Alfred might well have a heart attack, we must find the right way, and above all the right moment, but he didn't react the way I feared, after all he's getting old too, a touch of indifference came to his aid, no, definitely, nature hasn't done things too badly, and he said thank you, we'll wait until tomorrow to go and see him, people's temperatures go up in the evening, he'll be calmer in the morning, and he asked me to bring him the herb tea they drink every evening at half past ten, my niece stayed with me until half past eleven.

That evening confused with the one she spent ten years later with her niece in almost identical circumstances but apropos of Monsieur Alexandre's end, very distressing days which hadn't helped her poor brain, she's in an old people's home now as you know, her end seems to be never-ending, I hardly ever go to see her these days, it upsets me, she hasn't recognized me for years, really, nature, what bad workmanship, what a wretched thing.

Imagining himself in ten years' time, thinking back to this day, the everyday things, the people he'd loved, there'll be no one left but the person thinking back to what he imagined then, waste of courage, mind wandering, desire obliterated.

But Marie said to him, what is Monsieur thinking of, does he remember at this moment what he imagined ten years ago, surely not, we forget, look at me, my poor husband, the first one I mean, I can barely remember his voice, the color of his eyes, whatever Monsieur may say the imagination is two-edged, let him use it for his memoirs but in life it's a waste of time.

Imagination in place of memory.

Memory in place of imagination.

The days slimy.

Impossible anamnesis.

They'd finished the soufflé, I was in my kitchen waiting for them to call me but the bell didn't ring, there were still the endive and the cheese to serve, I was getting impatient and then I began to worry, all of a sudden I saw them both immobilized, sitting opposite each other, they'd had a heart attack, I headed for the dining room, I listened at the door first, I didn't hear them talking, I open the door, there was no one there, the table had been cleared, everything was in order, the clock said three o'clock.

It was at this period that she started being unable to sleep, she used to prowl around at night from her bedroom to the kitchen, she noted down on the slate whatever came into her head, she went back to bed and in the morning she couldn't read what she'd written, she quickly got scared, she effaced it with the sponge, or else . . .

Apparently they found on her bedside table drafts of letters she had taken out of the master's wastebasket, and cuttings from newspapers which mentioned, but I . . .

Impossible to hear yourself speak in this din, dangerous crossroads, why don't we go and sit in the square for a moment, it's going to be a nice day.

And indeed the first signs of spring were in the air, the blackbird this morning, the cold less cutting, the daffodils in bud, a certain resonance between the houses, a certain light, in short the ladies went and sat under the war memorial, a brand new bench, they put their bulging shopping bags down beside them and talked once again of that prehistoric story that had shattered everyone, they'd been in a real nightmare, they were suspicious of their neighbors, they didn't dare go out after nightfall, but it was all so allusive and mixed up with present day preoccupations that a third person who wasn't in the know wouldn't have understood a word.

That's the way life is in a little country district, the stranger is lost there, their habits have been formed since time immemorial, woe betide anyone who doesn't conform to them.

Like the life of people's brains, at that, a different organization, a different balance, the amateur can only find his way around them with difficulty, and she compared the brain to a soufflé, you put it in the oven at around the age of reason, it rises very gently, it swells, it dilates until it gets to the age of manhood, which varies with every individual, then it gradually sinks and ends up quite flat, or else burned, which was certainly the case with Marie and her master, what's going to become of them, I was only speaking of it the other day to Mademoiselle Moine who said that in serious cases where there's no family the mayor has to intervene but he'd never dare risk it after all the tales you hear about madmen barricading themselves into their houses, she could already see Monsieur Alexandre and his maid armed with shotguns refusing access to the castle.

As for Monsieur Léo, we have very few souvenirs of him left, that photo as a soldier, and a pair of trousers and a pullover in his wardrobe which have been there for thirty years, as well as the little drawings pinned onto his bedroom walls which he did as a child, and the painting of the harvest when he was a young man, and even his hairbrush on his dressing table had belonged to his grandmother, no one has touched them, he left us when he was twenty-five, at first he wrote from America, and then less and less, and finally nothing at all until the announcement of his funeral.

He loved the mountain, that blue one over there, oh dear, its name escapes me, but all you could see through the window was the little garden and the fields up to the forest.

Cut.

Work of trial and error, of fresh starts, of hypotheses, no trace on the slate, and yet words were written, they appear somewhere, the limbo of the discourse to be explored, noting down those scraps, then effacing them with the sponge, searching for a problematic, urgent redemption, step by step, keep hold of the handrail here.

She listened behind the door to the child reading, he stumbled at every sentence, the master gave a little cough, he poked the fire, he poured himself out a cup of herb tea, the little voice grew fainter, the old man said go on, then he rang.

Those voices that come back to you.

No longer finds any comfort in them.

A deep, inner joy that doesn't . . .

Make a note on the slate, leeks, washing powder, soap.

She went back to her stove, as if propelled by an old spring, but at that period it was a long time since she had cooked anything just for herself in her kitchen where we used to go and visit her at New Year.

What's marvelous is fritters with sugar.

She used to make her own tonic wine, using concentrated essence of quinquina.

A slightly unpleasant smell of clothes that had been worn, and of mold and frying, a crocheted antimacassar was fastened to the back of the armchair with double-pointed gilt pins to conceal a grease mark, maybe the uncle's head when he took his nap there.

And then, insofar as what concerns us, the end of a period of metaphorical tergiversations, of individual malaise, which had given rise to certain so-called poetic developments, all that was so long ago that when you leafed through the manuscript you were seized with vertigo at so much totally wasted activity, ah yes the end of an era, roll on the next one and to hell with our nephews.

Théo said, it was useless me searching through the papers, I didn't find the slightest indication of any dates, impossible to establish any sort of chronology, either Uncle had systematically muddled them all up, or more likely he wrote down several samples of his bizarre thought when he was relatively young, and all he did later was return to them as the whim took him, so no development.

What conjuring tricks he had to get up to but it was only fair to his uncle, after all he owed him his fortune, his education, his house, his place in society, do you really think he could ever have managed that on his own, or pushed by his parents, you must be joking, by the way what became of them, wasn't the mother a bit mad, it was congenital, yes, or else contagious, since the maid . . .

All alone in her kitchen, not a living soul to talk to, have you seen the price of oysters, where are the days when I used to buy them every Sunday, even so you can't live on cod the whole year around, what times we live in, in the old days it was Good Friday, that's going to be in two weeks isn't it, doesn't time fly, not nearly so cold, no, you'll be with the family for the holiday won't you, didn't Magnin fix you up a little room in your son's house.

Her daughter-in-law brought her her coffee in the mornings, really spoiled, she would have liked to stay there a couple of weeks but you can't impose yourself on people, people, what people, am I people, she answered, her daughter had planted her beans too early, they may get caught by the frost this year, she would put in some begonias.

The repetition of facts from one age to the next, this never-ending story, life is just a few years of drifting nothings.

Or the fruit of silence suddenly.

Entry deleted.

Concentrated his attention on those papers, a whole maniacal existence in which he recognized his own, page after page, the terrors of the old man who used to get up in the middle of the night to make a note of his obsessions, Théo's education, the bills to be paid, the remembrance of goodness knew whom, mixed up, when he was having nightmares, in an overwhelming confession of helplessness, the familiar illness, the fight, step by step, against its ascendancy, and the delirium finally recorded at the same time as the humble everyday duties.

Do you understand what you're reading.

No M'sieur.

Go on.

The mountain, that blue one over there, the smell of junipers and geraniums.

The whole so allusive that you completely lost the thread, then why go on listening.

She was standing behind the door, imagining Théodore one fine day dealing with the master's papers, invalidating page by page the legend the old man had woven around his family, his person, and his occupations, he too would get caught up in the game and then it would be his turn to use his own existence to pulverize that of his uncle, vanity too is contagious.

To pulverize, that's to reduce to dust.

Legend, something that has to be read.

These written words that appear somewhere, we'll get there in the end with a little method.

Step by step, this redemption.

So that everyone would have contributed to mixing things up, what an idea anyway to bring the packet of old papers up to date, would it have been Théo who had it, it's hard to see who else to attribute it to since we haven't had anymore news of Léo, and as for Alphonse, Alfred, and other Alberts, in short I can still hear the master saying to me, what do we know of the truth, where do you think it hangs out, down the well stark naked, poppycock, in the heads that their owners call cool, certainly not there either, the truth requires secret places to hide in, what did he mean with his secret places.

Doesn't time fly, yes, it'll soon be Easter.

That voice, even Marie's that you can hardly recognize, we really are going to have to appeal to Théodore but there's no hurry, patience, patience.

And if the great figures become blurred and the heart isn't in it anymore we'll find another angle.

In any case, when they came to tell him that the uncle had had a heart attack she immediately linked it to that of the brother, that was years before when everything was still in place, I mean in working order, the way of life in the gentlemen's house, guests, visitors, servants, the alterations, the improvements, the tenant farmers to deal with, the neighbors to be polite to, people just don't know the kind of worries that arise from this kind of idle life, you can call it that in comparison with the life of the laboring classes.

And taking advantage of a moment's inattention to get in a remark about it's just life, something like that, after all since it's necessary, but regretting it very quickly because there are some words that stick in your throat.

Or trying to mention the day and the time, that mild April, a pause in his absurd movement toward what.

Only too easy to epilogue on destiny, nothingness, the nothing-you-carry-with-you, and the illusion of accomplishing anything whatever.

Cut.

Or of the opposite movement, which reimmersed him at that time in the procession of masks, figures and symbols, a whole section of collapsing memory, what were they actually, those characters who so absorbed us with their worries, their copulations and their funerals.

Uncle Alexandre, that old crackpot.

The so-called nephews, those little hoodlums, cheap gigolos who went from one old man to the next for the price of their not so fresh youth.

Ugly soul, rotten to the core.

Those moments of truth, were they any better than the others, those of the fable, you might well ask yourself.

In short, the excellent Théo had great difficulty shaking off the master's chimeras.

It seems that Madame Marie gives him a helping hand when he needs one, she still has all her wits about her, and when he isn't sure where to place this or that event in relation to another she comes out with her opinion, which facilitates the work.

As for me, I can still see him, our drunkard, with his suitcase full of advertising leaflets, he had them in all shapes and sizes and on all subjects, he went and picked them up in printing shops and out of dustbins, a job that filled an entire existence, he used some for toilet paper, he used to distribute them very ceremoniously in the bistros against a glass of red, he'd completely lost his bearings, the local people used to laugh at him.

And when he was home in the evenings, he fed his folly by classifying his leaflets, the vacuum cleaner pile, the washing machine one, the electric iron one, the razors, the potato-mashers, the peelers, the crushers, the concrete-mixers, the beauty preparations, the health ones, the hygienic ones . . .

Try to disentangle reasons for false trails.

In other words, to find out why the manuscript is stuffed full of information likely to mislead anyone who consults it.

The uncle's motives in doing this.

Fundamentally a very ordinary story of an old artist whose imagination has deserted him and who is trying to get by with subterfuges, complications of form, fancy writing, pretensions to metaphysics and symbolism, why the hell do we have to go in for all that, Théodore said to himself, and nevertheless went on with his tidying up.

Until the day when he realizes that he himself has become this juggler at the end of his tether, and that the story of this contorted, concocted, controversial manuscript is now well and truly his own, Mortin reincarnated in his nephew, marvelous, you should have seen how . . .

Potbellied, my dear, hawking and spitting and not even clean in his person, ah, how right they are when they say . . .

Yes indeed, you wouldn't think it, that poor old man, but I tell you, haven't you noticed the way he looks at women, psspss, well it amuses *me*.

Radishes were in season now, and new potatoes and asparagus, doesn't time fly.

And, said Mademoiselle Moine, after all why should I bother my head, my sister-in-law isn't a princess, at that price I can't afford to buy more than one bundle, it was always one of my mother's principles . . .

To which Madame Dubard replied, I agree with you, brought up the way we were it mortifies us to see the way they squander money these days, I'm going to wait another two weeks, whereupon the other said, after all so am I, my sister-in-law isn't a princess, and she put the asparagus back on the stall, the grocer's wife was amused and told them they were right, but she has to keep a bit of everything for the townspeople who come for weekends, they don't care what things cost.

Lapse into second childhood, that's easy to say, he said, but I was the one he bored to death every morning telling me his dreams and I tell you he was foundering in it, and all his fancy writing, pretension, complication, administration . . .

Cut.

The thing is, I'll tell you . . .

Cut.

The thing is, what is there to say . . .

Cut.

The thing is that I, no longer the same, no, phenomenon, yes, overwhelming, what bad luck, poor child, so nicely, all of a sudden, his head, putrefaction, phoenix, a phoenix all right, but the difficulty . . .

These walls, lids, shackles.

As if the adventure, poor child, wasn't the same for everybody.

To pulverize, that's to reduce to dust.

Legend, something that has to be read.

Step by step, this redemption.

Yes but, well, me, those as deny it, I understand them.

The whole so allusive, alas, no other way.

Sweet April is on its way out, the harm has been done, the action is starting all over again.

No longer the same, easy to say, luckily there's the dream, and your method, you know where you can put it . . .

Do you understand what you're reading, no, go on, personally I'm quite willing to take up the thread again, just to pass the time, doesn't it . . . and his greasy little hat on his crown, looking for, to haunt the cemeteries, clever, to check there that he's really dead, next week, not to be able to hear, duty, duty, this alarming imposition, I agree with you that in one sense, until we have more information, taking the circumstances into account, let's see, adjusted his little pince-nez at the end of its little ribbon, and that's what after so many years of hard labor . . .

Sweet April, yeah.

Bad luck, yeah.

Dream, oh benediction, come.

The time when he suddenly appeared out of a pumpkin, we shall see, we shall hear, we shall, yeah, remake our phrases, the only way to liquidate them.

A grand phrase that would have to be relinquished so as to shine out beyond the frightful cemetery.

So Monsieur Théodore still aping, still applying himself to discover the reason, in all that crap, given that it was all chance, I don't mind, even though not so very pure, why some passages were so obscure, he makes a discovery when he puts on his uncle's pince-nez, but there, how to explain it, something kind of occulted by . . .

Traces of effacement.

Then, putting them on the wrong way around, something else occulted by . . .

Then just one eye for one lens and for the other, then the other eye for the other one, and for the first one, a staggering discovery, but how to explain it.

So perturbed that he puts himself not in Monsieur Alexandre's eye, but in his ear.

This time the discovery is indescribable, which shows that his pitch was not that of the conservatoire.

He must have suffered from a buzzing noise in his ears, he said, but can you be satisfied by that sort of evasion.

He became so cheerful it was enough to break your heart, he came out of his room saying it must be occulting an era that's just beginning, the snag of the ana-time in which I am still struggling.

Ah, these poets.

The blue mountain comes back and the smells of . . . ah, what was Monsieur Alexandre's nose like, possibility of nasal expression, he was so sensitive, so close to nature, all the more so as it turns out that his lucubrations were only produced a few days before his death.

And to come back to those little hoodlums, how many times didn't we catch them in the mornings, don't cut me off, fiddling around with each other, you should have seen it, not a bit embarrassed or ashamed, Madame Marie was quite right to say that it was their education, punishment, damnation, what the hell did it have to do with us, boys will be boys, that had spoiled them rotten, but the content, what do you make of that, with details to back it up, to give a bit of spice to his insipid pages, he was well aware of it, the old crackpot.

So then looked for the said details among the jumble of notes but could find nothing but entries crossed out, effaced, what a pity, we could have made some dough out of those revelations, although these days that sort of thing is a bit overrated don't you think.

And it's not exactly, the other woman continued, beside herself with fury, as if he deprived himself of the pleasure of stuffing it up his nephews' assholes, the old bugger, even so you aren't going to tell me . . .

Jesus, you ought to be ashamed.

In short, truth lies within other people, and apropos of assholes, on Candlemas, or Cometopass, or ComettoMass day . . . oh, I give up . . . I need, look, a dart here, pointing to her breast, and the opening should come down to here, and as for the length I leave that to you, but the other couldn't see very well, then he puts down his glasses and he wonders, is it a symbol, I've never appreciated that sort of thing either, but what can one do against the inevitable, a few days before his death.

Occulting an era that's just beginning.

Because death, what can it be the symbol of, eh, you can't answer.

Multiply its occurrences, that's all one can do.

Those of my uncle in any case, we haven't skimped on their number.

When for example I . . .

Théo gets back into his uncle's old harness and provides a sequel to that confused mass of notes, marginal comments, scraps and memories, and Marie, who spies on him, hears him, on the evenings when he's got very excited, cursing the dead man, a fine example of loyalty to his memory.

His uncle, his uncle, an old whoremonger neither more nor less, and the young man, he's nothing to boast of, even so it's about time the facts were put straight, what's all that ridiculous highfalutin stuff, hm, asparagus has gone down but eggs, what's the matter with them this year, maybe the Dutch hens are taking the pill, who can tell, it seems it's even worse in Denmark, dildos for children and . . . oh stop it Madame Buvard there's a young lady present, but she was having a quiet giggle, what about the darling buds of May, Mademoiselle, are they coming out, at your age I had a fabulous boyfriend.

When, one cold early morning in October for example, I was through the cemetery gate and walking along alley number three hundred and thirty-three, time immemorial, looking for that grave of that whom, good God, the aunt, her niece, her son-in-law, her daughter-in-law, the whole chrysanthemum tribe in the notebook, rustling, a smell of dead things, and when I say things, an old stump, an old asshole, in spite of the refinement of the decor that filth in his heart which messed up his Easter mornings, poor little angel, those posies of pricks under the lilacs, those poop-hole wallflowers, he was so very sad I give you my word, sniffling and snuffling, hawking and spitting, his false teeth in the little tortoiseshell box that the aunt or her niece or her son-in-law, well yes, eh, old age, he was well able to imagine Théo taking his place and sorting out the frightful pile of shit, excuse the expression, he might change the order of the pages but the ascent took place without anyone's help and it was fatal, fatal, d'you hear me, that little girl's voice, perfect diction up to the fatal pass, an image that comes down to us from time immemorial.

The lilies of the big sleep.

And incidentally, sleeping twelve hours a day like that, is it really hygienic, for twenty nightmares that almost kill you, he replied, a dream of mist over there pays dividends.

What do you feel at this moment.

An enormous sadness, an ordeal out of all proportion.

That manitou, then.

Eclipsed, as you might say, we'll make do without the Alphonses, the Alfreds, and other Alberts.

Well yes then, looking for that grave in the early morning he stumbles over a crackpot crouching among the chrysanthemums, is that any place to do your business, the fellow stammered his excuses, a string of farts, all the mythological tribe in memory of two or three individuals who were excessive but had been hit by the hurricane of the . . .

A missing link.

He had got up early one morning to avoid the flock of fiddlers, but is that any reason for shitting on the dead like that.

Especially as we need to revive this idyll, hey nonny no.

So poor old Marie was mustering her memories and, here, sit down there, told us that at eight o'clock she took him up his coffee, he always looked terrible in the mornings, sort of yellow, his face grayish-blue as if sunk in the end of an epoch, premonitory signs, we were trying to find that package of retouched photos where the grandmothers were going goofy, a question of corridors, marble balls, and metaphs.

Cut.

That dream of mist over there.

Cut.

Make it go down to posterity, from this date to that.

Fine example, it may well be, of loyalty to . . .

Impossible anamnesis.

We'll get there in the end with a little method.

We went to visit him, he'd got a lot weaker at the time, huddled up under the rug over his shoulders, the portrait of a grandmother above his armchair, by his side a little table with a pink-shaded lamp which lit up the bundle of old papers, he didn't touch them anymore but they kept him company, the maid, when he moved from his bedroom to the dining room, had been told to take those sheets and put them on the table where he took his meals, a nostalgic to-ing and fro-ing, even though his personality inspired very little sympathy I did sometimes feel sorry for him, quite wrongly as it happens, he was paying the price of his stupid vanity, things were returning to their proper place, could anyone wish him anything better in extremis than a clear, or more or less clear, vision of what he had been.

As for his brother, is this the place to mention him, I doubt it.

Abracadabra.

Poor Monsieur Théodore, he had all that trouble sorting out the filthy stuff of the dying man, it was no sinecure, used to collect newspapers, printed matter, advertising leaflets, catalogues, which he piled up in suitcases that cluttered up his study, they ought to have thrown everything away, but if amongst it all there had happened to be I don't know what, a . . .

Call me Dodo, if there's anything I can do for you . . .

Those attachments of the old boy, what could they have given him, a lot of trouble and nothing in return, he still spoke of them, spoke, that's saying a good deal, by the lamp that the maid moved from the bedroom to his big toes, a friendly sort of to-ing and fro-ing, under his whoremonger's rug.

Well yes, our fine mornings at the grocer's, our little suns and our tittle-tattle, a sadness that almost kills you, what shall we do with it when the day dawns, the carnival hours, the organization of the nights, shall we . . .

Lost in the hurricane of the pages.

Was it true that that was what made his head feel like a factory.

But the other woman was still thinking about her asparagus, no time to rush off to the cemetery these days, we'll get by without our dead, come on, dear, I've got my niece, she'll be getting impatient.

Two or three nieces, why not a dozen, while elsewhere there was a serious conversation about tomatoes, doesn't time fly, I grow them but I haven't planted any yet, what with this cold weather, the darling buds of May of our grandmothers, a sore throat that's what I've got, how do you manage about your fire with your legs, the nurse sees people at five these days, her house is all upside down on account of the builder fixing her up a little room in the attic, with me it's my heart, I'm going for my injection, and my husband, it's his liver.

The little woollies on the stall.

That music in the streets, it's new.

Ordeal such as no one has ever endured.

Closing the dossier he shouts out let him go to the devil, I have my own word to say, too, and I shall say it.

He has left the library, he has gone for a walk in the direction of the cemetery, passing by Magnin's and Thiéroux's and Dubard's, the track followed the marshland which was full of the white plumes they call cotton grass, and bulrushes, and sedge, the heathland strewn with wild orchids and juniper, the corn reaching to the forest, he arrives at the cemetery, or rather the site, there's nothing there, a marsh hawk perched on a dead tree trunk flew off as he approached.

Say it all over again, out of proportion.

He sat down on a stone, head in hands, despair too is absent from the roll call, what to do without its aid, mumble some memories, lost their trace, old track manhandled, old desire liquidated by the gales of the derisory.

Bah, let the water flow under the bridge, an' anyways, worries, I got just as many as you, trying to find a few moments of happiness somewheres, could be, they disappears, huh, he talkin' like a hick agin.

For a May morning, the beautiful chatter of a bluetit.

For a May morning, doesn't time fly.

Well yes, Monsieur Théo, I knew him well, your uncle, a man like they don't make anymore, you ought to have seen the way he got himself up, good God, who ever would have thought he was that age, wasn't a bit sorry for himself yet he was never without his worries, almost makes you think it must preserve them, my father, he was ten years younger, he died at the same time as him.

Or if he was mixing him up with the other one, but after all what does it matter.

Along the old track, his constitutional, Monsieur Théo, was day-dreaming about the mystery of things, the power of the spirit, the nature of the soul or vice-versa, all confused as he got older in a fog of signs and symbols, really as clear as mud.

Then he went back to his room to revise his reflections, because he is an eminently moral man and he cultivates that love of clarity which has done so much for the promotion of nature, the advancement of the pathways of the age, the mystification of power, the emancipation of hygiene, and the exaltation of old men.

The slate, always come back to that.

Other things to note than that accumulation of drifting nothings.

Take a hair of the night that bit you.

And in the first place, dismiss Théodore, he has no place in this cesspool, the man who speaks is responsible for what he puts forward, no maneuver, trick or evasion is acceptable from now on.

I, somewhere in that intolerable night, the ascent or recollection turns out to be mortal, and where's the benefit of it since the man who speaks, but who, no one so far as we know.

Or that he devoted himself to this ascesis, the doctor suggested in front of the corpse, in order to arrive precisely there, in which case no regrets for anybody, thus putting an end to the rumors concerning the death, they were still rife, you have to keep the dialogue going, and for the ladies it was something to talk about at the grocer's, find us another victim, we're in the market for one.

Otiose story that can never again be told.

What support from now on for this word, which can never run dry.

The maid mixing her notes up with his papers, the child falsifying the message by his awkward reading, evasions.

Repetition of facts that are no longer united by desire.

Impossible anamnesis.

But it had to be pursued at whatever cost, what did the means matter, if the drama turns out to be mortal perhaps that's where the benefit lies.

Oh, it wasn't that he was so much of a show-off, the maid added, on the contrary, between you and me, peace be on his ashes, fear was his daily bread, everything took on such proportions, a thoughtless word, a ridiculous little irritation, a broken glass, his nephew's future, the fate of his family, his responsibility as . . .

Entry crossed out.

His responsibility as . . .

Entry recrossed out.

And the anguish of what lies beyond the chrysanthemums, he couldn't avoid that either, as if, I ask you, the maid went on, eternal damnation was the price we had to pay for the dog's life we live which we could well have done without, don't you agree, personally I've always had faith in Providence, let it get on with it.

And then it was that constant harping on the murder, to ward off the evil eye, another version, then another, and another, a way of merrily, as they say, passing the time, the time that you still have to finish.

And anyway, was it very nice for Monsieur Théodore, but he counted for so little when all's said and done.

Right, since we have to go back to it, and seeing that we aren't the judge of the validity of anything, I'll tell you my own version of the death of that old man, it's years ago now, which gave Monsieur so much to think about, and maybe even helped him not to die like a dog, because I maintain, even if you do call me a great ninny, that there are some subjects that have more weight than others with regard to the serious side of life, even when you're on the wrong track like the people, look, whatever you may say, some people have class and others don't, which doesn't mean to say that they aren't all the good Lord's creatures, it's called natural inequalities, and you aren't going to tell me that a man who spends his time, especially after a certain age, on frivolities, or who's only interested in all that fucking business, excuse the expression, is preparing to die as decently as the one who meditates on his end, that's an opinion that no one could be against because unfortunately, whether we're the least bit philosophical or not, we shall all come to it, and whatever you may . . .

But what was the matter with Madame Marie with her morbid thoughts, she used not to be like that, is it a sign that she's come to the end of her tether, really, it makes me sad, such a devoted woman who's only ever thought about other people, ah, how right they are when they say . . .

Monsieur Alexandre came back from his walk, he went back up to his room and noted, rewrite version old boy's death one last time.

But something else was brewing beyond their consciousness, and to say something is to say very little, and consciousness, nothing at all, and to say, even less, well what then, shut your trap.

Take a hair of the night that bit you.

The left hand corner of the bistro as you go in.

The old man is sitting there with two others drinking his glass of white wine.

When I heard Théodore going into the salon I suspected him of being in connivance with the maid, who was the only person who knew that I kept my papers in my writing desk.

It was a Saturday, Marie at her niece's, and my nephew supposed to come and see how I was after that tiring soirée I'd given for the neighbors, a courtesy I'd postponed as long as possible, I was still in bed, it could have been . . .

At his bedside the doctor said, you will have to see this ordeal through to the bitter end, concentrate now, courage.

But however hard he tried the sick man's head was a vacuum, it's all beyond me, he said, I've gone over everything, ask my maid, she has witnessed all my efforts.

And the maid said, Doctor, can't you leave him in peace, what a way to cure people, give us your bill and go away.

But the doctor holds his ground, he continues, he says even so, isn't there a case for going back to such and such a point, yes, for instance, that meeting in the cemetery, could you tell me more about it.

Whereupon Mortin opens his eyes again, he says the cemetery, yes, everything started there, I can still talk about it, I always shall be able to, yes, could you move this pillow to make me more comfortable.

Marie and the doctor help him prop himself up.

And the master takes up the story where he had left it in time immemorial, he speaks in the voice he had when he was a good little boy.

I had a slate on which I noted down everything that had to be done during the day, and when evening came I effaced it with a duster or a sponge, and the time passed quite pleasantly, I mean that I didn't have to bother about anything other than passing it.

Days nicely filled with occupations, without a single minute's break between them to let the unpleasant memories infiltrate.

I had my work on the archives, as you know, all sorts of notes and documents relating to things of more or less interest, but do we ever know which of them may sometimes become interesting.

And a great many phrases either imagined or picked up here and there, I've always liked phrases, and in my classification I distinguished them from things, but on the whole I think there was a fairly normal balance between the two categories, the approximate equilibrium of my mind should have guaranteed that of the other.

I was much criticized for collecting all that stuff, especially by Marie, because the dossiers accumulated everywhere and she was finding it more and more difficult to do her housework, but what is housework compared to the relative peace of the soul.

Until the day when, getting up at about eight o'clock as usual, I go to the kitchen to get my slate and I see that everything I had noted down and then effaced the previous days had returned, as if freshly traced in my own hand.

I didn't ask myself the question, because I never find any answer to it, but I thought it was serious, and I decided to smash my slate into smithereens.

And my misfortunes date from that moment, my horror of memory, the slimy days from which you can only escape, and with what difficulty, by sleeping most of the time, is that a life, I ask you.

In my short waking moments I have got into the habit of going to the cemetery, and it has happened several times that I have fallen asleep there when I'd stayed longer than I intended.

The doctor listens, notes down certain details so as to be able to ask more precise questions later.

One year on All Saints' Day I went to the cemetery with a bunch of chrysanthemums to honor the memory of an old acquaintance, it was already crowded with people who had come to put flowers on the graves.

How old would I have been at the time, something like thirty, Marie will confirm it.

The doctor noted.

I listened to their very prosaic conversations, they hardly spoke of the dead at all but about the price of chrysanthemums, the little pot at five francs, in former times that was adequate, do you approve of useless expenditure.

Alley number three hundred and thirty-three, side-alley number seven hundred and seventy-seven, I was lost in that labyrinth, looking for the grave in question.

No one noticed me among so many people, I have never been particularly noticeable, dressed like all young men at that time, denim trousers and little American-style jacket with patches over the elbows, thick knitted woolen scarf.

The doctor noted.

I don't know whether you are in the habit of frequenting country groceries, you always hear the same remarks there, the weather, no seasons anymore, the bad harvests, the rheumatisms, the troubles children cause, that was more or less the atmosphere of the cemetery that evening, the everyday routine, in short, when all of a sudden I find myself face to face with a fellow who was getting on a bit, he was meditating at a family vault, he invites me to sit down on a nearby grave and we talk about everything and nothing until nightfall, the old idiot thought I was his dupe but I'd immediately seen through him, first his hand patting me on the shoulder, your worries will pass, and next stroking my thigh, and next, you know the sort of thing, the crowd had disappeared, liberties, and then he said, I shall say you're my nephew and you'll call me Uncle and we'll live in a beautiful house I own.

That sort of sadness, the doctor groaned, when shall we be free of it, dismayed at the trite nature of the anecdote, he had been expecting a revelation but it isn't Sunday every day.

Nor All Saints' Day every day.

A missing link.

And he kept interrupting himself, poor Monsieur Dodo, saying no, that wasn't what I meant, something else from such and such a date to some other date, something else was coming to light from beyond people's consciousness, something else, something else.

The look of an aristocrat racked by remorse.

But sleeping twelve hours a day like that, is it really hygienic.

Do-do, to bye-byes we go.

Whatever you do don't wake him up, he said, our treatment doesn't go beyond people's consciousness, we shall see later what his brain was weaving, that mass of notes and documents, that hodgepodge of drifting nothings.

Imagination in place of memory.

Call me Uncle, if there's anything I can do for you, my suitcase, your box of treasures, we shall get the benefit of them with the passing days, and that revelation they were expecting, psspss, you hear a thunder clap, devastation, cataclysm and the like, the Parca jabbering for a reality that has never stopped being imminent.

Do *you* believe in the . . .

Good God, said Madame Buvard, he gives you the leaping heebies these days.

On account of dying, on account of we obviously can't last forever, then what do you make of the future.

So many misunderstandings, and personally, his habit of never finishing his phrases gets me in such a state, it's like his head, he's only ever had half of it, and when I say half . . .

The underground passages are being hollowed out, exchanges now take place only in the opaque shadows.

Just one more little effort, said the doctor, this or that point, you remember, and the dying man spoke in the voice he had as a child, and the maid burst into tears.

I had a slate, yes, my aide-mémoire, on which I noted down, apart from the things I had to do the next day, phrases just as they came into my head, especially at night, and at dawn, when I couldn't sleep anymore I used to copy some of them out into my dossier of the phrases, not the things, do you follow me, that I needed to think about, sometimes for whole nights on end, to find out what they revealed, and I always thought that an invisible manitou, Marie can testify to that, was organizing somewhere beyond people's consciousness a sort of discourse which we might take for wisdom if we only bothered to pay attention, at what moments, my God, I really don't know, mine were those of insomnia, but there must be others for other temperaments, I imagine that a poet for example, in flashes, for they are brief, is aware of more of them than a man like me, and can more easily guess their secret meaning.

His lucidity is touching, says the doctor, and the maid between two sobs replies, it won't last.

Doesn't time fly.

June again, love-in-a-mist, betony, centaury, cow-wheat, its flowers, its crickets, its perfumes, but the heart was no longer in it, all the shutters closed.

Who will take account of our passionate innocence.

To rediscover time in one's innermost depths, what a sinister joke, might as well believe in the freshness of dung, go and discover the flowers it's composed of, how long will they go on making memory a substitute for eternity, nauseating dupery, but one enjoys being a dupe, doesn't one, Doctor.

Dupe, dupe, what do you mean by that, and who's talking of eternity.

To know who is speaking, said the dying man, that's another story and I'm very glad it is.

Memory in place of imagination.

And perhaps he had had some idea in the old days, who can tell, of utilizing his reflections in the interests of some great project, like many other solitary people who in their gray moments cultivate what they call hope, not realizing that there is the same kind of difference between it and the real as there is between . . .

The heart was no longer in it.

In whiffs, as you might say, the image of the old bistro where, centuries before, between two Pernods, were embodied the fabulous chimeras which for them took the place of the present.

The terrace with its balustrade, the fountains, the imposing main staircase, the tall mullioned windows, after his death they found them on the publicity labels of a make of chocolate, the manor houses of the region series.

Imagination in place of memory.

It was like his brother and his nephews, and their family house and the parties they gave there, I never saw the slightest sign of any of them, but Madame Cruchet didn't come from the district and the older generation had been in the cemetery for ages so how could we believe her, and what's more she was losing her marbles at the time she was being questioned, adding, on the contrary, he lived in a hovel, I've seen him there dragging himself from the kitchen to the crapper, he didn't even have enough money to pay a housekeeper.

The contradictions you find everywhere the moment you begin to think.

And that it's a great mistake if you don't take account of what happens to other people, you might perhaps see it more clearly through what happens to yourself, so many considerations which come easily to those whose weakness is contrition, or that the hand linked to the words it is retracing is no longer a suitable instrument, you can't hear very well, suitable for what, for the great project he probably had which consisted in conjuring up out of this mass of notes a truth that has never stopped being imminent, how can you tell.

He couldn't have been feeling very comfortable, said the maid, what with his insomnia and his nightmares, will you change the pillows.

How can you lead an existence between the dread of the cemetery and the horror of memory.

And not only his habit of never finishing his phrases, but that of not facing or of diverting questions concerning some of his convictions, an act of cowardice which won't have been of the slightest advantage to him, on the contrary, all his secret hopes of notoriety completely fizzled out and that just served him right, because what other way is there to see notoriety than as a consecration of the determination to assert oneself.

It might be wondered what she meant by some of his convictions, she had known the old man better than anyone but we wouldn't have got anymore out of her because she had been well trained, and after so many years she was still on her guard against betraying him.

And Théodore, rereading these notes in the evening of his life, could still only guess at the nature of the feelings of their author, that old uncle he had barely known but who had made him his heir, nevertheless specifying in a codicil that his drafts, as he called them, must never be divulged in any manner whatsoever but must stay in the attics of the house as if they were an integral part of its walls, and in the event of any break in the continuity of the succession a clause must appear in perpetuity in the deeds of sale to include this last wish of his, was it legal, wasn't it rather pure fantasy even though extremely touching, I grant you that.

June, its flowers, its crickets, its perfumes, all the shutters closed.

Through dying, among other dreads something like that of frontiers and betrayals.

Born on the borders of the trans-Arcidoine province and of Dualie, and never having known to which of these two territories he owed his origin, so confused is their history, he claimed to be martyrized by the feeling of being loyal neither to the one nor to the other, martyrdom however not necessarily being evidence of a cause generally recognized as being of prime importance, it all depends on the conviction of the victim, and what criterion, in this domain there are none.

What eloquence, said Théodore.

And Monsieur Dodo replied, eloquence, I don't know, but unless you know what it is to suffer you will never know from what innermost depths your words well up, nor how to judge them.

For indeed, the dead do answer.

Retrace his steps along the narrow track through the wood where the rushes grow, along the pond up to the bridge, then turn into the path that led to the old residence, who was it that used to own it, no one to rescue it from its ruins, a fine romantic picture but we weren't all that keen on that sort of thing and the marshes are insalubrious, when all of a sudden a young man appeared in front of us, you're the doctor, quick, take this shortcut, Monsieur has been taken ill, the telephone's out of order, we heard later that this adolescent's mind was deranged, day and night he haunted the confines of the manor house and claimed to be the servant, many people out for a walk have met him, he's allowed to be at large, he isn't dangerous, until the day he planted a butcher's knife in the old crackpot's back.

Like the day of the last fancy reception the landowner gave for the neighbors, that was how long ago, in short the cars arriving around eight o'clock and a young manservant showing them where to park on the terrace, but his remarks were so confused as a result of his great fatigue, and his age, and the hazards of a difficult existence, and heredity, to tell you the truth we preferred to leave it at that and let the survivors do the best they could.

So they were all barmy in that part of the country.

He kept taking a letter out of his pocket and reading it, or thinking he was reading it, putting it back and continuing his walk, though more and more slowly as a result of his great fatigue, and his age, et cetera, on the track by the pond where the water lilies added a romantic note, farther on the heathland and . . .

But that letter, can you tell us something about it, did his maid know about it, had any of his friends read it or what, it must have played some part in the deterioration of the poor man's character mustn't it.

Oh, can a letter cause such devastation, that doesn't seem very likely, yes, I know the saying about how words disappear but writings remain, I agree that you can go back to written words night and day during a whole existence but in my opinion the real agents of death are the spoken words you can't take back, it's precisely the things that disappear that leave a vacuum behind them.

I frequented him for years and I can tell you that it was a bitter disappointment after all that time to find him just as he had been when I left him, none of our feelings leaves us cold, I saw and heard him once again cultivating as if it were an orchid his stupid little despair which he nurtured until it became a veritable derision and the result on his mind was an irreversible sclerosis, that's nothing to boast about, especially not an artist or someone who claims to be one, when people are uneducated maybe there's a kind of deviation of the mystic sense which pushes them to take a delight in a state close to it but really, what good does it do, in the whole history of humanity the aridity of the soul has never been held in much esteem, and for good reason, I'm not saying that you can't make a divinity of death seeing that nature gives us abundant proof of it, it has always contained the seeds of the world to come.

The murder in the cemetery, a different version every time.

The conversations in the bistro, that dream for incorrigible babes in arms.

The hazards of a dreary existence which suddenly, at its last hour . . .

This imposition, invincible fatigue.

. . . at its last hour, is the main topic of all the tittle-tattle, one All Saints' evening.

What a lot of things Monsieur Dodo had in his suitcase, when he sometimes took them out for us we had a good laugh, we weren't hard to please, no.

At such and such a page a time to love, at another page a time to yield up your place.

And little by little, just like that, with the passing days, a sort of stupid litany which took the place of a chronicle for us, you see how very backward we were.

For indeed, the dead do answer.

Yes but that isn't all, ladies, she said, let's not be too softhearted, it's a question of knowing whether we are to continue with the classification as we agreed or whether we are going to leave it all in a jumble, it's my opinion that, given the leisure we have, rather than knitting for the poor we should be engaging in equally useful work if we were to finalize our benefactor's manuscripts.

Thus spake Mademoiselle Moine, not the aunt, she's dead, the niece, the president of the Dieudonné Foundation, after the death of

Théodore who, having no heir, had bequeathed his house to the parish, which he considered to be the best way to ensure that his uncle's wishes, as expressed in a codicil, would be respected, he had added a small sum to guarantee the expenses of the Foundation whose aim was to welcome tired intellectuals to this tranquil spot, the mayor, who at that time was young Chenu, had ensured that some modest funds were voted for the upkeep of the building and the conversion of the attic into a public library, in this way the town hall volumes were married to those of Monsieur Alexandre, and the memoirs of the latter would remain ad vitam within its walls, Mademoiselle Moine's idea of continuing the classification begun by Théodore, then to have it bound in calfskin by Mademoiselle de Bonne-Mesure, not the aunt, she's dead, the niece, who had taken up this delightful pastime, she'd already bound several of the Library's volumes, had at first been welcomed with enthusiasm by the ladies, but they were having great difficulty in continuing with the classification and were beginning to feel sorry for themselves at the moment when this narrative resumes, hence the president's remark which fortunately was made in the appropriate tone and manner, the ladies plucked up courage again and went on with the work, with what difficulty can be imagined, what they really needed was someone very much in the know but how to pay him, and then, when you think of it, maybe everything was for the best because the very fact that these laboring ladies had so little insight made them adopt a whimsical classification which would not be the least attraction of the volume once it was finished.

Bound in calfskin, but that costs a fortune.

Well, believe it or not, the last time I saw Mademoiselle Francine she offered to make us a present of both the leather and her work, it's true that she can afford it but we should never underestimate a generous gesture.

And how long is it now, more than a year, yes, since the volume has been finished, three hundred manuscript pages, incredibly thick, about thirty-five by twenty-five centimeters in its blond binding with Memoirs of Monsieur Mortin written on the back, and when you ask Mademoiselle Moine for it, because she also acts as librarian seeing that she lives at the Foundation, and incidentally she hasn't done so badly out of the deal, she lives like a princess in the founder's own room, she who used to be so impecunious, that's the least you can say, and when people who want to consult it ask her for the volume she tells them you aren't allowed to make notes of any sort, you'll expose yourself to legal proceedings, and that's also written on a label inside the book, it even makes you wonder whether it's in conformance with Monsieur Alexandre's intentions that the book should be read at all, but his nephew had taken it upon himself to interpret the codicil in the wider sense.

What's a codicil.

It's a supplement to a will.

And what does that big book talk about.

About things that aren't for children, go on.

One more detail, the volume is fastened to a desk by a chain so that no one should be tempted to take it away, but even without that it would be impossible because our president never leaves the attic on Thursdays, the day the library is open, and I can assure you that she keeps her eyes open.

Not that our library is much frequented, far from it, whether it was at the town hall as it used to be or at the Foundation as it is now, young people go to the cinema and the people of our age have the television, even so there are still one or two people who are faithful to the culture of literature, or let's just say to culture, for example our town clerk who's also a poet as everyone knows, a man of great merit, the ladies say, because what with all his woes, he's lost his wife, his son, and his two daughters, and even just recently his daughter-in-law, as if destiny had got its knife into the family, he might well have taken to drink like everyone else, but no, he . . .

What's destiny.

It's misfortune, go on.

He goes on, as before, with his work at the town hall, and reading the newspapers, and frequenting the library, and occasionally publishing sylvan or rustic or rupestrian odes in our local rag, but I think I've said that before, or was it apropos of Alexandre, which is no less touching.

Ah, these poets.

And there's also Mademoiselle Francine, she's no longer in her first youth, she's getting more and more like her Aunt Ariane, same kindly face, same corpulence, same walk, and also the tone of her voice, you might easily think you were hearing the dead woman but as for the social round, she's dropped it, she stays at home with her housekeeper and only very occasionally sees her cousin, Monsieur de Broy's nephew, and Madame de Longuepie who was a Ballaison, if my memory serves, if memory serves, I've said that before too, it's so humiliating to be reduced to harping on the same old . . .

It's funny, the gentleman's losing his marbles too, like you.

You don't say marbles to your uncle.

What do you say then.

You don't say anything, go on.

. . . harping on the same old memories, or something of the sort, don't let's commit ourselves.

But you, Uncle, had you read the book by Monsieur . . .

I . . .

Had you, tell me, had you read it.

I . . .

Why don't you answer.

It wasn't a book, it was notes, yes, I read them during his lifetime, and I found them mediocre and I told him so, that was why he never wanted to publish them.

But what did those notes talk about, were they stories, tell me, Uncle.

Stories, yes, thousands of stories.

Then they were for children.

You're right, Théo, I'll try and tell them to you but don't interrupt me or I shall lose the thread, well then, there was the one about the café of illusions, and the one about the down-and-outs, and the one about the manor house, and the one about the pond with the water lilies, and the one about the path through the wood, and the one about the underground passages being hollowed out, and hollowed out, and the one about the cemetery, and the one about the word that sticks in your throat, and the one about the lost letter, and the one about the so-called nephews, and the one about the law court and its sentence, and the one about the dethroned king, and the one about the murderers everywhere, and the one about the garden with the nettles, and the one about the knife, and the one about the dead children, and the one about the grief, and the one about the rats, and the one about the innocents, and the one about the journeys to nowhere, and the one about the town, and the one about the crossroads, and the one about the grief, and the one about the dead children, and the one about the lost letter, and the one about the murderers, and the one . . .

You've already said that, Uncle.

I've already said everything, my boy, but everything has to be said over again for fear of . . . and you shouldn't interrupt me, I don't know anymore now, too many stories you see, far too many, I don't remember them anymore.

The old eyes closed, the old head dropped, and the child called the maid who . . .

You understand, said Marie, he's old and ill, that's why we sometimes don't understand him, but I who have known him so long, I . . .

And I would come back from my walk, he confided to Théo, and go back to my notes, and I'd make a list of all the situations in which I could get it off my chest, but it became so difficult that . . .

Entry crossed out.

But Louis too, who'd known him well in the old days, Louis said none of that is of the slightest importance, don't let's worry our heads, Monsieur Théo was absolutely right to let the public have access to the book, and he remembered a particular morning when he had rushed into the kitchen, Marie had told him to wait in the salon, he'd been looking through some illustrated magazines and between the pages of one of them he'd come across a manuscript note which said roughly, if my memory serves, I distrust all my intentions, even my last will and testament, even though it was drawn up by a notary, is it really mine, I sometimes doubt my signature, as if the other, the invisible manitou was taking its revenge by fits and starts, that's the fate reserved for those as pride themselves on their lucidity.

This Louis, anyway, you might wonder who he was, but what was the point, like all the rest a relic of a situation that had become illusory.

A missing link.

Or, once again asking himself the question about Louis and that meeting one morning, he told himself that it was of no importance, a minor matter, a minor matter, he'd probably come to arrange a date for the move, the books, the kitchen utensils and the dog, what was its name, Léo or Dodo or something.

Ask Marie name of dog.

Even so it was the meeting in the cemetery that he came back to the most frequently in his moments of lucidity, the circumstances changed from day to day, as did the identity of the person encountered, sometimes he spoke of an old man, sometimes of a young man, sometimes even of a dog, which couldn't fail to be touching, unless he took it into his head to draw some philosophical or whatever conclusions from it, I've always had a horror of that, also of his propensity to see symbols in the slightest hazards of existence.

But we really weren't spoiled, what with the maid and Théodore, and you know how it is, the evenings are long in the country, so that the old crackpot's monologue sometimes entertained us, and there was the advantage that we could always leave the room at any time, he took not the slightest notice of our presence, a bit like an old record, if you like, which went on playing nonstop and in whose outmoded music we might discover contrapuntal details which had previously escaped us or which we'd forgotten from one time to the next.

At such and such a page he says what illness, I've never been ill.

At such and such a page he says old record, old record, contrapuntal my ass.

At such and such a page the maid asks where the corpse has gone.

At such and such a page Magnin is standing another round.

The holy water sprinkler hidden behind the counter which was being used as a catafalque.

And the family vault had become a puppet theatre where the ancestors' mugs appeared on All Saints' Day, jabbering for the delight of the faithful a dialogue of the dead in pure showbiz tradition, crowned by an Aunt Sally where you chucked pots of chrysanthemums, wham on Auntie Jéromine's phiz, wham on Grandma Estelle's phiz, and then that character, who was he, with his curé's hat, wham on his phiz, wham.

Even so he was sometimes amusing, was Uncle Alexandre, but it never lasted very long.

A candle was burning at the deceased's bedside.

A handle was churning up his diseased backside.

The poor man took one word for another.

His dossier in facsimile in the drawer of the deluge.

Cut.

This imposition, invincible fatigue.

Ah yes said the excellent Marie, what didn't he put me through with his drunken babble, no sooner was he back from the bistro than he started spouting for hours, his stories were only ever about putting an end to it, finishing it, cutting it short, yes but was it logical, either you talk or you keep your trap shut and there was me, great ninny that I was, listening to him and thinking he was unhappy, but just between you and me that kind of fellow never believes a word he says, I ought to have dismissed at least half of what he said or told him to go jump in the lake, especially on those occasions, what an idea, to drink yourself silly just because you've made a mess of your life, can you see me running around from one bar to the next.

The time it takes to transcribe a phrase.

June, its flowers, its crickets, its perfumes.

Ah, poetry, ladies, he was saying, our town clerk at the parish fête, do you even know what it is, and Madame Thiéroux answered sweetly, oh, Monsieur, all ladies know that, it's when people write verse when they're twenty, all our sweethearts did that for us.

Poetry, yes, it's something, but just imagine if it went beyond the twentieth year, where would that get us, but that poetry is addressed to ladies, there they were all agreed.

A really nice fête with a cavalcade and everything, pity it had rained but it's the same every year, and apropos of rain, snails, because her boy catches them in the hedges, sometimes there are a hundred or even two hundred, obviously she's obliged to cook them, it's a shitty job salting them, excuse the expression, and it takes such a time, after that you need a lot of garlic and parsley to make them really taste like snails.

Poetry, yes, but that kitchen was enough to make you sick.

She was fed up, just between you and me, with never being able to get away from her stoves, especially on fine evenings, sunsets, she could put them you know where, it's true, the condition of women, basically . . .

And that every time you had to say to yourself, we mustn't let ourselves get depressed again, there's a far more beautiful sunset elsewhere, unique of its kind, within everyone's reach, whence we derive the strength to overcome all life's sadnesses, just a little effort and you'll see it and all your troubles will pass, a bit like that old remedy, the Fountain of Youth, that Abbé what was his name used to make, you remember, well that's what poetry is, but as for the effort, in the first place it takes some making and there are days when it's easier to say shit.

Or else she was kicking herself for having got married, what the hell does that have to do with anything, she was in favor of free love and no children, or just love children that you put into a modern institution so they lose all taste for family life, and the mother can take an interest in politics and reform the man-made society we live in, men, the stinkers, good God, they bash up our cunts, our hearts, our brains, and, oh come now Madame Buvard, watch your words, there are a young girl's ears here, it was strawberry time, doesn't it fly, and the first cherries . . . blather, that's all pure blather.

And ass time too, yeah, and time for the first nettles, careful, you lovers, nature's all very fine but it stings, it stings, I remember one day my boyfriend had forgotten the rug, and me in the meadow stark . . . Madame Buvard, that'll be eight francs seventy-five, plus fifty centimes for the parsley, nine twenty-five.

But what does he do all day.

I can see him in the mornings, opening his shutters at eight, and then, toward nine o'clock, he walks around his garden, at that season he bends over a rose, and then over the honeysuckle, according to Madame Marie he's very sensitive to smells, and then all of a sudden he stops, he seems to be thinking, unless his intestines are bothering him, then goes on toward the well, always that well, I wonder what it inspires in him, you never know, he may chuck himself in it one day.

Rose time, goodness.

And then.

And then I see him going back to the house, and he comes out again around two o'clock, and then around five, and finally around seven, until the moment when his maid calls him in to dinner with her boozy voice.

Ah, because she drinks too.

She says she doesn't, but ask the grocer's wife.

What she couldn't understand, then, was what some other people said about him, that he spent his days in the bistro or elsewhere, let's not be too specific, led the dissolute life of an old vagrant, and when I say vagrant, picking up any old junk, never sleeping at home, or pretending to be a beggar, a low-grade salesman, a third-rate actor, a down-and-out and everything, how could you make sense of all these contradictions.

To which the other retorted, if you believe all the tittle-tattle you'll never make sense of it, and anyway what do you make of the passing of time, he might have led a different sort of life in the old days but have settled down now, the old rumors could still be around and getting mixed up with the recent ones, no difference in their nature and that's just as well, if we always had to be sorting out the old from the new in every domain nothing would ever take shape, nothing, d'you hear me, that's what civilization is.

Settled down, settled down, with his mug, does a man who's settled down have a face like that, look at Uncle Théo, at least he inspires confidence.

The horror of memory.

Or else a double life, why not, that would become interesting.

Cutting in from time immemorial.

The old rumors being mixed up with the new ones, poor Alexandre repeated, that's why my head feels like a factory.

And he went back up to his room and made notes, voices from all around, from before, from last night, from afterwards, I am their spokesman here, traces of effacement.

Surging back, the old myths.

Blather, that's all pure blather.

The time of larks and poppies.

In the mornings he used to go and pick bunches of flowers in the fields, do you call that normal at his age, preceded by the dog which used to disappear into the grass, sniffing out the traces of hares and sparrows, a charming rustic picture and a hymn to the far off times when nature, that old trap for halfwits, reigned over pure hearts.

Monsieur Théodore, even so, I used to say to him, couldn't you do some useful work, I don't know, well, gardening, planting trees, leeks, salsify, that would be cheaper for us, a packet of seeds in the spring, for the vegetables I mean, and there we are, safe for the season, instead of spending good money every day at the grocer's, a sou is a sou.

You remind me of my mother, he used to answer, and anyway, salsify, that muck again, they say it causes cancer.

Because a single word was enough to set him raving again, he used to come out with puns like in his father's day, his father despised all those larks and he called his boy a sissy.

Because personally, his illness . . .

Why his illness, why always harping on that, is it essential, we deplore his state, of course we do, but to have it shoved down our throats as our daily bread, what a bore, has he at least got a doctor, and anyway, let him get on with it, said Étiennette, ever since she's been working in an office and has her own car she hasn't been the same, you remember what a delightful girl she used to be, so discreet, so humble, so much the better for her in a way, but so much the worse for us, neither discretion nor modesty have ever been any use to anyone who wants to succeed but why bring up Étiennette again, I have a feeling that there was something about her on the tip of my tongue but it's gone, unless it was the fact of classifying those damned papers, maybe I caught sight of her name casually, or else it could have been the horrible episode in the cemetery you were just talking about, Mortin's body found dead on the grave, then we shall never get away from these retrospective visions, a fine method to make progress.

Because he was like that, Monsieur Thédore, enough good intentions to pave the whole of hell, unforeseeable reactions against his saturnine temperament which, in the eyes of a third party who wasn't in the know, could make him pass for cheerful or dynamic, so that the rumors about him were nothing like him, and as they always reached his ears they disturbed him deeply, making him ask himself questions and answer them badly, he would have done much better to withdraw a long way away from the tittle-tattle and gossip and take no more notice of what people said, his deeper nature would have taken the upper hand, and if it was of an irremediable melancholy, well then, he could throw himself into the well and adieu, and anyway why should we at all costs want people we like to be artificially healthy, that must distress them far more than accepting their unhappy fate, destiny is destiny it'll always have the last word, and it isn't by relieving people with pills, or pellets, or persuasion, that you'll make them any happier, personally, psychology . . . and then really, happiness, has anyone ever known what it was, and love confused with pleasure does that make sense, come now, reread the great authors and don't let's descend to this sort of concierge's talk anymore.

For indeed, the dead do answer.

Full of horrible photos of people who'd been strangled, or hanged, or had their throats cut.

Answer, but in a language of their own, something like that of the dream, that benediction, ah if only it would return.

Great ninny, not a word of truth in what he tells you, how do you think you can make a life between the fear of the cemetery and the horror of memory.

Or if that was what people call life.

Because you, then, you don't believe in the progress of science.

Dear Mademoiselle, one does not believe in progress, that's for idealists, one observes it, and furthermore it all depends on what we mean by progress, the sense it is given today is a shoddy derivative, its real meaning is of another order.

Oho, aren't we uppity.

A missing link.

He saw his maid going upstairs surreptitiously, reaching his study, entering it, the room was filled with a pink light, she goes over to the writing desk, ferrets through its drawers and the dossiers, jots something down in a notebook, steals the drafts from the wastebasket and, leaving without a sound, goes and locks herself up in her bedroom and writes in her concierge's language a journal consisting of a hodgepodge of reflections on existence, the fate of maids, religion, the condition of women and the cost of living, alternating with culinary recipes and accounts of dreams in which the poor creature's unconscious had a whale of a time, she's a . . .

The room was filled with a pink light, she goes over to the bed, puts the breakfast tray down on the bedside table and, before the sleeping man has had time to open his eyes, plunges the potato knife into his throat.

Why does she bring the breakfast tray, tell me, Uncle.

Because she's used to it, and so as not to arouse any suspicion in her master's mind, in case he was already awake.

What's suspicion.

It's the disease of the washouts, go on.

The room was filled with a pink light, she goes over to the bed, puts the tray of potatoes down on the chamber pot and, before the wide-awake man has time to say oof, strangles him with the . . .

Cut.

And to think that he had imagined that too, his maid murdering him, the old chucklehead, I knew him better than anyone and he gave me a pain in the neck with his suspicions about Marie, she changed as she got older, became shifty, went through his drawers, and was visited more and more frequently by a nephew who looked like a dubious character, he stayed in the kitchen with her for hours in the evenings, talking in a low voice, when her master asked her about him she said that the boy was in financial difficulties, he came to ask her advice and each time cadged ten francs off her, a sou is a sou, in short Alexandre had lost confidence in her, he was going to forbid her to have the fellow there, he'll have had time to make a plan of the apartment, as for the safe in my room Marie must already have told him about it ages ago, what's going to become of me it's giving me nightmares, must I dismiss this maid and get a worse one, it's frightful, I replied, you're getting ideas into your head, what's happening to you, Marie is the most dedicated of women, the most honest, but he didn't listen to me.

Murdered by his maid or by one of her nephews, that's a new one.

Repeat, I am dead, I shan't keep silent anywhere.

Repeat, to emerge from less than nothing.

Repeat, take a hair of the night that bit you.

And if need be we shall sleep twenty hours, he added, Uncle's stories will drive me bonkers, for he was still sorting out the papers and numbering them, I can still see him with his greasy little hat, his little pince-nez, coming back from the library, enough to break your heart, a drink here, a drink there, so charming with his story of the little elephant and the little soup tureen full of milk, rationing, he was completely pickled, we teased him, we stood him another round, his little moustache, his little ribbon running from one folder to the next, our youth in the café of illusions.

Café of illusions.

And how we used to dream of fame, and of the public weal, and of morality and poetry, what a thing that is, gentlemen, may it last beyond the twentieth year, well, in counting the people still cultivating it Monsieur Théo couldn't even come up with three names, taking old leaflets out of his suitcase he started reciting odes by what's his name, elegies by thingummy, and sonnets by a . . .

Betony, cow-wheat, cornflower, poppy.

Do-do, to bye-byes we go . . .

Old chimeras, everything is disintegrating.

The relative peace of the soul.

Oh, it's not that old mother Marie was a saint, no, she had set tongues wagging on account of her gifts as a witch, according to some people who went to consult her in her kitchen of an evening, speaking in a low voice about their matrimonial troubles, it seems she had second sight and used some bizarre methods to break down the defenses of the agent of trouble, if not actually to eliminate it, but no one can furnish any proof, thank God.

Or tie the heretic to the stake.

Seeing her so-called nephew to the gate and whispering three words in his ear.

Used to walk around by the cemetery to observe her master surreptitiously.

But when you think back to the last days of the master one thing is striking, the serenity he had achieved, no more aggressivity in his behavior, no more sudden changes of mood, or was it senility, maybe he had lapsed into second childhood, pee-pee, pot-pot, but all that is such ancient history, at all events one impression remains with me, that of relaxation, isn't that your feeling.

Oh, personally, you know, I barely knew him until he was in the hospital after the murder attempt, he was under sedation and everyone who has just had an operation reacts in the same fashion.

In short, it's all as clear as mud.

And come what may.

As for confusing one funeral with another, alas, you know what memory is, we shall all be in the same boat, the procedures don't differ much and the same goes for the deceased, not to speak of the survivors, no one could reproach the poor nephew for being a bit vague about the subject, and also . . .

. . . for being a bit vague about the subject, and also about that of the facsimile notes, perhaps that was what he had meant to be but he'd forgotten it when it came to delivering the documents to the Toto or Zozo Foundation, some such name, we'd have to go and check on the spot, the ladies who had been classifying the notes may well have taken the originals for reproductions or vice-versa, why attach so much importance to details which don't have any, and what's more . . .

. . . which don't have any, and what's more, do we even know whether the famous volume in this so-called library, probably no more than a shed tacked on to the church youth club, has as its author the old man in question, or whether it isn't something quite different, the archives of the parish or commune or God knows what, always supposing that it exists, personally I consider that that story of the chain attaching it to the desk needs to be taken with more than a grain of salt, once again let's not have preconceived ideas but let's go and see for ourselves.

Like the questions of the codicil too, you know as well as I do the unimaginable imbroglios created by wills, which more often than not are rewritten, recast, lost, stolen, interpreted, et cetera, do you realize what a mess you're getting yourself into, trying to get things straight, to me it all seems childish if not worse.

Monsieur Théo used to say, speaking of his uncle who used to drive him silly with his doubts about the value of his rough drafts, that, depending on the day, he used to pick out a random remark from the pages of his hodgepodge and then comment on it interminably, taking neither account of the domain it came from nor the time he had made it, so that the next day he might come across another remark that invalidated the previous one which he would then comment on again without comparing it with his previous day's assertions, so that a third party who wasn't in the know might have accused him of senility, but that for his part he didn't see it that way because the common run of people don't understand the first thing about the contradictions of a mind which, the more vigorous it is, the more enfeebled it appears, so that he clung to the table at which they had both been seated listening to Monsieur Alexandre monologuing, convinced that he was witnessing an unparalleled manifestation of lucidity, so that he had also convinced himself that it wasn't chance that made his uncle put his finger on this or that thought when he opened his manuscript, but that a subtle and absolutely consummate mechanism, even though it wasn't apparent, had been functioning both in the writing of the notes at a time X and in the revision of the same at a time Y, no material indication needing to be taken into consideration in order to authorize any kind of value judgment concerning the equilibrium of the forces present, so that when all was said and done he could only consider that anything whatsoever that came from the pen or the mouth of the old man deserved his closest attention.

Poor Monsieur Théodore, you can understand how he finished the way he did.

And it was also he, incidentally, who, thinking he was doing the right thing, probably imagined the existence of a second maid who succeeded Marie, so as to put people off the scent when they began to study the dead man's memoirs, which second maid was supposed to have searched through the master's papers to find inspiration for her own journal, and, knowing nothing of Alexandre's past except by hearsay, may not merely have confused the facts and the names but may furthermore have surreptitiously interspersed her own writings in inverted commas with those of Mortin, whence a possible explanation for future exegetes of the mental troubles he allegedly suffered from and of the disorder that reigned in the dossiers, because it was impossible for him, for Monsieur Théo, to allow people to think Marie capable of such an action, the evidence of the survivors could only agree about her integrity.

Then what of the rumors about her gifts as a witch.

A missing link.

Or only existed in the mind of an ill-intentioned person, who didn't come from hereabouts, or quite simply in the mind of the unfortunate uncle.

Voices from all around.

But the explanations after the event could only diminish, if not reduce to nothing, the importance of the writings in question, to see things from the analyst's point of view would in any case have been aberrant, a text worthy of the name only being what it is by a kind of grace which cares nothing for the latest craze.

Preceded by his dog which disappeared in the grass, the child used to go and pick bunches of flowers in the mornings.

A magnificent phrase which will have to be repudiated so that we can glow beyond the frightful glossary.

Step by step, this redemption.

. . . for the tourists, those disgusting swellings, you remember, she's still there, poor thing, she takes up even more room on the sidewalk, she doesn't exactly come into the flyweight class, she's getting even fatter as she gets older and she doesn't wash herself anymore, can you imagine the stench she trails around with her, it makes you feel sick.

And the other didn't know what to do with her lettuces which were going to seed, she didn't dare eat strawberries on account of urticaria, she didn't want to have anything to do with cherries on account of her intestines, she was hesitating between a tin of sardines and one of tuna fish, in the end she settled for a packet of rice, that's still what goes down best, as you might say.

Because with this craze for leaving town, the tourists are always asking me whether I know of anything for sale, only the day before yesterday I told one that the hut behind my orchard was going, well, it's already been bought, where's it all going to get us, this flight into the countryside, as the papers say.

A slate, yes, on which he notes down whatever comes into his head, and when morning comes he effaces it all, but the words stick in his throat so he retraces them.

Until the day when his hand is no longer capable of following his thought and he chokes once and for all.

But the master rebels against this prediction and repeats, no, I shall never keep silent, confusing speaking with tracing words on the slate, and he stuffs himself with remedies for rheumatoid arthritis, how stupid, you know what I think of pills and other expedients.

And of psycho-posology, or posolo-psychagogy, or menopau-chatology, in short, that's all for the moment.

What's the moment.

It's the shit you find yourself in when you're hoping to get out of it, only to fall back into it at another moment, go on.

The implausible story of Uncle Alexandre's pince-nez which it seems he only needed to put on his nose in order to see a pumpkin turn into a phoenix, a rabbit hutch or a wheelbarrow, a monumental staircase which led you up to the seventh heaven, in short his usual verbiage which with the passing years took on a clinical form as if a dream, I mean the sort that saves, could be the fruit of expedients or procedures.

Monsieur Théodore went back up to his room and noted down a thought relative to the mistaken ideas of the most distinguished minds, then he reimmersed himself in his reading.

His reading, his reading, we know what that was, old books of spells dealing with magic, witchcraft, alchemy, which he attributed to his uncle to put that idiot of a maid off the scent, tormented as he was by the pledge he had so lightly made to devote the rest of his life to Alexandre's dossiers.

Or if the old crackpot, looking as if butter wouldn't melt in his mouth, had devoted the rest of his life to the accumulation of notes relative to those matters which were as scabrous as they were esoteric, how can we tell, the so-called bound volume that's supposed to be in our library, just try and find it, it's only a fable that was given credence by some people who have never set foot in the Foundation, or who were making fun of Mademoiselle Moine.

Attached to the desk by a chain.

Ask Marie habits Alexandre and obsessions Théodore, intolerable confusion uncle nephew.

The slate in smithereens, it really made her laugh that anyone should make a drama of it, the dog had broken it by tugging at the string attaching the sponge to it, a puppy, playful like all puppies, the slate had been lying on the kitchen table, it had fallen onto the floor and got broken. Marie had replaced it the next day.

One day plus one day, the details change, you don't realize it, and then in the end you don't recognize anything anymore.

One day plus one day.

He was walking in a garden he didn't recognize anymore because an invisible manitou, et cetera, the kind of mawkishness that sets children dreaming but then that dream, where is it, and how can we gain access to it without cheating, something, a detail, a nothing, must have got lost en route.

A drifting nothing.

Something like the soul, or that kind of vagrant wind, the notion of which should one day be reconsidered with the seriousness of a child, well yes, we'll come back to that, and people will be most surprised to . . .

Most surprised, and suddenly overwhelmed.

And Monsieur Théodore, who thought he was making a discovery, was rubbing his hands like Punch after he'd given the policeman a good hiding, that would have been a sight worth seeing but there weren't any spectators.

Or that he must have been very blind to believe himself so enlightened, and what followed, in short, that sort of cheap rhetoric.

No spectators, but an ear that it was quite impossible to disregard, maybe it was the soul in question, in short that sort of *petitio principii*, at least he wasn't confusing it in order to get himself in good with what they call conscience, that old trap that is so aptly named, the science of . . .

But that at all events it was out of the question to be able to sleep when, like him, one had the task of seeing this beastly classification through to a successful conclusion.

Adieu the twenty hours of sleep, and the dream, he wouldn't find it in his bed.

Knock knock knock, Marie at the door, she was bringing his breakfast, she enters and is stupefied to see the master at his writing desk where he was sleeping like a log, he opens an eye, he says he's going to sell his bed, she says you're losing your marbles.

To sell his bed, yes, so as no longer to be tempted to sleep but to stay glued to his desk, why not attach yourself to it with a chain while you're about it, so as to find there and nowhere else the relative peace of the soul, relaxation, repose, ecstasy, or God knows what, he launched out into his verbiage again and Marie pulled him by the sleeve to where she'd put his breakfast and kept saying a good hiding, that's what you need.

Or that nature had really done things very well, to lapse into second childhood would be the salvation of anyone who has lost his soul, the only place for dreams, the nursery of chimeras, and carry on papa with your pee-pee, pot-pot chirruping.

Cut.

He did indeed babble a bit, the excellent man, when people asked him the question, why do you go on keeping your records, taking notes, making your rough drafts as you call them, he replied habit, habit, you know what it's like, and then if he had confidence he would reveal some touching little secrets about his need for company, how his papers played the part of confidants, and his need for a hobby, even when he was very young he always had to have some little work in progress, a little painting, a little sonnet, a little thingummy, adding in a very low voice, as if he were confessing to some horrid failing, I used to have gifts, yes you wouldn't think it but that's what people used to tell me, but uniquely in this domain, don't worry I never understood the first thing about mathematics, or sociology, or important things, just as well, because if that had been the case they wouldn't have got me any further than I am at this moment, there must be something strange about my character, I really don't know what to call it, but it would have prevented me from ever in my life finishing anything.

Enough good intentions to pave the whole of hell.

And then he took another sip of white wine, and he smoothed his little hat and his little moustache, and pff, once again he started jabbering adorable little things about nature, sunsets, the little mice, the coupons his mama had to have when milk was rationed, everything he could have said if he hadn't been what he would have liked not to be.

But well, obviously, we stood him another drink, and then he was enough to break your heart, mixing up helter-skelter little clichés about art, and feeling, and poverty, and the hic, pardon me, trouble you had with the taxes, and the invisible things that, hic, pardon me, what was I saying, on the occasions when it didn't all finish in little sobs.

Ah, the café of illusions, it certainly heard some things, our youth, as you might say.

Or our resignation, our colossal failure, pff, another little glass of wine.

And why not when all's said and done, said Louis the waiter, to end up like that or any other way is all much of a muchness, the hardest part is to accept it, after that you forget, but he was a drinker too and there were times when we couldn't follow his arguments, did he mean to accept one more round, we never had much difficulty in doing that, or to accept our colossal failure, in that case you go on thinking about it until the end, you cling to it as you do to a life belt, or to accept the fact of saying what you didn't mean to say, or of not saying it, in which case everything has to be started all over again, that really can't be what existence is all about, unless . . .

A missing link.

Another thing from beyond people's consciousness.

One thing's certain, Magnin added, and that is that we shall all have been in the same boat, and that's comforting, it proves we're interested in the ties that unite us and not merely in our own problems, as unthinking people claim, but did he mean comforting in the sense of resignation to our collective failure, or in the sense of necessary rebellion, which incidentally in both cases implies more rounds until the end.

The little corner on the left as you go in.

And he came out again to walk around his garden where the grass, the leaves, the perfumes, and the birds, were suddenly of the same nature as things said, everything was confused in an illocalizable murmur as if the eye, the ear, and the nose were merely one single means forged by the manitou in question to make unthinking people fall into the trap that is so aptly named.

To say it all over again, yes, that was the program, but just imagine the state of that old man who had never succeeded in anything, not even in becoming Dodo's heir, could you reproach him for losing his marbles over it, or seeming to be crushed, depending on the days, conscience is all very fine, duty, giving your word, but strength, what do you make of that, he replied, gabbling, though, we'll get there in the end, hic, pardon me, with a little method.

Or if the formula say it all over again had been whispered in his ear by an evil spirit who had dedicated itself to his downfall, because in any case, he himself had never said a thing.

Or if, by dint of repeating the crackpot's formulas, he had ended up taking them for his own.

Good God, she'll drive us bonkers, said the other, but the maid didn't take any notice or didn't hear or only so badly, she was no longer of this world, dedicated as she had been all her existence to the man who had died.

And I'll have some beans, too.

Doesn't time fly.

That old fritter they want to get us to take for the memory of Aunt Marie.

Impossible anamnesis.

What about your writing, then, is it progressing, they asked him, knowing that he was hoping to make something of his uncle's hodgepodge, he adopted a contrite air and made out that he would no longer have the strength to see it through to a successful conclusion, at the same time boasting of his failure so as to authenticate his work.

Authentic, authentic, isn't shit authentic, where do you get all your excuses from, and anyway that way of cultivating other people's fiascos, *we* are real artists.

Regress to before the flood, which is the time they still live in.

She thought she could remember, but it was all so long ago that he told her he couldn't believe it, so much of the arbitrary about this work, when you think of how serious great books are, the reflection they demand, the method they impose, he didn't feel up to it anymore but she wasn't exactly sure what he was talking about, his confidences were rare and she wasn't a woman who allowed herself indiscretions, but outspoken as usual, she added curiously, when you try to bite off more than you can chew you only get what's coming to you.

Well, that's another new one.

And in any case, who's talking about respectability.

Or that he might have told Théodore, the wheel has come full circle, everything is more or less clear to me today, or at least the essential, I can't wait to get out of it, which he did anyway a few weeks later by means of the knife we have spoken of, planted not in his back but right through his heart, he didn't miss.

Suicide camouflaged as murder, which represents a fair amount of perversity.

But then that changes everything, said Madame Buvard, how the old slob must have hated his nephew to want to get him convicted, what do you know of the sequel.

The other replied, Théodore, personally I never saw him, nor anyone from his place, it was his maid he had a grudge against, or else someone that I don't know.

Someone she didn't know.

The room was filled with a pink light, he went over to the bed where Marie was sleeping like a log, he searched her drawers, but he bumped into the chamber pot and knocked it over, the maid opened an eye, she gave a little cry, he bound her with a rope and gagged her with a scarf, then, thinking he heard a sound in the corridor he escaped through the window, taking a notebook with him.

She recounted her adventure in the disturbing, monotonic voice of a sleepwalker, and then started all over again *da capo*, like an old record playing nonstop.

Death waiting for her at the corner of the pillow.

Years later, when we were remembering these details, I did my best to get them to admit that it was a question of something quite different from either facile repetitions or word play, they didn't take any notice and called me an ignoramus, as if drama could only be the fruit of a logical argument.

And analyzed the whys and wherefores, and finally decreed that poetry had no existence outside a certain system or method.

Or as if to do away with the pillow would at the same time banish death.

Ah, if it was a question of poetry, then we understand your . . .

Cut.

Let's have a think, she said, and let's proceed with a little method, one, leeks, two, potatoes, three, radishes, four, lettuce, five, washing powder, that makes five plus four, nine, plus three, twelve, plus two, fourteen, plus one, fifteen, you owe me fifteen francs, but she'd got the wrong columns and was taking the numbers for the prices, and started adding it all up again.

As for the rumors about the maid, you know these hayseeds, a lot of thickwitted beasts, bastards, backbiters, vultures, if they don't like the look of you, right away they accuse you of being a damned soul, I imagine that Marie, being so compassionate, forced herself to listen to her neighbors' tales of woe and gave them advice their husbands couldn't stomach, hence their vengeance.

That room sealed off from every gaze.

Familiar images developed in it which were immediately replaced by others, and others again, incessant movement, those of the necropolis, hypotheses about the history of the place, those of childhoods, those of cataclysms, those of monsters, those of clouds, of roads, of skies, of circles, of heads, heads everywhere, that neurosis, hypothesis about the origin of evil, which gave tragic relief to the slightest appearance.

Carrying, dangling from a string, the parcel containing his bones, that's where we've got to.

Find elsewhere the reasons for that fierce determination.

Apart from the vestiges of a ravaged conscience.

That letter addressed no one knows to whom.

My dear nephew, I'm recovering, I'm waking up, I renounce you, disinherit you, loathe you.

An end to tergiversations.

I went back into my tomb, where I'm awaiting the resurrection of the dead.

To pass the time, and to earn two or three sous, I'm guarding a herd of pigs near the cemetery.

In the evenings I go back into my hole where believe it or not I reflect on unheard-of things, I who thought myself dedicated to perpetual repetition.

The smell of my livestock never leaves me and it's given me a new soul, the miracle has occurred.

I have found my slate again, I no longer note down regrets on it, but other . . .

And then immediately efface them.

In touch with putrefaction and decomposition, hence oriented toward the future.

A wonderful thing, now it is I who am expected, waited for elsewhere, remember the parable.

This ridiculous attempt at evasion will have been necessary in order to discover where the beyond resides.

The beyond resides.

Residence assigned to what cannot have one.

Which is to tell you, my dear nephew, that I am in possession of all my faculties, which were so frequently doubted by people like you.

Find another way of formulating the unformulatable.

Say ah, say oh.

Ah.

Oh.

This ridiculous attempt at anamnesis will have been necessary to discover where the immemorial resides.

The immemorial resides.

Which is to tell you that finally, deprived of all my faculties . . .

That business of the pigs, could it be an inspiration.

I get up before daybreak, awoken by the revolting stench and the grunts of the pigs around my tomb, they want me to open the cemetery gate for them.

For in fact they are parked there for the night.

Just imagine the state of our necropolis, hygienewise, that'll discourage the All Saints' Day fans.

I get up, then, and I go out, and I go and open the gate, jostled by the animals who squeal as they rush outside.

My task consists in not letting them stray and overrun the crops.

A missing link.

Can anyone imagine the picture, heavy with symbols.

Around ten o'clock I break my fast with a beetroot, and I meditate, with acid belches.

My God, how many belches and acidities will have been needed.

And beetroots.

Cut.

To give the impression of structure, that old trap for the unwary.

Let us cast our pearls.

Epicure and Saint Anthony.

Afflux of reminiscences, cave canem.

Apropos of dogs, he must have died in the tall grass, he'll be eaten by my pigs, it's not my business anymore.

So we've arrived at detachment.

The moment that word is out, back comes desire.

The hermit and temptation.

On the slate, the progression of desire, we'll never make an end of it.

Toward midday I pick up my beetroot again, and when I've eaten it I doze in the heavy July sun, difficult digestion, while the pigs wander all over the crops, then I have to run and chase them out.

To touch on the question of the master and of the wages, there must be a master who will remunerate me, new complication, where does he live, what is our relationship, probable link with the parable, you see dear nephew I'm not leaving anything out.

The cemetery swineherd.

They'd call me Popo, being lacking in imagination, but I should have inner resources which it would be better to conceal, to make the pleasure last longer.

That of jabbering one last secret while one still holds the floor.

Unless it's already too late to mention the pigs, maybe not knowing how to fit them in.

Unless we give them all a name to replace the dear departed, there'd be Théo Dodo Louis Alfred Alexandre et cetera, as well as Marie mother Magnin mother Chenu and Étiennette for the sows, would that be appropriate, maybe a bit too obvious.

The harvest, doesn't time . . .

Blue chicory among the corn.

As for detachment, no progress in spite of the fable.

But the grave, I'm keeping that, from now on it is my inalienable property.

Return to the fold very gently, go through the gate, alley number three hundred and thirty three and so on, all things considered it's no sadder than anywhere else and there at least no one will have the nerve to come and turn me out.

See about linking this episode to the rest.

A fine assembly of drifting words in honor of what is no longer imperative, but bah, all that savoir-faire is just vanity.

Time, that old fritter for incorrigible babes in arms.

Between two lines effaced, between two words that have become inaudible, that of resurrection.

The mountain, that blue one over there.

Children sliding down the hill on a sled.

A verbena in the garden.

The piano on the veranda was playing a waltz.

Arches covered with fairy-roses.

A needle in his heart.

Abracadabra.

When recovery is achieved, in spite of everything, start all over again with the seriousness of a child, with no other aim than pleasure, but what to do with the old man struggling on his pillow, speak to him, he can't hear anymore, wholly occupied in gathering his strength for the fatal pass.

Or find a different voice, which would reach him as if it were an elixir and which would suddenly return him to what he called his destiny, nothing other than his original state but without the artifice of time, an ineffable plunge into the water of the dream in which he had always moved.

Conscience, absurd fatigue, obstacle to any culmination.

The new law.

And, without overstating anything, the certainty of having finally been restored to poetry.

A different voice which must take over.

The only object of my efforts, to make the present minute last, or let's say to abolish it.

At distant intervals a reminder, a friendly sign, in order to test my regained strength.

The grocer's wife was seen today at old mother Buvard's funeral in the midst of all the sorrowing ladies, the deceased was a kindhearted woman in spite of her vulgar eloquence, we discovered that she had been wonderfully good to her neighbors when they were in trouble.

There was a heatwave, the dead woman was loaded onto a delivery van because she was poor, but the plastic wreaths around the bier were perfectly adequate.

Difficult to follow the new-style service at the church, the curé was the only one who was singing but on the other hand he said some sensible and consoling things.

Madame Thiéroux didn't go so far as to greet mother Magnin but she did turn up, though, in memory of the deceased.

And at the cemetery the widower stood in the shade of a cypress tree so as not to get sunstroke, which showed he still had his wits about him, nothing is more distressing for a congregation than unrestrained grief.

The cemetery overlooks the cornfields, everything was suffocating in gold and blue, it was almost worth it for such a sight.

The new law.

A window open onto the night.

Crescent moon, July on the wane, the harvest will soon be at an end.

A different voice, but all of a sudden, like a dew, the love of what has been said.

Start all over again with the seriousness of a child, I listen to the singing of the Théo that I was, old Dodo is dead and I think back to his worries and his aversions.

Something else is being prepared beyond people's consciousness, it had to be reshaped first, we have been at pains to do so.

Get back into harness again, with other aims.

The fear of what time immemorial conceals is far away, the old forgotten myths can be tamed with a little patience.

The house and its surroundings no longer have their former aspect, they have shaken off the obsessions of the occupant who deformed their appearance.

To bye-byes we go.

He wouldn't have been loved enough, that old bird of ill omen, but he had had a presentiment of something without managing to find its formula, I shall reread his notes and put them to good use.

What a lot of tergiversations in order finally to set foot on the land of the dream, which he sought but never attained.

He'll be dead before August without having paid either the interest or the principal, but another moral will take account of his passionate innocence and I shall be its author, with all due respect to the good fabulist.

Here was the field that was opening out to the survivor.

The route from the room to the well is now a path that crosses the garden diagonally, it's bordered by box trees on the left, and farther on there are daisies in the summer and dahlias in the autumn, on the right is the kitchen garden where Marie methodically grows leeks, parsley and tomatoes.

Arches covered with fairy-roses.

A needle in the heart, which has caused us to pass from one age to the next.

The piano on the veranda.

It's enough to have a phrase to transcribe.

And what is proved by the phrase, whose meanders and modifications avoid straight lines, if not that it doesn't trust them.

The love of what has been said comes back to you without warning.

And come what may.

At distant intervals a reminder, a friendly wave, I'm not afraid of nightmares anymore.

A new law requires a new fable, let's wait until it takes shape with the passing days.

Because saying and resaying are two different things, the material is expensive, a little patience 'fyou please.

The lilies of the big sleep.

Finally restored to poetry.

A verbena in the garden.

All regrets stifled, task accepted, to recompose as a defense against anguish, no matter where it may come from, that unforgotten dream, then finally leave it far behind, an old ceiling cluttered with birds and flowers in the taste of a bygone age, and progress toward the inaccessible, without landmarks, without erasures, without notes of any kind, unattainable but present, which must be believed in for fear of never dying.

● ● ● PASSACAGLIA

So calm. So gray. Not a ripple in view. Something must be broken in the mechanism, but there's nothing to be seen. The clock is on the mantelpiece, its hands tell the time.

Someone in the cold room must have just come in, the house was shut up, it was winter.

So gray. So calm. Must have sat down at the table. Numb with cold, until nightfall.

It was winter, the garden was dead, the courtyard grassy. No one would be there for months, everything is in order.

The road up to it skirts some fields lying fallow. Crows fly up, or are they magpies, you can't see very well, night is about to fall.

The clock on the mantelpiece is made of black marble, it has a gold-rimmed face and Roman figures.

The man sitting at this table a few hours earlier, found dead on the dunghill, wouldn't have been alone, a sentry was on guard, a trusty peasant who had seen no one but the deceased one cold, gray day, must have gone over to the slit in the shutter and apparently distinctly saw him put the clock out of action and then sit there prostrate in his chair, elbows on the table, head in his hands.

How to rely on that murmur, the ear is deficient.

A courtyard surrounded by old buildings, paved and clean, rectangular, with on the north side, at the entrance that's to say, a pinewood gate and two clumps of pink hydrangeas, with on the south side between the barn and the pigsty, set back a bit, an iris bed at its best in the spring, to the west the dwelling-house, to the east a young elm wood, in the center a fountain, circular basin the worse for wear, spout the shape of a chimera.

The story would seem to have begun a long time before this, but talk about prudence, talk about vigilance, it looks as if only two or three episodes have been revealed, and that with some difficulty, the source of information being permanently deficient, that almost inaudible murmur interrupted by silences and hiccups, so that you might well have attached no importance to it and considered that the whole thing started at the time when the clock was put out of action. Which side to take.

He had sat down at the table one spring day, he'd just come in, outside everything was blazing with sun, a bunch of irises in his hand which he dropped, a sudden fainting fit, and then after a period of insensibility picked up, put in a vase which he placed beside the clock, only a very few hours separated this season from the following one from which it was reasonable to presume that, if it was a question of irises, this particular variety was a late one, you couldn't hear very well, perhaps orchids, a bunch of wild orchids in high summer when the fields were flowering with all sorts of plants, he'd been seen coming back with his harvest, what sort of a man was he to decorate his house with flowers like that, solitude deranges people, inexplicable passions, manias, you never know, prudence.

Strictly speaking there was probably only the neighbor whom he posted as a sentry on certain days, not giving any reason for his mania but the neighbor being handsomely recompensed wasn't complaining, he kept watch, smoking his pipe, relieved by his wife who used to mind the goats and knit, bending over her needles, her hands forever active, she doesn't remember to look up and doesn't notice . . .

So calm, so gray. The corpse is lying flat on its stomach on the dunghill and it seems that the neighbor's child on his way back from school caught sight of it amongst the elms, touched the inert body lightly on the shoulder and then apparently rushed home to his mother, night was falling, the father was working in the kitchen garden, they called him, they went back to the scene, that was it all right, he was already stiff.

He stays there with his head in his hands, strictly speaking it isn't a malaise but what you might call a fit of abstraction, for hours, numb with cold, then he gets up and walks round the garden without bothering to open the shutters because night was falling, he's caught sight amongst the elms of the child coming home from school, may have waved to him, apparently walked round the well trying to get rid of obtrusive memories, crossed the lucerne meadow and made his way towards the maize-fields, they'd already been harvested, it was winter, after that it was beetroot and then you came to the forest.

So the neighbor and his wife and child went to identify him, it was dark, with a torch, and when they had certified the death the man said let's take him home, you take that arm I'll take the other one, they dragged him to his bedroom and put him down on the bed, the woman was perspiring, the next thing was to declare it at the town hall and the man said I'll go, we'd better lock the house up till I come back, you go back to your kitchen with the kid because he was hungry, this wasn't the first corpse he'd had to cope with, the wife and child went off, he shut the door, the key was in the lock, he turned round, focused his torch on the front of the house where all the shutters were closed, not the slightest sign of the accident, there'd been no witness and no one supposed to know that the owner had come back this gray winter's day to inspect the premises, had put the key back in the lock and opened the door again, you never know, prudence, and then went over to the village.

The road leading to it skirts some fields lying fallow. Crows fly up, or are they magpies, you can't see very well, night is about to fall.

Something broken in the mechanism.

In the book he was leafing through there was an old-fashioned illustration, the sort he adored, queer fellow, inexplicable passions, the murmur was getting weaker, brooding over his cheerless days, the conversations with the doctor, the comings and goings in the paved courtyard, the solitude.

The difficulty for anyone who has cut across the fields is to find the road again a couple of miles further on, the paths are nothing but mud at this time of year, and then flooded meadows that you have to skirt round on the left, then the marsh on the edge of the pinewood which is a very strange place, full of birds' carcasses and feathers among the brambles, when nature reclaims her rights in the middle of a cultivated field she's more awe-inspiring than she is in a primeval forest, and then turn right, and there's an old quarry, prickly hedges and bits of soft, ploughed ground which are difficult to cross.

The neighbor was going down to the village one cold gray day, he was on his way to tell the mechanic that his tractor had got stuck in the mud in a field and that nothing happened when he pressed the self-starter, he'd been tinkering with the engine all the previous evening without the slightest success, hadn't a clue, the mechanic would come up with his breakdown van, one more bloody expense to add to those of the summer for the same machine.

The neighbor the previous evening had been tinkering with his engine by the light of a torch and a storm-lantern which he'd first put on the seat of the tractor and then balanced on the nearside front wheel.

But the goatherd bending over her knitting had started visibly when he came up, he'd teased her saying something like you must have a guilty conscience, you couldn't hear very well, the woman had laughed, toothless mouth, cheeks as red as a lady-apple, little eyes of different colors, they say she's pretty wily.

Went over, then, towards the forest by way of the mud paths and came to a halt because of the exceptional level of the water in the marsh, had to make a detour of something over half a mile to get to the wood and coming out by the pine-knoll apparently caught sight on his left about a hundred yards farther on of the tractor stuck in the mud and then coming along on the road the mechanic's breakdown van. An instinctive step backwards. Fear of being seen.

Then went back to his reading, for hours, numb with cold, in that enclosed room, it was a dark night, no one unless he had his nose right up against the slit in the shutter would have suspected that he was there in this season, the goatherd had long gone home with her animals, the neighbor too had come back from the village, it was winter, it was beginning to rain, the first drops could be heard hitting the cobblestones in the courtyard.

That corpse on the dunghill.

Something broken in the engine.

The grassy courtyard today, no trace of the old cobblestones but the proportions between the buildings are still harmonious, very little change unless it's a corrugated iron shed on the north side, a few more young elms to the east and fewer stones on the cover of the well, nothing much, if you didn't know you wouldn't have noticed anything but a conscience can't be prevailed upon to cheat, he'd had his day, the solitude which was supposed to be inconsiderable had become intolerable, the old-fashioned illustration in the book, through the enlarged slit in the shutter anyone outside would have seen distinctly that cold room in the lamplight and the reader leaning his elbows on the table, he's stopped moving, the hands have fallen off the clock-face.

Then they came with the mayor and the doctor, the door was still open, and they saw the man sprawling over the table, the book had fallen on to the floor, they decided to lift up the corpse which was already stiff, they put it as best they could on the armchair by the fire, huddled up, askew, they would wait for it to become more malleable, thanks to the cold it hadn't started to smell yet, the neighbor's wife prepared the bed, they would put it on it for a few hours just time for the formalities which would be simplified as there was no survivor, in the drawer in the table they found a will to be given to the coroner, they wondered what on earth could be in it, the buildings weren't of any value, one more ruin in the district which already had its fair share.

The sentry seems to have seen something over by the elms, apparently waited, watching the path leading out of the wood to the barn, but nothing appeared, apparently went to look, not a sign of anyone, night was about to fall accompanied by its phantasms, who knew that evening how far their enticement might go, you had to be on your guard, not flinch.

There'd been that great friendship with the doctor, for years, they couldn't do without each other, walks in the forest until nightfall, conversations by the fireside, boring things like that but they understood perfectly well, they'd gone halfway along the road together and suddenly one died and suddenly the survivor was a stranger to himself, lost all interest, there'd never be a fire in the hearth again.

The peasant stationed at the corner of the hedge explained that he'd seen the mechanic coming with his breakdown van, he was going along the road towards the marsh, and he'd wondered whether it wasn't the neighbor's machine again which had seen better days, he'd bought it secondhand the previous year and had had nothing but trouble with it, which only goes to show that nothing's ever as good as new, anyway it was sheer stinginess, he knew him, even when he was quite young, you couldn't get him to part with a sou, he needn't go complaining then, as for the mechanic, he isn't grumbling, he makes his living out of breakdowns, apparently he waved to him, he had his apprentice with him.

A few pictures that needed amplifying, extricating from their dross, obscuring until the moment when, having become interchangeable, their profound difference would give rise to a world of aggression and rout, that was the task he'd set himself at this very table, in this cold house haunted by years of insouciance, here everything took on the accents of nostalgia and on some evenings of terror, phantasms of the night that leave nothing of memory's suggestions intact.

Working on marginal notes.

But the doctor continued, he had gone to the master's that day in the morning round about ten o'clock to spend the day with his comrade, even at that time he hardly had any patients left, practically retired, he hadn't found anyone, sat down on the terrace, on the south side that is, behind the house, he couldn't be seen from the gate, thinking that the master must have gone for a stroll in the wood by the marsh or in the forest and would be back before noon, the peasant who claims to keep guard on certain days must have gone down the lane at about half past ten and not seeing anyone in the courtyard must have walked round to the kitchen, gone in and put a duck that the maid had ordered on the table, he apparently stayed some time in the kitchen and searched the drawer in the table and even the big cupboard in the dining room where the master kept his papers.

So calm. So gray. Crows or magpies fly up, startled by the noise of the breakdown van going down the narrow road. Leaden sky, traces of hoarfrost.

At his table in the cold house the master going back to his book was making a marginal note by the side of a murmured phrase, you couldn't hear very well, shadows, phantasms of the night, the story will never come to light, no visible flaw. Something broken in the mechanism.

But his maid at about seven in the evening went into the dark room and said as she lit the lamp that's you all over, don't tell me you were working, it isn't right to daydream like that, will monsieur kindly allow me to lay the table, she pushed his papers over to the left, he got up and poked the fire.

A few pictures to extricate from their dross in order to discover beneath their weft disorder, distress, and then progressively a lull, so many years of this work, shadows never so dense, phantasms reduced to hiccups, night would only come impromptu when it was no longer desired.

Told the story of his death that he had imagined in detail, amplified over the years, tragic or touching according to the evening, by the fire, the bottle of spirits on the table, so that the doctor fell asleep to the swaying of the hearse while his companion introduced into his memories new episodes which would be the object of comment the next time or which would be deleted from the definitive version shortly before he went to bed but his dreams recast everything, upset the order and it would take the narrator till tomorrow and even longer to restore the verisimilitude to his story.

The sentry had seen the mechanic go by, he wasn't going towards the marsh but in the opposite direction, the doctor before he settled down on the terrace had walked right round the house, he'd tried to go in through the kitchen but the door was locked, it was probably the maid's day off, it was harvest time, the terrace which faced south was already stifling at that hour and the doctor opened the umbrella in the center of the iron table, he lay back in a blue-striped deck chair, he had taken the book with the old-fashioned illustrations from the room and was looking through it when it seems that the man with the duck called out from the courtyard, the doctor would have answered and the man must have gone up to him and put the bird on the table.

As you went down from the terrace to the river you crossed a garden in tiers, on the top level on either side of the steps there were rose beds in the middle of which a pedestal formed the base for a vase decorated with mythological bas-relief, each bed had a box border, and yew-trees occupied the angles of the squares, a balustrade separated this first level from the next, in which ornamental lakes replaced the flower beds, the center of each being adorned with a fountain, at either end were orange trees round a bust of a satyr or a tree-nymph.

At his table was making a marginal note by the side of an empty phrase on happiness to be dispassionately revised, as if in all logic . . .

The maid brought in the soup, the master helped himself absent-mindedly, he'd got up to his removal from the town, hundredth repetition, when there was a knock at the outside door, he goes to open it, it's the child bringing a duck, he gives him a couple of sous for his trouble and the child leaves, he calls the maid and gets her to put the bird in the fridge, after that she cleared the table and the master was noting in the margin of the book . . .

A handsome façade on the garden side, six windows upstairs, slate roof and turrets of the same material flanking the corners of an almost stately home in which the neurotic, stingy owner was moping.

So calm. So gray. Crows or magpies fly up from the beetroot field and go and perch on an elm.

The master on the terrace at the iron table was writing his memoirs, he'd got up to his removal from the capital into a largish village on the hill or by the forest, you couldn't hear very well, the doctor was walking up and down in the lower garden, autumn weather, blueness of the air.

If I'd known, he said, that all that effort was going to have such a miserable result, writing my memoirs for a monthly magazine, but the doctor comforted him, it was just as good an activity as any other and it even had an extra something, the literary aura, there was nothing to mope about, a good many existences he knew of finished in a less satisfactory fashion, he definitely had everything he needed and the leisure, that was important, leisure, what would he do without the delightful fireside chats, without the care his maid took of him, in short hundredth repetition on the terrace one fine autumn day, they'd got to the coffee, the doctor was just about to fall asleep and his companion was calculating the cost of building a greenhouse at the bottom of the French garden.

Or else alone, sprawling over the table in that cold room one winter's day, the fire out, door open on to the grassy courtyard in the center of the dilapidated buildings, the wind was whistling in the elms, the neighbors' child was home from school, night was failing.

Then she said monsieur could at least mend the clock, I never know the time, my alarm's always slow, to which he replied get your alarm mended, I know, ask the doctor after all, an old joke, the maid went back to her kitchen, she would be dishing up at any moment, he went back to his reading.

Those years spent waiting for no one knew what and then not waiting for anything anymore, in the end people started making fun of him and mothers used to tell their brats that they'd get the old man to eat them up if they weren't good, his hat on his head and his leather boots, were they yellow or red, you couldn't quite tell, he was going towards the marsh again and disappeared round the corner of the quarry.

He had long pondered over this story of the corpse and had given it his assent, though still hesitating about the time and about the child but they weren't of any great importance, a dunghill, what could be more suitable.

He had arrived one gray day, had come in through the kitchen, hadn't opened the shutter because night was about to fall, he had crossed the big room and seen the faded bunch of flowers and the book on the table, must have decided to postpone his reading and gone out again into the courtyard, then walked round the garden and saw on the dunghill . . . everything perfectly logical, no discrepancies.

Was writing his memoirs between two inebrieties, source of information deficient, the period in town and meetings on the promenade, springtimes are so short, those endless removals in pursuit of no one knew what and now nocturnal terrors, murmured appeals, phantasms that loom up in spite of the lamplight, infinite distress.

From one year to the next these great changes in depth.

The marsh with its birds' carcasses.

The goatherd had gone out round about ten o'clock with her flock, six pepper-and-salt-colored animals, she'd gone limping down the lane leading to the marsh, her camp stool under her arm, her black shawl on her head, the dog was frisking about by her side, a ratter that snaps at the animals' hocks but doesn't know its job, they've disappeared round the corner of the quarry, it was bluish, glacial December weather, hoarfrost, frozen mud, the mechanic coming from the opposite direction with his breakdown van apparently met them a good deal farther away than the marsh, which was hard to explain given the pace the old girl was going but these things happen in the country, a few moments' inattention are enough to confuse your sense of time, even perhaps to change the pace people walk at, you've just seen them dragging their feet or dawdling along the road, a few moments later you can't see them anymore.

She stopped for a second to get her breath, looking in the direction of the village which you can't see from there, a gently-sloping field meets the horizon, crows or magpies flew up and perched on an elm, lapwings were foraging in a ploughed field, others going over towards the marsh, the little dog started barking when it saw the breakdown van appearing about half a mile away, movements are as rare as noise in this part of the world, it ran something like twenty yards, the old woman called it back and started walking again, the breakdown van then disappeared round the other end of the quarry where the road slopes down again, the goats which were beginning to graze all along the lane started off again too with sudden little jumps, strings of droppings and bleats.

In the garden the doctor after he'd walked round the flower beds settled down in his deckchair and started to read the old-fashioned book with a pastis in his hand, the duck man arrived by way of the lower garden which gives on to a little gate, he'd come from the direction of the marsh because he said to the doctor I saw the mechanic coming up with his breakdown van, the neighbor's tractor again I'll bet, why does he always buy such junk, he'll never change, a wasp fell into the glass of pastis, oh, go and get another glass you know the way, it was probably then that the man went into the kitchen and he comes back with his glass saying how is it that the maid isn't there, it isn't Thursday so far as I am aware, it's explained to him that she's at the postman's funeral, he'd been found dead on the dunghill three days earlier, the duck man said I thought as much I mean that he'd finish like that, he was drunk from morning to night, because this was the first he'd heard of the demise on account of his recent rounds on the borders of our region, he's a breeder and calls with his van every Wednesday to take or deliver orders, corn-fed, very good poultry, he was sipping his aperitif and saying it's strange, just think with all this scouring the countryside there are times when how can I put it I get the feeling that I'm not there, I sometimes think I'm somewhere else or it's another time of year, just like that all of a sudden, only the other day I was driving along a road in the middle of winter, it doesn't last but should I do something about it, what do you think doctor, the doctor replied watch your liver and come and see me, I'll take your blood pressure.

The feeling of not being there, yes, something broken as if what he'd just said had happened at some other time or that he wasn't himself at the moment of speaking, God how complicated it is, or that because it's such a long journey, because he does it so often or because he doesn't pay enough attention or that anyone could do the same journey blindfolded anywhere else with anyone's van, come and see me the doctor repeated, and they sipped their pastis the one tormenting himself on account of this strange illness, the other blinking in the admirable light, the blueness of the landscape in the distance, the forest on the horizon, the fields of rapeseed and the green walnut trees.

The master must have got home at about one o'clock, he walked up the different tiers of the garden and saw the two of them on the terrace, after greeting them he too sat down, poured himself out a pastis and was amazed to find the doctor there at this hour on this day, he hadn't done anything about providing lunch but never mind, they'd have yesterday's leftovers with a good salad, the poulterer must have left at about a quarter past one and the others went on drinking for a good half-hour, the master said he'd been down to the marsh and had seen the breakdown van, the doctor smiled, no doubt about it you really are a happy lot, the only thing that happens in a whole morning, a tractor stuck in the mud or I don't know what and everyone's talking about it as if it were a great event, because he'd met another neighbor on his way there.

Then fed up with waiting for the two drunks the servant came out on to the terrace and said monsieur is served, an antiquated expression that amused the doctor, the duck will be burnt and it won't be my fault.

In the glacial room was leafing through the book, December evening, the clock was showing the maid's time, the rain was beating down on the cobbles in the courtyard.

An April shower, the garden swamped, the plan for the greenhouse on the lower level, two notes from a blackbird resuscitated his childhood, everything would start again in the spring.

That murmur interrupted by silences and hiccups.

Then the other man left and towards the end of the day someone apparently saw him over by the marsh, they heard about it at the café where conversations intersect and intermingle, anyone who isn't really listening doesn't follow what's being said and with the help of the booze everything merges into a sort of monotonous drone which is always the same, come winter, come summer, so that you could . . .

Or the goatherd on that pink and blue morning may have branched off a good way before the quarry and gone down the road to the village, probably sat herself down in the sheltered corner between the orchard wall and the neighbor's barn, out of the wind, and started knitting while the ratter was frisking about in the stubble, he can amuse himself with a mouse, an insect, a shadow, with his own tail, sometimes he suddenly starts rushing round in a circle as fast as he can go, another circle, another half one, he stops abruptly, sniffs at something and then goes running up to his mistress who gives him a little slap on the nose, he'll never learn anything, the goats are grazing the hedge, the old woman stands up and shouts, she waves her stick threateningly, she limps off and drops some stitches in her knitting.

And on her way home she met the master coming back from the marsh, he apparently said isn't it cold, have you got proper heating, she answered yes or no, you couldn't hear very well, you could see her make a vague gesture, you could imagine her lady-apple face and her toothless smile, too far away to catch the details, they said something else to each other for maybe another minute, he pointed over in the direction of the marsh, you could see them part, it must have been one o'clock, time for lunch, the sky was already becoming overcast, rain soon, how can we count on a normal season these days.

Leave nothing of memory's suggestions intact.

Night again, close the shutters again, that lament again, it'll never come to an end now, in the inner ear, which is why you can't properly hear the eddies on the surface.

Even so it was something, that tragic end on a dunghill, they'd told the doctor who contrary to the deceased's expectations had shown sincere grief, he's quite distraught, he stands there in the middle of the room, he can't take his eyes off the corpse huddled up in the armchair, the neighbor's wife pushes a chair over to him, forces him to sit down and goes into the kitchen to heat up some coffee.

But the neighbor's child had so much imagination, a highly-strung child, impressionable, that it seems he took the scarecrow for a corpse, either it had been blown onto the dunghill by a gust of wind or the master had put it there, and he didn't apparently go anywhere near it but went and told his parents who, once on the scene . . .

Phantasms of the night and of yesterday and tomorrow, death at the slightest deficiency in thought, like the scene of an interior with a window opening on to the desert, the void from which you protect yourself by inescapable domestic pursuits.

The sentry posted behind the wood apparently saw someone coming up and walking round the house at daybreak in this humid cold that goes right through you, he'd moved so as to be able to watch the door into the kitchen, then nothing, went up to the building, walked round it, no sign except for a pair of secateurs left on the bench on the south side since the autumn, already rusty, which he put in his pocket.

The sentry, a wily peasant who claims he suffers from nervous disorders which are difficult to control.

And the other person, this had been going on for years, who was watching the master from a window . . .

So calm. So gray. An old pigeon was tottering along the roof of the barn. There's a puddle in the middle of the grassy courtyard. On the south side a little cluster of leafless plum trees.

The doctor like an old pigeon was shuffling round the courtyard of an old people's home or else pushed by a nurse was catching cold under his blanket, the master used to go and see him and between two nose-drips the old man mumbled his apologies or memories, you couldn't hear very well.

When suddenly the maid appeared and said don't try and make out you were working, I saw you at the window on the lookout.

The time is out of joint.

The mother in the carriage leading to exile. Then in the little suburban garden they'd chosen. Until the day when the page had been turned and you could no longer imagine her other than covered with daisies in her young girl's dress.

The sentry posted at the corner of the wood rubbed his eyes at daybreak and saw the carcass of an animal on the dunghill with its feet in the air and its belly slit open.

On the bit of bloody lawn where the neighbor's child was playing, unspeakable anguish, when all the ghosts from elsewhere have emigrated for the last time into the innermost recesses of memory.

In the margin beside an empty phrase.

Tainted with mildew they either dragged themselves along in great masses or hoisted themselves up the girders or dived down into the cellars through the trapdoors.

Source of information deficient.

Through trying to catch that murmur between two hiccups he had at first managed to make his hearing more acute so long as youth had lasted but once he was over the bend it had gradually started to diminish and resulted not long before the aforementioned period in solid deafness, internal crackling, dizzy spells and headaches but by exercising all his willpower, like a streetcorner musician, he had reconstituted a kind of passacaglia.

So calm. So gray.

On his way down from the master's house where he had delivered his duck the man had landed up in the ditch with his van and he had been trapped underneath it for a good hour until the children on their way home from school discovered him and went and told the gendarme who told the mechanic and the two of them with some others were struggling to get the thing out, heave ho, finally they managed to release the driver, all he had was a broken leg and the neighbor offered to drive him to hospital, the man was groaning like a woman, you'd never have believed it, him being so tough, the doctor who doesn't practice anymore except when the occasion arises said that it wasn't all that marvelous the way they dealt with you at the hospital, that in this sort of case a thorough examination was indicated, his head might be injured too, next, that's to say that evening in the café, the mechanic was explaining the sort of maneuvers he goes in for each time, this wasn't the first, with his breakdown van, but you didn't know whether he was talking about the van or the tractor, too far away, deafening noise of all those voices and of the pin-table, makes you wonder what the regulars got out of it but calm and reflection are not very highly prized round our parts, noise intrudes into even the most remote domicile in the form of wireless cacophonies, sweet songs, and other parasites.

In the meantime the garden under its white mantle, sudden snow-showers and squalls, was secretly preparing its silly little surprises, its stereotypes, its childish joys . . .

In the cold room the book fallen on to the floor.

Or the secateurs left on the bench.

Or the memory of the maid like an astringent for traditional purposes.

Crows fly up cawing, bad sign, you wondered what sins of commission or omission you had perpetrated, conscience never clear, the doctor on the terrace raising his eyes from his newspaper said remember that flight of crows was it January or February, this or that calamity apparently hit the village, adieu to all the optimistic projects . . .

Crows or magpies.

Hundredth repetition.

Those pictures to extricate from their dross.

As for the goatherd she fell asleep counting her stitches, her flock wandered over to the marsh and impelled either by greed or curiosity ventured into it and got stuck, the lame woman only caught up with them much later, night was falling, when the mechanic went into the café.

While the master who thought he was alone got up out of his chair, went over to the fireplace, hesitated for a second and then broke the hands of the clock, the act of a maniac, it was only the next day apparently when he was himself again that he did what he could to stick the hands back on the clockface so that the maid shouldn't know.

And the other man, leaving the slit in the shutter walked round the wood again, passed the dunghill again where the scarecrow was lying with outstretched arms, took his little boy's hand again and they both went off towards the pasture-land, pale, pure sky, hoarfrost on the blades of grass, ice in the potholes in the road, real winter weather that shrivels you up under your jacket and grips your skull in a vice.

Goats getting stuck.

What to do with all these snippets.

Bit by bit the traces of the olden days faded from his memory, names, words, as if the immense wave of exile . . . or the fact that . . . nothing and no one anymore, gray shadows heralding the night, he'd end up taking refuge behind the stove with the dishcloths, a nice quiet corner, dreaming of bacon soup and scratching his groin.

And the other man, leaving the slit in the shutter walked round the wood again, he saw someone running over towards the marsh, how could he follow him, night was falling, he takes his little boy's hand again and passes in front of the dunghill on which the dead cow stands out as a sort of light patch, they'll be suspicious, so and so must have killed it but they can't find any excuse to question him, why have it in for the cow, it died of cold, no trace of any injury, and the farmer's wife who kept saying such a good milker.

An old jealousy, the father explained, he'd kept company with the farmer's wife when she was a girl and amongst neighbors . . . or something like the suspicion people had had that he used to water his milk, shame and hate are involved and he poisons the cow instead of the farmer.

Goes up to the corpse, cuts off the udder with his penknife and throws it into the neighbor's barn as he goes by, it was dark, you could see a ray of light through the kitchen shutter, not a sound.

That mutilated corpse, with its bloodstained trouser fly.

That they must have been illuminated in those transitional days by something other than the light of judgment, a way of foreseeing with serenity what was to follow because it's long, it's deflected for ever, now, what's the use of trying.

The town promenade. False perspectives between the trees. Floating whitish loves through the narrow openings of imaginary doors invited you on Sundays to the accent of Te Deums. That fermentation up to the grave, no reason to be surprised at the cleanliness of corpses so soon, so soon.

The servant takes the soup out and comes back with an udder on a dish. They start chewing. Milk runs down their chins and thin trickles of blood.

To come back to the goatherd she said as she brought in the coffee, I saw her waiting for the van to arrive, she stopped a long time on her way pretending to be getting her breath but you know her, she's a wily one, and the fact that she hadn't taken her dog would you say that was just by chance, not at all, while the master was remembering having seen the hound frisking about in the stubble, the doctor concluded that nothing we see has failed to be imagined previously.

The story will never come to light, no visible flaw.

And thinking later in the cold room about what he had casually asserted that he could now only envisage by snippets he sat there prostrate in his chair, a puppet, hands hanging, nose reddened, with as if on the reverse side of tears that ridiculous and painful laugh that turned into a hiccup, no possible explanation unless . . . and once again the servant came back, lit the lamp and said you aren't going to tell me.

Working on marginal notes.

He pulled himself together after the coffee and produced his page of memoirs, trying to find an anecdote, all the afternoon, the light was going, when the maid came back with the soup, monsieur is served, according to a fixed rhythm, expressions that hark back to the flood, same arrangements for piano solo, but what's happening, nothing, nothing's happening, the carriage was leaving for exile with its contingent of down-and-outs, they'll get there one day, they'll draw the curtains at daybreak and find . . .

In the heated room the two friends glass in hand are evoking memories. Fine china hanging on the walls, old furniture shining as a result of the maid's assiduous polishing duster, a well-to-do house, no urgent needs. Outside the light is going, the clouds are gathering, it'll rain before nightfall. The last hen in the yard goes into the henhouse to roost. The guinea fowls can be heard crying. Crows or magpies fly up from the neighboring field and go and perch on an elm tree. A tractor comes out on to the road from the ploughed fields and disappears round the corner of the quarry. On the neighbor's side, the sound of the axe on the chopping block.

As if the account of these multifarious instants . . .

And the other, abandoning the slit in the shutter, went limping back to her herd, whistled to her dog who was running round in circles in the stubble and tells how as she was on her way back from the pasture-land she saw the breakdown van covered in blood, she took the long way round by the lane but later she had time to notice on the dunghill a flight of crows like in the year of the death of her poor mother, and after that behind the wood a shadow, always the same one, you couldn't quite tell, that went running away towards the village, all this boded no good.

Because you had to make hay while the sun shone, quick quick before it goes, make use of the slightest lull as if the little bit of time granted . . .

On his way down from the master's house where he had delivered his duck the vanman took the road leading to our county town, the characteristic troubles he suffers from and which will soon force him to give up driving, advised by his doctor, in the first place they distress him and then they make him stop a couple of times en route, he explains a few days later that he had had the impression that he'd been going along the road in the opposite direction with no recollection of when he'd been that way before.

The master is on the terrace taking the clock to pieces.

The ornamental lakes reflect clouds that don't seem to be in the sky.

In the margin beside an empty phrase about happiness made a note, pleasure of false discoveries.

But the dream remodeled everything, upset the order, and it would take the testator till tomorrow and even longer to restore the verisimilitude to his document.

What to make of these snippets.

Go back on to the terrace, you can see the dunghill from there.

That mutilated corpse, with its bloodstained trouser fly.

And the other man leaving the slit in the shutter retraces his steps, walks round the wood and sees the scarecrow, the dummy, stuck on a bush, he takes it down and throws it on to the dunghill, the mechanic who was passing with his breakdown van called out something to him, you couldn't hear very well, the man continued on his way down to the marsh, at the bend by the quarry he sees the doctor, he goes towards him, about fifty yards separated them, and when he arrives he realises that there isn't anyone there, he goes back up in his van to make his usual journey with the usual mirages.

The town promenade. Floating, whitish loves through the narrow openings of imaginary doors.

The sentry apparently saw him come out of the room and go running down the road, he was looking for the doctor who was there in front of his eyes dropping off to sleep, he went looking for him as far as the marsh, he made his way through the mud, up to the pinewood where amongst the carcasses the white, white skeleton was swinging, he sat down underneath it, he opened the book at the appropriate page and found in the margin a note he didn't understand, so much effort put into this exegesis, and disappeared just before night fell into that rising mist, then the sky clears, he had to go back, back to the snores and take up the thread again, the sentry will never put a foot right.

But he said straightaway that it was impossible, he was parked with his breakdown van right under the scarecrow, no one had touched it at that moment, it must have been later, at nightfall, well it was that particular moment that the neighbor's wife had been talking about, he had apparently gone behind a hedge to urinate while the other was cutting down the scarecrow, but on the dunghill, no he hadn't put it there, he'd taken it with him, even though from a distance you couldn't quite tell, he seemed to be holding his little boy by the arm.

Holding his little boy by the arm to get him across the marsh like a doll, the kid wasn't touching the ground, you could divine the two of them in that mist at nightfall, they landed on the other side, the pine-wood, amongst the birds' carcasses, an image that remained graven there, in the book, then the whitened skeleton hanging on the bush with for tutelary divinities those beaks, those shrivelled up wings, those breastbones, those skinny feet, it made you tremble, you came back to it, the page was never turned.

Hundredth repetition.

The sky was becoming overcast with little clouds that didn't seem to be reflected in the ornamental lakes.

Or the watchful echo in the recess of the barn repeating word for word the phrase murmured at half-word intervals caused the syllables to overlap and the indiscreet ear to retain . . .

To go back the way you came, turn, return, revert. Murmurs, divinatory formulae, tedious repetition.

In the cold room, an old rug over his shoulders, the master alchemist of the nothings that enabled him to survive was leafing through the book, making marginal notes, picking up the magnifying glass and daydreaming over the shape of an outline, of a piece of calligraphy, of a white patch he discovered over the water in the lake, dissipation of a haze, semblance of a line, survival of a word, his existence as you might say cut off, cut down, one level lower, fashioning spaces in its own image, so as to be able to move without collision, like an old-fashioned and obstinate skater in the sempiternal morning of his mania.

On the road that goes there a black mass is advancing, at first either crawling or rolling, you can't see very well, and then upright like a wall, silent, the fledglings fly away, the field mice disappear, a velvet edifice that all of a sudden fractures and frays, it's a flight of crows, the fields are grayish, the sky has faded.

On the road that goes there a black mass is advancing, it's a very tall man, you can't see very well, coming this way, you think you see two men one on top of the other, coming this way, you see it's a peasant and a scarecrow, he stops, the fledglings have relapsed into silence, the man goes into a vineyard and sticks the dummy in a bush, he ties it to the stem with a rope, it stretches out its arms, its head is hanging, it looks like a corpse that's already stiff.

In the quarry a shape is moving, it's crawling up to the ridge, a gentle slope, it's stopping, or watching, it digs itself in, it reappears farther on, rolls down to the path below, then drags itself along for fifty yards, there's time to see the night fall completely, later the man will be found lying on the dunghill, his arms outstretched.

Turn, return, revert.

The sentry dozing behind the wood heard a branch crack, he opened an eye, the night was clear and glacial, he got up, cocked his gun, crept in amongst the trees, saw a ray of light through the slit in the shutter, went up, glued his eye to the slit, the master was putting the clock out of action, come back to inspect the premises, no one would be there for months, the house is shut up, everything is in order.

Afterwards he told the goatherd that the master had come back to inspect the premises, light through the slit in the shutter, he had gone over but must have fallen asleep again in the meantime because there wasn't anybody there, the house is shut up, everything is in order, when suddenly the child came up shouting something, you couldn't hear very well, it was before nightfall and while the neighbor's tractor, which makes such a din, was going by, the child was on his way home from school and had apparently seen on the dunghill . . . his mother had questioned him before she put him to bed but how could you rely on the brat, he has too much imagination.

He remembered the former layout of the premises, the courtyard surrounded by old buildings, not much more, but in the interior a table and a mantelpiece with a little black clock in the place of honor, gold-rimmed face and Roman figures, he'd never seen it going but perhaps heard, heard, on what occasion . . .

An old pigeon tottering along the roof of the barn.

You could also hear the glug-glug of the fountain in the middle of the courtyard as far as the road to the marsh but nothing from the north, the barn side that is, a louder noise was needed to awaken the echo, a curious fact when you think of the slightest sound reflected back in the other direction even a branch cracking, even a murmur, or if the doctor only spoke of it years later, not remembering the distances anymore, a sentimental old dyspeptic, his friendship with the other man null and void ages before.

Inexplicable passions.

When the morning was well advanced, went the rounds of the buildings, keeping his ears open for the slightest sounds that insinuated themselves at this hour above the birdsong, sometimes found the sentry asleep under a shelter, woke him with a tap on the shoulder, he muttered a few apologies and went off to drink his coffee, the master continued on his rounds, inspected the remotest corners and very often tried out the barn echo by uttering a groan that came back to him as something quite innocuous, evanescent phantasms, then he too went home and the maid who was singing softly in the kitchen brought in the coffee.

Was noting in the margin beside an empty phrase.

Sprawling over his table, loss of consciousness, the doctor gets busy and with the maid carries him on to his bed, when he opens his eyes he starts talking about the flight of the crows again, while the servant was making one last cup of beef-tea for this caricature, the word would be written, salutary for the incarnations to come, a warning, she brought the beverage but he'd given up the ghost, the doctor was sobbing in the next room, it was all over.

There was nothing left of the false mystery of the night.

In town they were remarking on the event, they said they'd known him, they were amazed that they'd lost sight of him for so long, they recalled some acts of his childhood and youth which ought to have made them smell a rat, was it believable in this day and age, practicing magic or whatever it's called, the schoolmaster said that it was still traditional somewhere or other, he'd studied, all sorts of ridiculous words, fetishes, the evil eye, amulets, and one thing leading to another very old memories of our parts, we weren't too clear whether they were grandmothers' tales or children's nightmares, it seems that they were still dormant in people's consciousness, well and now that thing what d'you call it appeared today, there were proofs, a real danger for the population, we were at its mercy, sorcery or Middle Ages what is it exactly, a group of sadists who made books of spells and love philters, it was enough to make you tremble.

The other neighbor, the woman who sells fruit and vegetables in the market, that little stall in the corner on the right as you go in, not all that fresh, she's always smuggling in bad tomatoes or over-ripe fruit, started to say that her little girl had been odd for several months, she was always at Mass or in the cemetery and didn't look well and no appetite, they questioned her, she answered yes when it should have been no and things that didn't follow like for instance some tale of a pin in her pants or her catechism book hidden under her pillow, such a gay child and from one moment to the next she became moody and overscrupulous adding I think to everything she said or starting to cry because she'd make a mistake in giving change at the grocer's or what's more serious asking her father questions about death and babies' corpses and the life everlasting, you can imagine my husband, he tells me about it in the evenings, he's sure the child ought to see a doctor, well those things down there that aren't normal come up here, a sort of influence like the flu or foot-and-mouth disease, that's what she said.

Or like the plumber for some time now all the pipes he repairs are blocked in the same place, he can go to it with his eyes shut, and a sort of fungus the like of which he's never seen runs all along the drains or sink pipes or I don't know what, and what's even more disturbing is that it's always at the same moment between eight and eight-ten that his customers telephone him, he can't keep up with the demand, he saw his colleague in the new part of the town and he says the same, there's something fishy behind it all.

Or other signs that people wouldn't have noticed in normal times like two people talking to each other who keep stumbling at short intervals over the same word.

This question of talking or of keeping quiet, of being precise or not, of saying too much about it or not enough was apparently more or less what the schoolmaster was pointing out in his lecture on tragedy except that then we wouldn't have understood anything mysterious thinking that it was a question of a specialist in French who had to do his job conscientiously like everyone else, not suspecting I repeat that the thing in one sense making all due allowance concerned us all and that it was only our naivety that prevented us seeing thank God the appalling abysses on the brink of which we play around with our slightest word, yes this affair brought us right up against something of this sort, this man had a power, he acted covertly without ever getting mixed up in anyone's life.

Whereas other people described these subtleties as nonsense, the master had always been an impostor and went on sowing discord at the same time as he was giving himself airs, they quite bluntly reminded each other of the dishonest things he'd done as a young man, not just telling lies but the shady schemes he'd been involved in, do you remember that so-called antiques business, all the articles were new fakes neither more nor less.

Or that none of it had anything to do with anything, they were imagining things, you had to let everything find its own level and life goes on, none of this makes us any wiser or any richer.

People we don't know go past on the road in their car, they stop outside the neighbor's, we see them talking to the wife, then outside the other one's place but there's no one there at this hour, then go off again still very slowly, they're certainly looking for something, when they pass a man on his way back from the fields.

They were to find out little by little that he sometimes entertained people from the town but never the same ones, different cars, someone seems to have carried his curiosity so far as to take their numbers.

And so without anything having apparently changed, the work goes on, the worries and little joys typical of these parts, in short, life, nevertheless it looked as if some profound mechanism had been set in motion which would undermine the foundations of our edifice, that laborious accumulation of straws in the wind, no power could oppose it, no resistance.

Or other signs that we wouldn't have noticed in normal times.

That story of contagion and foot-and-mouth disease had put them on their guard, where would all this lead us the plumber added, we'd have to institute proceedings but there wasn't any accused, against whom to take action, it was just simply that strange events had followed one another like the blocked pipes and that cat that had eaten her kittens, or irritating ones like a supplementary tax on agricultural machinery which hadn't been published in the local paper because of some intrigue or other, in short trifles which assumed dramatic proportions, this concurrently with certain remarks . . .

So the neighbor and his wife and child went to identify him, it was in fact the postman panting on the dunghill, a hereditary disease which becomes aggravated with age, they had to take him home somehow, luckily the mechanic was passing with his breakdown van, they called out to him, picked up the unfortunate man and laid him down in the car, they took him home and his wife immediately said it's happened then I knew it would, when he goes off like that in the morning to the bistro it always ends up the same way but what got into him to go up to the marsh, what got into you she asked the sick man, he was practically out for the count and couldn't answer, all the time carrying him up to the bedroom with the mechanic, there wouldn't be anything to do there but give him his medicine and wait, she was used to it.

He could have seen it all from his window, it looks onto that side, but at that sort of time he's often going for a walk over by the marsh, the maid wouldn't have heard anything though, the kitchen faces east, and yet the noise of an engine in that remote part where no one ever goes by . . . as for the doctor he wasn't there yet, it must have been about ten o'clock, spring weather, the morning mists had not long dispersed.

Careful, you never know.

On the table a bunch of dried flowers made in the autumn of thistles and hemlock, the sort of country occupation at the time of year when people start living indoors again, chilly evenings, a fire in the hearth, a smell of mildew and tepid ashes, pleasant hours spent meditating on the book which was still there this glacial night, open at the page with the engraving, when suddenly a window bangs, the wind sweeps into the room, there was no one there.

Impossible said the sentry, I've just seen the master arrive to inspect the premises, he walked round the garden, he went in, didn't open the shutters seeing that it was so late.

Alchemist of the nothings that enabled him to survive.

The neighbor went down to the village to tell the mechanic that there was a tractor stuck in his field, whose was it, no driver, a model that didn't come from our parts but a recent design, no one had heard anything, the ploughing season was over or hadn't yet begun, he'd alerted the others who had no idea, no one knew what was going on.

Or that the previous evening they apparently saw a tourist tinkering with the engine of his sports car by the light of a torch or a storm-lantern, then he went off in the direction of the forest, the wife apparently said for a townie he seems to know his way around I'd never have believed it, the kid was there too, he doesn't go about with his eyes shut and he said that the machine was a German or American make, in any case red with a black hood that was torn, the mica or plastic that takes the place of the back window was missing.

In the direction of the forest but he branches off before, goes down a mud path and comes out at the marsh, gets out of the car, observes the exceptional level of the water and makes a detour of a good half mile on foot to get to the pinewood, therefore not an ordinary tourist, he knew the region but why go there in the middle of the night.

As for the goatherd she'd been home for ages, six hours at the very least, at sunset, unless in that season she didn't go out at all with her livestock, it's too cold and she's completely crippled with rheumatism, the nanny goats stay in the shed, yes that's probably it, remember to ask the neighbor since you can't get anything definite out of the witch, she'd be capable . . .

Dissipation of a haze, semblance of a line.

Immersed in his reading, hours and hours, numb with cold, couldn't even make out the shapes, night was falling, couldn't even make out the lines, sleep, it was then that the woman after she'd taken her goats home went back to the crossroads, she must have lost something, a knitting needle, her handkerchief, kneeling on the ground, fumbling in the stubbly grass, the mechanic apparently saw her on his way down, he stopped his machine and asked her through the window if he could help her, she stood up, she laughed, toothless mouth, little eyes of different colors, they say she's pretty wily.

She must have seen the corpse on the dunghill, she must have been within three feet of it because on her way home she followed the hedge, the master who was closing the shutter called out goodnight to her, she didn't answer, could she be deaf too, a very prevalent infirmity in our parts, especially the women, unless he didn't say anything, he'd only just woken up, still in a sleepy haze, one day less in which to brood on all those snippets, he wouldn't go to bed until daybreak, would spend the night wandering between his room and the kitchen.

The good days were over.

They would come with the mayor and the doctor, they would certify the death, the body was already stiff, trousers and shirt stained with dung, he must have fallen and dragged himself there, in fact they find both the appropriate traces and the red and blue checked handkerchief on the gravel, the goatherd is by the fireplace, her different-colored eyes are ferreting about the room, she says I saw him just a short while ago before dinner, he was sitting on the bench watching the sunset, a habit of his, he never really saw us at those moments he was dreaming or was he asleep, the doctor trying to do the right thing heated up the coffee for everyone, outside the barn roof was gleaming in the cold moonlight.

But when they discovered the will what a business, it was the doctor who came across it while he was sorting out the papers in the top drawer of that kind of chiffonier in the right-hand corner of the bedroom as you go in, yes what a business, he sees this is my last will and testament written on a blue envelope and he immediately thought that he was the only one who had any sort of right to open it in his capacity of intimate friend of the deceased, then he hesitated, it occurred to him that he didn't know what the legal position was but his affection for the dead man got the upper hand, telling himself that the document might fall into the wrong hands he opens the envelope and finds a second one inside it and then a third, whereupon he said to himself careful now, there may be something important in this, he couldn't explain his feeling to the lawyer and yet God knows he didn't pass for a particularly cautious character nor for one given to dramatising things.

So he gave the envelopes to the lawyer who said this is a special document which is a matter for the magistrate, we'll pass it on to him, which they do and the complications begin, you'd need to know the proper terms if you didn't want to put your foot into it, in short six months of beating about the bush to make sure first of all that the deceased person was in his right mind and the experts hesitated given that everything seemed to be so bizarre but the witnesses especially the maid were able to certify that he was indeed of sound mind, next the will named as heir a nephew who was dead who had himself left as heir a nephew who had also died in the meantime, now by God knows what process of deduction the testator must have foreseen that this was how it would be, in short little by little they arrived at the certainty that the doctor was the only beneficiary in the deceased's mind, why not quite simply have mentioned him, with, what was more, a description of the property such that you might well wonder whether it really existed at all, the dead man had spent his life establishing a system of affirmations and negations that was undeniably logical and unassailable, to avoid, it seems . . .

As if his existence had been cut off.

The neighbor said she'd seen the goatherd walking along the hedge and the master close his shutter but that at that moment a sports car had gone past on the road and braked suddenly, a man had got out of it and gone over to the scarecrow's bush, he probably wanted to urinate, she'd paid more attention to the car which you couldn't see very well but whose headlights were so powerful that they lit up everything as far as the barn, then the driver got in again but this is where people's imaginations take over and make them start questioning everything again, she declared that the scarecrow had disappeared, she swore black and blue, a moment before, the dummy had been silhouetted against the sky, she'd even said to herself really anyone might take it for a man, such a good imitation.

The tourist seems to have gone down to the village again and stopped at the café, he ordered a Pernod, the waiter noticed his rubber boots all covered with mud and asks him where on earth he can have been or merely thinks where can he have been, he looks more closely at this black mud to which a bit of the marsh grass is still sticking, no doubt about it, the visitor must have some special interest down there but what can it be, nothing to do with property in any case because the ground belongs to the commune, that's why no one gets anything out of it, the marsh could be drained and the surrounding fields made viable again, it seems that in the past all the land round there was under cultivation, that's typical of our times, so much waste both political and otherwise, don't tell me that the government doesn't do all this on purpose so as to have to get its staple commodities elsewhere, fiddles in exchange for God knows what advantages for the foreigners, we were in a bad way, and that the master who knows all about past history also said that there'd been a manor house on the hillside, there's no trace of it now, unless it's a tumbledown wall and the remains of an underground passage which as a child you wondered whether it wasn't Roman or Visigoth, not at all, only three centuries old, though that's not so bad, all this to say that our forefathers weren't mad, they picked out that spot which is superbly exposed and extracted their provender and wealth from it, we'd be curious to know that lord of the manor, who was he, as for the mud-bespattered fellow he drank his Pernod and left.

In the sempiternal morning of his mania.

Yes in one sense there was something puerile about that friendship with the doctor, you might have wondered, hearing the two of them, apart from the hawkings and scrapings of old bronchitics and the senile rambling, whether you weren't dealing with children their remarks were so foolish, they told each other everything including their dreams, something which to say the very least is insipid, or else how many times they'd urinated during the night or something their mothers had said or memories of their loves which once again took shape or the opposite after a Pernod or two, certainly it made interesting listening, not counting the quibbles and arguments of the yes you did no I didn't order, all day long, giving you the impression . . .

Phantasms of the night and of yesterday and tomorrow.

Pictures to extricate from their dross. Profoundly integrated night in which every deficiency will have its alibi.

Practices that were either magical or that dated from the Middle Ages, the schoolmaster said you're all mad, how can people worry about that sort of thing these days, it's all faked, exploiting people's credulity, have you ever seen conjurers producing pigeons from up their sleeves, well it's the same thing, sleight of hand that's all, to accuse that old dyspeptic of being dangerous would be to do him too much honor and what have you got against him tell me that, the ridiculous things his neighbor or the plumber get up to, the troubles some people have when spring's on the way, they'd do better to look after themselves, a good depurative and getting up early will restore them to health, do you suppose science is just a lot of rubbish, ignoramuses, that's what you are, but he went too far, the schoolmaster, in his indignation he went too far, people began to say that he was in league with the master, so much interest in our suspicions meant he wanted to give them some substance, we aren't all that stupid.

In that cold house haunted by all the carefree years, phantasms of the night that leave nothing of memory's suggestions intact.

That mutilated corpse, with its bloodstained trouser fly.

The apprentice when he came up with his boss to get the tractor going again apparently saw an enormous amount of crows on the dunghill, you couldn't quite make out, why worry, something or other putrefying, they had to get a move on, get this out of the way before the heavy day ahead of them, it was harvest time so it wasn't as if they were short of work, agricultural machinery is in a bad state of repair and every day something goes wrong for one farmer or the other, something broken in the mechanism that he'd been trying to tinker with the previous evening by the light of a storm-lantern but not knowing anything about it and hardly seeing more he only made things worse, there they all are from early morning with their vehicles at the mechanic's.

As if the chronicle of these countless instants.

And it was the same morning that the neighbor's oldest apparently came to deliver a duck and not finding anyone at home must have gone in by the kitchen, behind the house that is, it remained to be seen why he might have hung around there or even in the room, you could suppose anything you liked, we hardly knew him, he doesn't speak but you find things out about this one and that, every morning when he goes to work, he's a day laborer, he glances round the house but only as he goes by, he doesn't stop, not since the time he was surprised by his father at the slit in the shutter, it must have been winter, the house is shut up, everything is in order.

He goes into the kitchen which most of the time isn't locked, so few people go by along the lane and how can you mistrust your neighbors they're a decent lot, the maid has gone shopping in the village and won't be back till eleven, as regular as clockwork, the master has gone for a walk down by the marsh, the man puts his duck down on the table and almost automatically opens the drawer as if he'd seen something in it that time the maid was looking for small change, he finds some bills, nothing he was hoping for, then encouraged by the serene atmosphere of the house this summer's day goes into the dining room which is next to the kitchen, the door had been left open, goes straight over to the drawer in the big cupboard where the master kept his papers, opens it and doesn't find anything or perhaps hasn't time to search because he sees through the window the doctor coming through the little gate, he only just has time to go out and if the doctor sees him he'll calmly call out from a distance that he's left the bird on the kitchen table.

But the child had been present at the massacre of the duck, the old woman went at it with might and main then plucked and drew the bird, singed it, tied it up and said to the child seeing that you're here you might as well take it to the master you'll get a tip, I've got my goats to milk, the boy took the corpse and carried it to the kitchen where the servant wasn't, what to do, he puts his parcel down on the windowsill and pushes the shutter back, a thoughtful child, when suddenly the doctor who can't see very well from a distance and is for ever thinking himself the victim of everybody's indiscretions calls out what is it, who's there, the kid skedaddled, didn't even want to wait for his tip.

As for the poultry dealer no contradiction, he could perfectly well have gone by with his van and the doctor as he was alone said wait for the maid she isn't back from the village yet, here, come and have a nice pastis with me that'll revive you, a stupid thing to say to a driver but the doctor belongs to a generation, doesn't time pass, in which drink hadn't yet become anathema nor had anyone pointed out the connection between its misdeeds and speed on the roads for the simple reason that people didn't go so fast in those days, more often by bike than by car, a cyclist zigzagging or catching his foot in his chain, nothing funnier, now he's come a cropper in the ditch and the entire contents of his little trailer emptied all over the road, the children run over to pick up the palmipeds, they had a good laugh and said to their mothers when they went home to lunch that day, lovely spring sun, we saw the poulterer he was drunk again, all his ducks on the ground and him in the ditch, we put everything back in his the cart and he went off pushing his bike, his wife'll beat him again.

Meanwhile the kid who could see them tippling together goes into the kitchen, puts the corpse on the table and opens the drawer he'd seen the maid take the small change from, he offers himself the tip, that's the explanation, not realising that she knows how much is in it and when she doesn't find the right amount she'll suspect as much but you aren't really going to panic over one franc and the boy had a right to it, just simply tell him next time that he isn't supposed to help himself.

But the maid when she came back from the village went straight to the drawer to empty the small change from her handbag into it and sees that the bills are all out of order, she re-counts the money she keeps in reserve, there's nothing missing, on the other hand something has been taken, she won't mention it to her master, how could anyone imagine a child would be interested in it, it wasn't the younger one who'd put the duck on the table and the neighbor's oldest wasn't there at the time, early spring, sowing time, he'd been taken on some twenty miles away for a couple of weeks, the servant later discovered that the slaughteress had entrusted the bird to the farmhand telling him to put it on the kitchen windowsill and not forget to push back the outside shutter.

So calm. So gray. At his table in the cold house making a note marginal to a murmured phrase, you couldn't hear very well, the story will never come to light, no visible flaw.

So at about seven the maid went into the dark room, she lit the lamp, he asked what's the news in town, she replied that she'd met the postman and his wife with their little girl, they'd had a chat, he was very pale, still not recovered from a serious illness, his wife cut the conversation short saying he's had a touch of bronchitis he's got to be careful, a customer had told the servant all about it, the man suffers from fainting fits and falls down all over the place, the last attack was serious, he's going to have to give up his rounds by the marsh and he'll retire earlier than was foreseen.

So that the next day thinking over this conversation he doubted the validity of the doctor's suspicions, the body, because was it a corpse, seen the previous day on the dunghill and which had disappeared a few minutes later couldn't have been that of the postman who only goes out now on his wife's arm, the other man answered that he had never been able to stand the postman and that he was possibly not the only one, that business of his health might well be an act, nothing in his looks or behavior had seemed suspect to him, it's true the doctor is getting on, his judgment's going.

And if it was an act why did the wife minimize her husband's condition, bronchitis at his age doesn't put you on the retired list.

For in fact the body or was it a corpse seen by the master had disappeared a few minutes later, when the maid is asked she declares that she heard the sound of an engine and the goatherd the same except that she didn't see anything on the dunghill even though she'd gone by it, did monsieur really see it, because he can't see very well from a distance, or perhaps mixed it up, this in the doctor's opinion, he didn't say so straight away, with a vision of a scarecrow with outstretched arms which had almost shattered him the day before, they were still laughing about it at this very moment.

The neighbor's child goes up to the body, touches it lightly on the shoulder and rushes home to his mother.

Huddled up in an armchair, he was already stiff.

Go on then, tell, said the doctor.

And the other started again on the story of his death, adding details sometimes difficult to reconcile with the old ones but his correct logic which was typical of our parts made him fall on his feet, with this reservation however that the dream remodelled everything, upset the order, and that it would take the narrator till tomorrow and even longer to restore the verisimilitude to his tale.

A fire in the hearth, fine china hanging on the walls, the bottle of spirits on the table, the two friends sank themselves in the interminable tale, in spite of everything, that listening ear and that courteous behavior were a godsend to the talker, he'd got up to when he moved away from the town, hundredth repetition, dismayed by the inconsistency of his plans and that kind of quest for one didn't know what, so many years to wait, in the end people were pointing at him in the streets, the ogre who eats naughty children, do you think it's possible to go on like this, my memoirs you can well imagine I gave up believing in them years ago, and for what, good God, better to keep ourselves busy with this garden, what would you say to a terrace overhanging the river and put the greenhouse not down below but behind the barn, the doctor helped himself to another little glassful, the sort of questions that the other man asked himself didn't interest him anymore, moral ones that is, but that voice, its inflections, the slightly inebriated subtlety of the arguments and the profusion of both funereal and rustic images still appealed to him or let's say soothed him pleasantly, he was going to get sozzled, a friendship is based on mutual admiration and his for the orator wasn't shaken.

But what can be said about friendships that suddenly break up. Better to die together. He heard the maid muttering in her kitchen that she would cut out their Pernod. Already an hour and a quarter, life is becoming impossible.

And when they'd finished the duck, went and sat out on the terrace and when they'd drunk their coffee were just about to fall asleep in the spring sunshine when the poultry dealer emerges through the outside gate, he's crossed the garden and is hawking his wares. You won't say no to a little glass. The fellow parks it on a chair and starts yakking, something about mirages on the road, memories that fade, peculiar sensations, you couldn't hear very well, which makes the doctor say you want to watch your liver, come and see me, very strange yes, as if he'd just been saying . . .

It was quite obvious that it would have been pretty childish to give any credence to those tales of magic, what does it mean anyway, nevertheless strange relationships do arise between things or to be more precise how to put it, yes, unusual relationships like that cat that ate its kittens and the fungi in the pipes, apart from what someone said about the words that everyone stumbled over on the same day, it would be interesting to know which but they don't remember, they don't remember, and then, too, the parallels that people drew between these incidents and certain attitudes of the master who couldn't do anything about it, solitude confuses you, inexplicable passions, what sort of man can he be to live like that between his maid and that imbecile of a doctor, seems he's writing his memoirs, be interesting to see that, when just having to check a bill at the grocer's is enough to send him more or less round the bend, when he has to have at least three goes before he can explain that a tractor's got stuck in the mud down by the marsh, three or four goes, he doesn't remember which day it was or whether it was the boss or the apprentice that came with the breakdown van, nor whether it actually was the neighbor's vehicle, nor whether it was in the marsh or in the quarry, in short enough to make the toes of the woman he's talking to curl up in her shoes with irritation, she says that when she sees him come in she prays to heaven that two or three other people will come in behind him so as to have an excuse not to listen to him, if only his solitude could shut his mouth but no, you can only hope that he has a good heart attack, that at least would put a cork in it, that sort of christianery.

The other neighbor the one who sells fruit and veg in the market said that she was out for a drive on Sunday with her husband and her little girl the one who's getting a bit strange, they'd gone the long way round by the town and the forest and were coming back along the lane, they come to the hamlet, our two or three farms, at nightfall, when she distinctly saw the goatherd open her window and put a teapot out on the sill, they stopped their car to give the child time to urinate behind the hedge, that was when a white shape came down from no one knew where, stretched its arm out towards the pot which it took and then pff, disappeared, enough to freeze your bones, the mother made her kid get back into the car instanter even though she'd only done the half of it and through the dark night they went back to the village, the headlights weren't working neither were the sidelights, her husband couldn't understand why not, he'd just had the mechanic check the lighting system.

And that the master had always been an impostor, without ever getting mixed up in anyone's life he acts in secret, those people who come to see him, different cars each time, always leave by night and as if by chance the next morning we discover . . . or someone says he's seen . . . mark you he's on the best of terms with the goatherd, gives her his lucerne for her goats for nothing.

So without anything appearing to have changed . . .

Again high summer, again former images, how many years, to be able to have the wits one had then, not know anything about today, yesterday's phantasms are in their place, this season hasn't followed the previous one but is perpetuating itself from one break to another, so that a phrase formerly murmured at harvest time has just been said tonight or that last spring such a question will only find an answer with the next bluebells, how to get our minds going again, who has just spoken, who has just kept quiet, torn to pieces from one end of the trajectory to the other, a child's skull caps a senile face, the mouth is still saying I love you while the bell is tolling in the ear.

Now the goatherd coming away from the slit in the shutter apparently saw in the half-light the farmhand running in the direction of the marsh, she went back somewhere near the orchard to look for her knitting-needle, a storm-lantern in her hand, she bends down and sees blood on the road, no doubt about it, a car has just come round the corner of the quarry and is branching off towards the village, when suddenly a cry makes her jump, an owl coming out of the barn or perhaps startled by the car's headlights, all this in the space of barely a minute, how to take it all in.

What to make of these snippets.

It was in fact the farmhand that evening, the neighbor repeated it in the café this morning, he's just asked him to clean out the shed and the lean-to, he's employed to do all the odd jobs at his own insistence, he's not a bad man and we all have to live, yet some people refuse to employ him, the neighbor maintains that he's a thief but that isn't where the shoe pinches, it's a straightforward story of a deceived husband that's what it is, before his marriage but it's much the same, even though the wife has always denied it and still does deny it, in short when they found the cow dead in the byre the boss felt a bit awkward vis-a-vis the neighbor in that he'd trusted the farmhand, the fellow had taken him in, as if revenging yourself on a poor animal . . .

What to make of these snippets.

They saw the man again holding his little boy's hand, they were passing the scarecrow and the child was pointing at it, they went up to it and the father picked his son up and holding him with outstretched arms said touch it you'll see it's only straw, the child touched it lightly on the shoulder and started yelling, the farmhand went by at this moment, the two men conversed for a minute, you couldn't hear very well, while the child walked round the bush looking up in the air, not too reassured.

Phantasms of yesterday and tomorrow.

From one year to the next these great changes in depth.

Would undermine the foundations of our edifice, that laborious pile of straws.

They saw the master again at his table bending over the old-fashioned book but summer was back, you could hear the maid muttering that she would cut out their pastis, the doctor on the road shuffling along like an old pigeon was going to come and lunch off a duck, already half-past eleven, the clock on the mantelpiece is slow, the ornamental lakes reflect the clouds that don't seem to be in the sky, it'll soon be siesta-time and the plans for the terraced garden then the story of the removals from the town and elsewhere, hundredth repetition, to find yourself in the evening in front of the same aperitif . . .

When the maid questioned the neighbor who claims to mount guard in the absence of the master he replied that he hadn't seen anyone in the morning but in the evening on the other hand a sports car had stopped on the bend and a man had got out to urinate behind the hedge probably, he hadn't seen him go off again because his wife was calling him, she wasn't well and couldn't milk the goats, he had to do it for her, but the maid interrupts him saying that it was in the morning that the envelope had disappeared from the drawer, of that she's certain, while she was in the village, and that it couldn't have been a child who filched it unless of course he'd been told to do so, this thought often occurred to her, the child wasn't excluded then, next the neighbor said he'd seen the farmhand going out of the barn that morning, now he remembers, but the servant said that he'd never been in the kitchen, didn't know what the drawer contained.

And again winter, the frozen mud, hoarfrost and ice in the holes in the road, the house is empty again, everything is in order, between the bare elms the sentry sees the blue line of the forest, the pinewood, the quarry, and the bend, nothing is left of the false mystery of the night, the master will come to inspect the premises and sit down at the table long enough to brood over his memories, outside night had fallen, the barn roof was shining in the cold moonlight.

Leave nothing of memory's suggestions intact.

That they apparently saw, then, don't interrupt me, in the early morning a corpse on the dunghill, it must have been five o'clock, and it seems they thought it was the master because he had taken to drink, no more difficult than that, now there was nothing to justify this deduction, there were neighbors and other drunkards but things take root in people's minds and no way of getting them out again, anyway who's people, something more explicit was necessary, and anyway why corpse, it could have been a body which would get up a few minutes or a few hours later, a fainting fit, drunkenness not indispensable either, quite simply a loss of consciousness.

But the strangest of all was that obsession which always brought you back to the same images which because they had been evoked over the space of several months in the conversations of all sorts of people were no longer prepared to be forgotten, claimed their pound of flesh, in short would become living and not dummies anymore, but to the detriment . . .

A new reality which we wouldn't have wanted and which made a clean sweep of all the rest, victory, what slaughter, just about all we had left was a table to eat from, a writing desk to pass the time, and a servant who even though she wasn't . . . but that's not the point.

So calm. So gray.

That room where he worked, I can still see it with its whitewashed walls all cracks, its well-worn, innocent furniture, the big cupboard used as a sideboard where the servant put away the crockery that came down from grandmothers, blue patterns or birds on branches from which tulips and orchids were sprouting, six chairs round the table, a ramshackle wing-chair covered in leopardskin, a mantelpiece on which pride of place was taken by the clock that didn't go, through the window a little garden with plum trees and moss roses, a rainy spring, vague yearnings.

The garden too but at different periods, of changing aspect, multiple, really, so that the surroundings in which it evolved are hardly ever the same, which would explain . . .

That that day in the room into which he'd just gone when he came back from the town, wintry weather, steely blue and glacial, frozen mud on the road, crows flying up cawing, without opening the shutters because night was about to fall he'd made a fire in the hearth and sat down at the table, had taken the old-fashioned book and started leafing through it then had become drowsy and fallen asleep with his head in the hollow of his arms.

That the neighbor who calls himself a sentry, not knowing the meaning of words, and who plays the part of caretaker in the master's absence, going on his usual rounds notices a light through the slit in the shutter but for some unknown reason doesn't go and see what's going on and when he's got home, a hundred yards at the most, tells his wife that the master has come back to inspect the premises.

That that same day perhaps the caretaker's child or the neighbor's child on his way back from school sees on the dunghill by the orchard something like an outstretched body, he goes up to it and then runs all the way home.

That they'd thought for a long time that it had been a question of a fainting fit, he'd got up or rather dragged himself from where he fell to his room where the maid when she came back from the town had given him first aid while they were waiting for the doctor whom she'd sent a child to fetch.

When suddenly he jumps, he'd dozed off in the deck chair, looks round and sees in the mossrose walk the good doctor who's given him palpitations, a few moments later he tells him the dream he's just had, bad digestion, the other man was at his last gasp on the dunghill and the assembled neighbors explained his fall by the presence of the scarecrow in the bush, hardly logical, the poultry dealer appeared at the gate and maintained that it didn't take more than that to give rise to mirages on the road, the detours of the unconscious are strange but to explain what or foresee what, you could imagine anything, great freedom, wasn't that the domain of poetry, in the soft light of the setting sun, the garden is resting, the blue line of the forest marks the horizon and the servant on the porcelain tray decorated with birds and tulips brought in the aperitif, you won't say no to a little glass the poultry dealer is asked.

When suddenly the postman at the bend in the road comes upon the goatherd and her flock, he only just has time to brake, his moped skids and he's in the ditch with all his mail dispersed, he told the neighbor a few moments later that it was a spell the old girl had put on him, impossible normally not to see her with her filthy quadrupeds, she'd come out of nowhere like a devil, I tell you this magic business isn't all moonshine, she brews herbal teas at nightfall, it seems that someone saw her only yesterday putting her pot out on the windowsill and a white shape coming down from the roof, but how can you believe that poor stupid postman, he'd had one too many and that's all there is to it.

When suddenly . . .

But he continued on his rounds inspecting every barn, every hayloft, every hut, you have to keep your eye on everything with these vagrants in the neighborhood now, where can they come from, it's my opinion that some of those young hooligans from the town, we don't need to look any farther, have got into the habit of going poaching and even highway robbing, an organised gang, that's the youth of today for you, vindictiveness and violence, didn't they attack the postman the other day not a couple of steps from the grocer's, grabbed his wallet and his sheepskin jacket and then ran away down the street round the corner.

Turn, return, revert.

And when the maid brought in the aperitif the poultry dealer had got as far as the business of the tourist in the sports car, he'd been seen first in the village and then at the quarry and then on the road to the marsh a couple of steps away from here, I wonder what on earth he can be up to, that's three days he's been hanging around the district, hasn't said a word to anyone except to the waiter when he ordered a pastis, don't you think that in such cases we ought to tell the gendarmes, he could be a spy or something, they say there are some prowling around the neighborhood at this very moment still it's none of my business, suddenly adding this remark with some agitation, the idea had just occurred to him that the master might see in his observations a connection with what people said about certain visits received here, different cars each time, the master was trafficking in God knows what.

On the dunghill something bleeding, the apprentice went over and saw a red rag, he looked up and saw that the scarecrow was disintegrating, its cap had fallen off too, all the straw was coming out of its trousers, he cut it down and patched it up as best he could.

Something red, it looked like horse-meat, here come the crows.

Muttering incantations with every step, the old woman was making her way towards the quarry.

And suddenly the whole countryside disintegrates, corpses are strewn all along the meadows and roads.

Plunged in his pettifogging apocalypse.

The old woman in her kitchen sitting by the fire was watching her soup. Iron pan, chimneyhook, blackened grate, gridiron, and tongs. The table was laid for three. The old man came in from the fields and sat down without a word. Their grandson came back from school and went out again to play with the dog, a short-legged terrier that he got to jump by holding up a bait, sugar or biscuit. The wind was blowing in the elm tree and on the grassy bank that runs along the courtyard, it started a runnel of water zigzagging above the wooden pail, the tap drips. Above the kitchen garden corseted by its trellis you could see irises and peonies, clusters of leaves and beanpoles.

And suddenly the whole countryside disintegrates, corpses are strewn all along the meadows and roads, the farmhand came back from the marshland carrying a carcass, with his burden in his arms he moves warily so as to be able to deliver the object intact to the master who is waiting for him on his doorstep.

Then when the meal was finished cleared the table, sent the child and the old man to bed, night was falling, the wind had dropped, on the motionless elm tree that white shape that from a distance you'd have taken for a carcass, perforated and frail, the old woman put some freshly-picked stalks to brew in a pot, night was falling, a crow was still perching on the motionless elm tree, then cleared the table and sent the child and the old man to bed, the farmhand arrived at the master's house with his burden, she put her receptacle out on the windowsill, that white shape that had come down from the roof . . .

Put the brew out on her windowsill, night had come, the master was wool-gathering looking at the stars when suddenly a white shape that from a distance you'd have taken for a carcass, perforated and frail, came gliding down from the neighboring roof on to the shrub that a storm had stripped of its dummy, you could see it in the headlights of the sports car at the bend in the road, the apprentice was getting out when suddenly . . .

Profoundly integrated night.

The doctor seems to have gone out at dusk, making his way towards the master's house but for some unknown reason branched off at the quarry and plunged into solitude, night had come, the crickets were scraping away in the grass, flashes of light appeared on the horizon, that's what they call summer lightning, when suddenly he sees a huddled-up shape on the ground a few yards away, he goes up to it and recognises the goatherd, she says she's looking for a knitting-needle, she is in fact shining a torch over the ground.

After which the woman apparently said that it wasn't the doctor she'd met at that hour but the farmhand, he was coming away from the neighbor's house, the neighbor had a sick cow in the byre, the epidemic was gaining ground, they were going to have to kill some of the cattle.

The old woman going home by night without attracting attention, she must have come out again on her own with the excuse of going to look for that knitting-needle, the evenings are long, what could she do without her handwork, but the farmhand had seen her down by the marsh, had posted himself behind a hedge, she was spying out the land all around her . . . after which she retraced her steps and came upon the apprentice who was putting the scarecrow back in the bush.

Or that that story of the epidemic had been invented by the poultry dealer who wants to sell his wares and tells them anything that comes into his head, people are stupid enough to believe his rubbish.

The maid lit the lamp, pushed the papers over to one side and laid the table.

A perpetual crime, perpetrated for years in this cold house, not a sound, the master is away, eyes everywhere spying, and ears pricked.

At his table bending over the old-fashioned book making a marginal note beside a hollow phrase, it'll come in its own good time, when suddenly the maid comes bursting in, what a way to go on, staying in the dark like that, she lights the lamp, he hides under his jacket the torch he'd been shining over the book, he'd been seen through the slit in the shutter.

Afterwards hours of pondering over all those snippets, there was nothing left on the page of memoirs but blots and graffiti, his life had emigrated elsewhere.

In the elms or the pinewood, in those carcasses everywhere, scintillations, nocturnal silences, dispersed, in disorder, irreparable, the book open at the old-fashioned illustration, the clock that doesn't go, infinite disarray, words adrift like so many disavowals, pursued even into his dreams, the only history he would have now would be written, his only breath would be literary.

It was perhaps at this moment that the poultry dealer appeared at the gate, towards evening that is, the master became calmer, he asked the fellow to sit down and he let him go on about his obsessions, the doctor apparently said watch your liver, come and see me.

Blots and graffiti.

Other themes would emerge from disordered nerves. Working on marginal notes.

When the farmhand had left the barn, it might have been half-past eight, night was falling, the last glimmer in the west, the line of the forest almost black, the terrace was deserted and the house had all its shutters closed, you could hear the frogs down by the marsh, it had been a hot day for the season.

Of that dreary, monotonous year.

Escaped notice who in some people's minds seems to have played his part and triggered off the mechanism.

When she got to the quarry the old woman put her folding stool down on the grass and got on with her knitting while her bleating beasts were bouncing about in the beetroot, the dog was amusing itself snapping at their hocks when the farmhand appears at the bend, he goes up to the woman and points at the wood with the carcasses in the distance, she nods, counts her stitches again, and then the sports car comes up from the opposite side.

A never-ending story of exile that the master called the exodus, undertones of distress, that flight from generation to generation, bloody or burlesque episodes in stations with trains about to leave, a lament that comes to light in the least of his remarks, incurable injury, that primeval territory under the pile of perfunctorily packed luggage, a whole hotchpotch of failings and compromises, a quivering voice that had never managed to run dry, the sick man's remorse, a ham-acting mea culpa enough to disgust you with people's confessions.

The mother in the train taking them into exile.

That murmur interspersed with silences and hiccups.

Source of information deficient.

Another theme that has emerged from disordered nerves, that of the adopted child.

The doctor was waiting.

When suddenly the scarecrow made the master jump.

You see he said we were partners Alfred and I, I mean Rodolphe, in some business goodness knows what, I wasn't cut out for it and quite shamelessly left him to struggle and maneuver so that the partnership was dissolved in the same way as it had been formed, as the days went by, that's years ago now.

A new situation.

You see he said I was stuck with the child, how old could he have been, about fifteen, I always thought of him as 'the adopted child,' feeble in both mind and body, his mother had entrusted him to us not knowing what to do with him, we didn't either, we gave him little jobs to do which he always made a mess of.

But that period was no better than the present one and insofar as I can be objective about it had no more of a future.

As for knowing what sort of a father I was, better not to speak of it, let's say a sort of prop or bean-stick only less fragile but the combination can't have been very pretty, we'd made our home here and the days passed just as they'd dawned in a sort of . . . and the days passed without passing, without a calendar and without passion nothing happens, we were in this uneventful house with the wind in its old tiled roofs . . .

That would be years ago now, when Alfred or Rodolphe not finding me to his liking anymore gave me the sack or years since he died having previously liquidated what he called our situation, so far as I can remember we were on our beam ends, it comes back to me by fits and starts, especially in my sleep, a whole series of irritations which seemed like great problems to us, people are quite right when they say that it'll all be the same in a hundred years.

Because I was well and truly alone, I only saw the adopted child at mealtimes if then, he continued as he had in the past trapping rats and hens, I neither heard him get up nor go to bed, he must have slept in a barn, not very tactful on my part to ask him but I can't think where else he could have hung out unless he preferred a hedge or a ditch or a dunghill, sometimes he smelt, not very tactful to tell him so, there was only one thing I insisted on, that he should have a tub on Saturdays, and then I used to soap him, I nearly scrubbed his skin off, it couldn't do him any harm.

The farmhand had just gone by.

There was only one thing I insisted on, that I should soap him myself in his tub every Saturday or more or less, with neither calendar nor passion I sometimes made a mistake and I felt less alone at those moments, I have his skin under my hand, I soap him all over without exception from A to Z which naturally took us by way of P, and maybe even concentrating on P, to tell the truth it's less a chore than a pleasure, or if in my haste to be less alone I soap him twice a week attributing my miscalculation to the absence of a calendar.

I only insisted on one thing, to soap him myself in his tub every time he smelt and that was often though I told myself that you have to be careful, we never know what the P has in store for us in a situation like ours, isolated as we were in that house and its outbuildings including a barn where he might possibly have slept.

With neither calendar nor passion.

A situation that I could have wished for or preferred without having had a previous one, something like the plums that fall into our mouths or the gift-horse that you must never look in the tooth.

A house and its outbuildings, isolated, which it would appear I had made my home and into which the idiot seems to have fallen like the proverbial plum, I didn't really look, I let him bed down in a barn or a hayloft, no rights over him, sudden duties that I hadn't exactly been looking for, there I was involved in a situation without a future that was the very image . . .

In short, a situation.

It was a bit tricky for me at the start as I didn't know the proper way for a half-father or let's say a half-adopted child to behave, should I I wondered soap him in his tub when he smells, should I ask him where he hangs out, seeing that I had only the remotest recollection of his previous situation or let's call it mine, that partnership with Édouard or Rodolphe in which without responsibility I must have let the calendar shed its leaves while I was thinking of God knows what for years and years.

His life having emigrated elsewhere.

Telling myself that without passion.

Having only the remotest recollection of my previous situation, the one that preceded the partnership, a thing that might have been able to enlighten me about my duties of the moment but just you try and fight against that sleep, what else can you call it, in which memories of a situation which was perhaps not our own come back to us by fits and starts, what sort of a hornets' nest have I got myself into again, but of the presence of the idiot I could have no doubt.

Other diversions such as butterfly-watching or weeding the meadow, yes, we did weed it, an incredible diversity of plants to the square yard, I used to try and remember their names and inculcate them into my protégé.

Against that sleep.

It was I, then, who because I had inadvertently smiled or belched gave the impression of being Rodolphe's partner, things hang by so slender a thread, I who had been seen sitting down to a meal maybe or crossing the garden to open the gate to the visitors.

Because I very much liked having visitors or what we used to call visitors, given that Rodolphe's interest in me might very well have made me succumb to suggestion, might have pushed me into the channels of the imagination so as to see me smile or belch at some creature of his kindly invention who was actually no other than the cook or the postman, I shall never be grateful enough to that Rodolphe who liked me so much, Édouard I mean, what tact, all this because the tedium that oozed out of our life was so dense that you couldn't see more than a few feet in front of you, the cook or the postman could hardly be told apart in such a fog, all he had to say was here's another visitor you see how spoilt we are, none of which implies that I only belched in the presence of these underlings, that was just an example.

When I got up in the morning the idiot was already out and about, he was ferreting around in the courtyard half-dressed, his hair all over his face, from a distance a certain elegance, the elegance of youth, from close to, his eyes absorbed everyone's attention, so sad, in that vague cretin's paradise or is it a hell, the same for everyone, I've known a lot, a place we have no access to, though after all I don't really know the first thing about it, my need to become sentimental may well have falsified all my notions about other people, he had a cretin's eyes that's all, too far apart and they didn't go in the same direction, the proof that my story about paradise is worthless, at that rate there'd be one for the left eye and one for the right eye.

Ah no it won't have been goodwill that I lacked but peace yes and perhaps when my previous situation was resolved and I found myself alone with that child I hoped I might finally find it but no, nothing, how could I confuse it with the sort of treacle I was sinking into unless that is in fact peace, unless that is the big sister of goodwill.

Two mechanisms in slow motion.

I watched the idiot amusing himself in the courtyard, he was making mud pies and I suddenly saw him breaking an arm or a leg or losing an ear, quick, I called him so as to see him smile at me, a recourse I didn't have with the broken plates but the day he stopped smiling at me, wouldn't that be the end of him, not wanting to stay with me, not wanting his tub anymore, and there he is gone to find other suns, other adopters, other mud pies.

People are right when they say that it'll all be the same in a hundred years.

As poor Raymond said when he died and landed me with the cretin, something to fill in the gaps in your existence, think about his future, make him take his tub, and those jams he didn't have time to finish, I'm speaking about Raymond, I had to boil them up again after the funeral and we were still eating them years afterwards, just imagine the pleasure, I had to start all over again from scratch, the child kept asking, that they were the plums from our garden, that Edmond and I had picked them, that we'd bought a preserving pan and that he died like that in the middle of a glut of jam, so depressing that I sometimes couldn't even finish it, while I was washing up I used to think about the pleasure we'd have had if we could have eaten it together, I'm talking about Rodolphe, to keep telling the child with such patience that it was the plums from our garden, are you listening, picked do you remember with Uncle Nanard, I'm talking about me, who went with you to buy that great big preserving pan in which Uncle Momolphe made the jam which if he weren't dead he'd be eating with us today, then to sick it up in disgust because of brooding over the funeral, terrible heat, a smell of the cemetery in our perishing fruit, poor uncle on his bed looked as if he was winking, that sort of thing, all the time telling myself that it would all be the same in a hundred years, what is jam, what is death, it would all pass as the days went by.

Ah no, goodwill.

As for the housework, scrubbing washing up or tub, I admit that I came to terms with it, the head or whatever it is that we call by that name does its work of preservation, how many memories came back to me then thus restoring the balance of the situation which without them would have been dangerously inclined towards sleep, it was thus that a session of pea-shelling could sharpen my judgment to the point of making me take action in time when the idiot was in danger, this by the detour of the snippets which one thing leading to another had brought me up to that particular day, and to the exact hour and second after which my cretin fell off the ladder or swallowed the sponge, a thing that I ought to have deplored without my little bits of housework.

With neither calendar nor passion.

And anyway it wasn't as if we didn't have any more visitors, I've always liked that and some did still come at longish intervals, a red letter day for us both, my heightened sensitivity made me turn to look in the direction of the valley at the precise moment when at the far end, down there, miles away, the visitor in some sort of vehicle or on a velocipede or even on foot came out of the forest, it was someone for us no doubt about that, we took up our positions on the terrace and watched his progress, an ant at that distance, and I said another visitor you see how people spoil us, who can it be, the road keeps winding, here a copse, there an old wall, the visitor got bigger and bigger, the child asked what's a visitor and I'd start all over again from scratch, it's someone who comes in a car or on a bike or you might say a vehicle or a velocipede or even a person on foot who comes to see us, why to see us, because people's eyes need to look back so that their hearts can be happy, what's a heart, ah a heart, my boy, a heart is . . . but who could it be, the visitor was getting bigger and bigger, it was a sports car.

An old-fashioned sports car, we'd taken up our positions on the terrace where we could start all over again from scratch, what's a year, years, all the time keeping our eyes on the visitor, watching him from one bend to the next, I was preparing my words and phrases, a deck chair, the last bend any minute now, only a hundred yards, only fifty, the sports car was going to stop, it did stop, the visitor got out of the vehicle.

In the excitement that gripped us three times a year.

We who had been preparing soft drinks, a deck chair, words and phrases for a visitor, clean hands and adopted smiles.

Recalling various snippets, talking about Momolphe again, doing the honors of our old roofing tiles, of our jam and of our funerals.

The happiness of semi-cretins when they're breaking the crockery or washing their Ps.

Now it sometimes happened that the idiot would get lost in the wood and I'd go looking for him ringing a handbell, he'd come running as if I were the lost nanny goat, associating with him will have been the source of a good many discoveries.

Now the visitor drank his soft drink and at the same time recalled Momolphe, he could still hear him, such a good man, how come he hadn't heard he'd died, hardly believable, as proof I brought a pot which we ate of jam.

How much goodwill I needed, I repeat, not to say at every twist and turn, I must be playing the fool or snoozing, things just don't happen like that, an unconscious misapprehension may well have led me astray all my life, my love of word-spinning which would have invented the child and the visitors if they hadn't happened to be there, coming out of the forest, while I was absentmindedly passing by, pondering over Momolphe's inheritance, that bundle of trouble he grudgingly bequeathed me . . . or that they weren't in the wood but at every twist and turn of my sleep, becoming embodied as the days went by so as to claim their share of the inheritance, as if poor Alfred with a simple wink had foreseen my snub and traced with three pots of jam the path I should have to follow.

Interspersed with silences and hiccups.

We used to go shopping in the village, going down by the shortcut between the blackthorn hedges, the child made bouquets of lucerne and I like an old nanny kept on saying what's lucerne, imagining that one day he'd come to his senses and leave me standing with the shopping bag, I was wrong about that as I was about all the rest, my goodwill was that lousy stuff you have in the corner of your eye when you wake up, it'll take me to the end of my life and even longer to get rid of it, that sort of sadness, and when we'd get to the grocer's we'd buy some sweets and I'd let him suck them while I imagined the day when without him I'd be dragging my feet from one shop-window to the next and end up at the bistro by forgetting what had brought me there, so that love if that was what it really was yes I could have done without it but there you are, it isn't every day that you make a hash of the jam.

So that when I'd finished my shopping I would meet the idiot on the pavement, he'd finished his sweets, we went on to the bistro . . .

So that when I'd finished my Pernod I would have another to reimmerse myself in a previous situation where without Momolphe or the child . . . the waiter asked me what's the matter Monsieur Nanard.

And that taking previous situations into account you might call that happiness, three potatoes in a shopping bag and a cretin sticking to you like a shadow but something tells me . . .

It'll pass the waiter kept saying, it'll pass Monsieur Nanard.

Now with neither calendar nor passion . . .

For Rodolphe too came to forget at the barcounter, that's how his mornings passed, blind as I was, I find his inheritance no light burden, every day we'll be tracking his obsessions in the dregs of my cup.

Now one evening when we weren't expecting anyone a friend of Rodolphe's came to see him not knowing he was dead, hardly believable such a good man, I never stopped repeating what's a visitor but you must have something, we chatted and watched the idiot silhouetted a very long way off on the west side, a certain sweetness, and taking lost situations into account you might call it happiness, an insipid taste to things, a feeling of having done your duty with every fart you let, with in the background that landscape like a Japanese screen with no perspective, old empyrean, an old boat that carries us along like dejected schoolboys, they've failed the exam.

We can't have been gay but the evening went all right even so, you must have something, he enquired after the idiot, you know he sleeps in a barn but which one, and you Monsieur Édouard will you spend the night in my modest abode, it was a good opportunity, no, someone was expecting him.

Or the pleasure the idiot and I had in prolonging the curtailed visits, if so and so stayed we'd spend the next morning cosseting him, tell us about your wife and daughter, he answers that his daughter is at a ball, a splendid creature and everything, as for his wife she hasn't managed to cure him of the empyrean, that paradise of dejected Japanese, admitting this to us in all modesty.

So we were weeding the meadow shoulder to shoulder, a tedious occupation that gave me the opportunity to repeat what's lucerne, what's chicory, until it was time for the tub or the postman but there wasn't a postman anymore, when I pondered over the time of stillborn aspirations as if the present, that cowardly solitude, already governed the past, for I haven't always been alone, the team Edmond and I formed proves that, we created a situation, I sometimes remembered in the evening that there was a button to be sewn on or a doubt to dissipate, I'd go to the bottom of things, scrupulously, methodically, and often he sent me about my business, until the day when I no longer had the joy of pleasing him, into what hornets' nest, while pulling out a root, conscience to make you giddy, that's the result, but this made a lot of situations at the same time and very late into the night I was still going over all the details of the past, no one to call me to order, as if my love for the cretin increased the distances tenfold and that at the height of passion the other was no more than a shadow, an ant disappearing down the road, going into the forest . . . a telescope, quick a telescope before my last attachment fades away.

Well yes then he used to get up in the morning and hang about in the courtyard, his hair all over his face, a certain elegance, I still have in my eyes the sight of his emotion when he was watching the clouds, in my nose his smell of the byre and in my ears his voice which opened my mind to the empyrean of the Japanese and of cretins, the sadness of situations without a future.

The hour when I ponder.

Mechanisms in slow motion.

The misery of this situation, the last one, to prolong it until death ensues, forget all vanity, all propriety, go back by easy stages to the Japanese paradise and inscribe myself there on top of a mountain, stay there forever, or under a little bridge watching the river water flow, three immutable wavelets.

He handed me the soap and my hand happened on his P, the innocent began to stiffen.

Here, I said to the visitor, if you'd like to watch, and I led him to the washhouse, it was time for his tub, the adopted child undresses and the session started, I'd whetted Monsieur Edmond's appetite, just you wait and see, to relieve the tedium of that evening, make the cretin have an erection, waste of time, the presence of a third party put him off, we had to give up.

A sorry nature.

That we haven't yet found the words, all this time, to do without nature, a phrase that would hold everything together, we'd say it from the morning on a full stomach until the evening when as the sun was setting we'd say it again with a stale mouth, no more need for either sleep or pleasure, a nourishing, soothing phrase, a panacea, while weeding the meadows, washing other people's Ps, nutritious, absorbable, enlightening, until the day . . .

And that day the idiot would appear like a seraph in that landscape with no perspective, his limpid eyes finally both looking at the same object, his plastered-down hair, his impeccable jeans, the elegance of the sky, and he would keep repeating to us the phrase that would suddenly open the doors of further empyreans one after the other, we would pass from one to the next . . .

That phrase.

Still not found.

You understand, he said, still not found.

Working on marginal notes.

The scarecrow was lying on the ground and the master went up to it, touched it lightly on the shoulder, on the jeans, it would have to be put back in the bush, haven't got the heart, it would have to wait on the dunghill, incalculable distress, would only appear in dreams now, which barn had he slept in, nailed to all the surrounding trees, no more sleep, from the bedroom to the kitchen he pondered over the phrase that would save him, waste of time, nothing left but to let yourself go under, night had come, the rain was pelting down on the cobbles in the courtyard.

Huddled up in an armchair he was already stiff.

You understand, he said, love, if that's what it was really I could have done without it.

Death at the slightest deficiency in thought.

Here, without a calendar.

The idiot must have gone out in the morning, he hadn't come in for his coffee, the neighbor apparently saw him by the river upstream from the pinewood, what was she doing there, a long way from her usual haunts, the master hadn't reacted, the child must be fishing for bleak, he'd been seen the previous day tying a hook on his line, he used to go off with the farmhand or on his own and stay out for hours, but rarely later than noon, his stomach would be gnawing at him.

Not to remember anymore, intermittently, the color of his eyes or a gesture, the child would be no more than a shadow, an ant disappearing into the distance.

He must have gone out in the morning, the goatherd apparently saw him over by the pinewood but the doctor poured himself out another glass and said . . .

From one year to the next these great changes in depth.

He must have gone out in the morning, he'd been seen the previous day tying a hook on his line, the farmhand said that the goatherd apparently saw him upstream from the pinewood, what was she doing there, the master hadn't reacted busy drinking his aperitif on the terrace when suddenly the maid had appeared and said monsieur is served, an antiquated expression that amused the doctor, he asks her by the way who moved the scarecrow but she didn't know, the kitchen window looks out on to the other side.

Must have come back round about one o'clock, he'd been all over the surrounding countryside, left at dawn, hours searching the wood, the quarry, the ditches, the copses, that only left the marsh, he saw the idiot being sucked down into it, only one hand . . .

Impossible, he'll be back any minute now, his stomach's gnawing at him.

But the image claimed its pound of flesh and the idiot was being swallowed up, the master came running, now only his head, only one hand that the master grabbed and heave-ho pulled towards him, bracing himself against the tree with the carcasses until the morning when the doctor sees that his fever is abating and at the sick man's request rereads the text of the memoirs, the drama transcribed word for word, the child is at the bedside, he'll have his tub later, you see he said really yes I could have done without it.

No visible flaw.

Turn, return, revert.

Profoundly integrated night.

It was the evening the visitor had been there, after he'd left, the idiot had gone to bed, the master was walking up and down between the bedroom and the kitchen, the frogs could be heard croaking outside and there were intermittent flashes of summer lightning in the sky, window open on to the garden, everything is in order, in those days the house was never shut up and there was no question of any project other than to live in it, happiness, an insipid taste to things with the feeling . . . walking up and down between the bedroom and the kitchen, I can still see him, a certain elegance, with that cold, hunted gleam in his eyes, he was talking to himself volubly and dramatically then suddenly stopped short, looked at himself in the mirror and restrained something like a hiccup, a strange person, no one had ever known him to have any attachment other than that to the idiot and later the doctor, a muted friendship, something broken in the mechanism, did they ever enjoy a single day of real gaiety together, when suddenly the corpse with its bloodstained trouser fly appears in the doorway, the master retreated and collapsed on the bed, the goatherd went up and touched him on the shoulder, they'd come to identify him while the doctor read in his papers word for word the murmured phrase.

An interval of half a word.

Pictures to extricate from their dross.

He must have wanted to use the chainsaw, must have pinched it from the neighbor, started it up and the thing does a sort of side-slip, the cretin makes a wrong move, the terrible wound drains him of his blood. He collapsed on the dunghill clutching his groin. There was no one in the house, the maid shopping in the village and the master walking by the marsh. It was apparently round one o'clock that they found him at his last gasp under the bush. The child bringing the duck seems to have made a detour through the wood, seen him injured and unconscious with that red patch spreading and spreading, he runs home to his mother who comes and identifies the inanimate body.

I can still see the woman going up to the corpse with a storm-lantern in her hand, she bent down, touched it lightly on the shoulder then raised her head up to the scarecrow with its arms outstretched in the bush, the torch lit up the ragged jeans from below, a red rag had just dropped, she picks it up and her oldest put it back as best he could, they went to tell the master and then they pick up the body and carry it into the bedroom, they put it down on the bed, it was already stiff, the maid kept herself busy heating up the coffee, the master was leaning against the mantelpiece sobbing and the doctor . . .

After which followed the description of the funeral, hundredth repetition, with for its basic theme paternal love or whatever it was that served as such, an ambiguous savor, disordered feelings to say no worse and which one more glass of Pernod would have sunk in God knows what, well yes nature, we'll have heard it in all its versions the business of the tub and the soaping, spiced this time by the bleeding wound, a scarecrow's despair, an unprecedented defeat, in short enough to start you daydreaming.

Whereupon the doctor leaning over the corpse plucked something bloody out of the wound which he said was the pièce de resistance, a movement of the mandibles and a clicking of the tongue, plunged back into the hole and brought the manuscript out intact, a real miracle, put on his specs and reread the phrase in which the other found a bitter taste, our predators have been at work, all that was left of the poor body was the skull and one hand clutching the communicant's little chain, that sort of jaded image which nevertheless had a poignant note for you, the time of merry shipwrecks, ah how young we were, all this to come back to the man walking through the twilight hoisting up the dummy, velvety flight, spreading clouds, a bad sign.

The child bringing the duck had made a detour through the wood, he'd seen the idiot cutting down the scarecrow and had run up, they'd carried it over to the barn, put it down in the recess, I can still see the red rag that had served as its belt, its frayed jeans, its jacket quartered on its prop when suddenly night falls, you couldn't see the outlines anymore, the straw sentry might well make anyone retreat, then the child went back under the bush where he had deposited his corpse and took it to the maid who took a couple of sous out of the drawer, here, this is for your trouble, she put the duck in the fridge.

Something bloody.

It was quite some time before this that the story must have begun but there again how much prudence, how much care, divergent elements, everything to be approached from a tangent, and to get what out of it all, insipid snippets, a shagged-out procession of exiles of every shade and hue . . .

To stifle the murmur.

From the cupboard the doctor took the jeans and the red rag to make the scarecrow, nailed the bits of wood together then got some straw and stuffed it into the gear hanging on the gallows, it was the time of the starlings who devastate the cherry trees, the time of plans for the garden, the time of visitors and of friendships without a shadow . . .

The master has gone back to his reading.

Liliaceous plants against a wall, tufts of poisonous weeds in the corseted little garden, the bench on which she's sitting with her knitting on her knees, she's not asleep, she's staring at a point over on the other side of the well, the goats remind her of the time, she stands up abruptly, straightens her apron and limps down the lane behind her flock, the dog was frisking in the stubble.

The man took advantage of the old woman's absence to creep into the kitchen, he opened the cupboard, the sideboard, went and looked under the bed, came back, was searching a chest when a cat started miaowing outside, the intruder jumps, no one in the garden, he goes out hugging the wall, he's disappeared.

The master has gone back to his reading.

He emerges from behind the bush, he's coming this way, he's holding the red rag and he puts it on his head, you could see the blood running down his temple, he collapsed onto the terrace.

He emerges at the corner of the house coming from the cold room, holding the red leather-bound book, he sits down on a chair, he starts trembling, it was quite late in the season, not a single leaf left on the elms, that icy north wind whistling in the courtyard, he stays for hours staring at a point over on the other side of the barn, night was falling, he jumped when he heard the doctor call, the doctor was no longer of this world, his thoughts were elsewhere, endlessly repeating things.

Passed his hand over his forehead and said I saw him coming towards us holding that red thing, acknowledged us from a distance and going down the path by the fountains kept looking right and left at the busts of satyrs or wood nymphs, disappeared behind the orange trees and reappeared here, he wasn't expecting to see the doctor, after that he couldn't remember anymore, and yet I was there he kept repeating, we were drinking pastis, all I can see now is the rag on the ground and the mud-stained boots, came back from the marsh, someone was lying down and being given first aid, after which the cold room crossed and the bed, someone was at his last gasp, try and remember . . . he was answering it could well be, other details, I'll have another look, the lamp on the table, yes, the clock on the mantelpiece, the door . . .

To go out into the garden at night, count your steps to the well, come back the way you went and then branch off towards the little party wall, four or five yards up to the bush, on a moonlight night the scarecrow would have made you jump, they'd stuffed it with straw, the neighbor's jacket and trousers, the farmhand's cap and the red scarf that had fallen on to the ground testified to the child, he'd tried to put it back but he wasn't tall enough, he'd pulled the dummy down by mistake, it's on the dunghill now.

Death at the slightest deficiency in thought.

For the night to get up, light the lamp, all the shutters closed, the clock makes him jump, someone had just come into the kitchen by the tradesmen's entrance, there's a red patch against the wall, he went up to it holding his breath, it was the neighbor's child, he'd left

his purse in the drawer, you gave me a fright said the master but the child was a long way away, someone was pacing up and down the room, the neighbors had just gone out, the coffee was getting cold in the coffeepot, he sat down in the armchair as if he were repeating that funereal farce, through the slit in the shutter was keeping a watch on the scarecrow which all of a sudden collapsed on the dunghill, the corpse of the idiot or of the duck man, farmhand's cap and bird's beak, the breastbone broken, slashed by a penknife, he took his head in his hands, the clock made him jump.

Or in the wood where the carcasses were, very early in the morning, to forget that dream, you could hear the goats bleating when suddenly the child disappears in the marsh, someone is laughing unpleasantly, he turned round, the echo from the fountain . . .

For the night to get up, count your steps to the kitchen, the child had been present at the massacre, a precise contour with that hole in the groin.

For the night to get up and make a note in the memo book of an image which disintegrates as you write it, snippets, that problematic past, the old toothless mouth, the clock face, those two hands forever knitting . . . the clock made him jump, the doctor had just left, an ant at this distance, the visitors at that time, the idiot in the morning his hair all over his face, the blue line of the forest, those interminable glasses of pastis and the crows' flights, a fainting fit, then nothing anymore, night was falling.

So calm. So gray. Making notes at his table. Outside, those fogs from one season to another. You go back to the marsh, the hanged man's tree has gone. The old woman hardly ever leaves her fireside. Things are unsaid, people are asleep. What else. The doctor in his flowery frame looks as if he's working. The maid out shopping . . .

Then he made a new will.

I the undersigned in the cold room, hemlock, clock out of action, I the undersigned in the marsh, goat or bird's carcass, I the undersigned at the bend in the road, in the master's garden, maleficent old woman, sentry of the dead, satyr, scarecrow, in a van on the route deviated by the evil eye, plaything of that farce that is called conscience, no one, I the undersigned midnight in full daylight, overwhelmed with boredom, old owl, magpie or crow . . .

To get up at night, go back to his notebook, make his will again, be overwhelmed with boredom, open the door, go out, fall into a reverie waiting for the old herdswoman of the dawn who disappears, gray and limping, into the wood, the sentry has gone off to get some sleep, the day may break, the pink and the blue, a morning, go back into the cold room and put the clock out of action, the action of a maniac, from one season to the next, night again.

As for the sentry, he'd fallen asleep in the corner of the barn, you could see him sitting there, his head slumps forward, dawn, that old herdswoman of dreams, will come and shake him, her flock shake themselves and she disappears round the bend, day is about to break, people are opening their eyes again, the nightmare fades, they'll be catching up with it, picking it up stitch by stitch all day long and in the evening they'll plunge back into it until the following dawn, gray and limping, her goats the color of dust and ashes, chimeras.

I the undersigned the sentry of the dead, at the crossroads, at the confines of such gray lands in the notebook, at the top of the elm tree whence the poor quality of our land becomes perceptible, nothing but stones, I the undersigned on the dunghill, in the goat shed, at dawn, at twilight, it must have been before clocks and all that rubbish of measuring and know-how . . .

There follows a description of the assets but in such a way . . .

As if his existence had been cut off.

The doctor in his flowery frame.

On an October morning or was it November, the elms have lost their leaves, the harvest is over, beetroots and pumpkins are piled up in the courtyards, the doctor is on the terrace. His hat on the grass beside him. In the midst of the clumps of rotting flowers you can make out a statue that has fallen off its plinth. Farther off, what used to be the main entrance, one side of the gate is missing, the other very much the worse for wear. The van stops in front of it, the man gets out, it looks as if he's going to come in but then he changes his mind and walks round the little party wall. The master emerges from behind the house, coming out of the kitchen. He's carrying a tray that looks heavy, objects piled up on it, you can't quite make out. The fog coming up from the river spreads rapidly, you can't see anything at all now. You can hear the doctor saying sit down, you can hear the word marsh, the word bend, but the words very soon become blurred, there's nothing but the sound of the axe on the chopping block coming from the neighbors', then that too disappears.

Until nightfall.

Sitting at that table a few hours earlier, found dead on the dunghill, a sentry was on guard, he had seen no one but the deceased one cold, gray day, must have gone over to the slit in the shutter and apparently distinctly saw him put the clock out of action and then sit there prostrate in his chair, elbows on the table, head in his hands.

NOTES

Passacaglia is as short as anything that Pinget has previously written. But it resumes in an extraordinary way the themes and motifs of his previous work. SB

Passacaglia is an amusing book, but it is also terrible. MC

The virtuosity of Pinget's attempts to reconcile the demands of the imagination with those of the intellect is sometimes astonishing, and it is the tension resulting from this continual conflict that produces humor. Pinget plays upon his own scepticism regarding the situations that he invents, so that in all his books, sometimes within the space of a single phrase, the reader is pulled violently in opposite directions. ACP

If we allow ourselves to be caught up by this book, without bothering too much at first about solving its little enigmas, we find that these perpetual enigmas make us want to read on, as they do in a detective story. And then we discover a work that goes much farther than all these enigmas put together. Pinget's tour de force is that, starting from the most concrete elements, he makes us think about the most serious subjects. AV

SB: Dr. Stephen Bann: Article in 20th Century Studies, Dec. 1971: "Robert Pinget: the end of a modern way."

MC: Madeleine Chapsal: Review of Passacaglia in L'Express.

ACP: Anthony Cheal Pugh: Introduction to Pinget's Autour de Mortin. In Methuen's Modern Texts, 1971.

AV: Anne Villelaur: Review of Passacaglia in Les Lettres franfaises.

RP: Robert Pinget: Letter to the translator.

The object of *Passacaglia* is to exorcise death by magical operations with words. As if the pleasure of playing with the vocabulary could delay the fatal issue . . . RP

Passacaglia perpetually hovers on the edge of nothingness, as the operations of the mechanical universe are called into question: "Something broken in the mechanism." The "cogito" still confirms existence, but on the edge of an abyss: "Death at the slightest deficiency in thought." SB

Much of Pinget's work consists, explicitly or implicitly, of a dramatization of the situation of the artist who no longer believes that conventional fiction is capable of giving real imaginative satisfaction, but who is nevertheless propelled by the need to find a means of projecting his imagination into situations that can better be presented within the novel format than any other. ACP

Pinget is pointing out that in fiction there is no standard of truth, not even a relative one. An original version of an event is not necessarily truer than a subsequent one—and vice versa. ACP

The dimension of Pinget's work has been that of every novelist: the world in time. But the unerring direction of his language has led him to the end of the world, the end of time. Hence the structural role of his progressive introduction of apocalyptic imagery.

. . . The act of stopping the clock, which is an initial and recurring motif in *Passacaglia*, suggests the removal of the temporal coordinates of the Newtonian universe. As a result of this act, the God/author is identified not as the efficient cause, whose creation runs like clockwork from the primordial decree, but as the conserving cause, whose constant intervention is indispensable. SB

The return to spoken language and the abandonment of the rhetoric of accepted literary style . . . is a feature of all his writing. . . . We must adjust our reading technique, if we are to appreciate fully Pinget's style. This involves retrieving the "childish" habit of allowing the vocal organs to form the unpronounced sounds. . . . Moreover, if the reader adopts this mimetic reading technique consciously he will also be able to assume a certain critical distance, or a more sceptical attitude to what he is reading, that will allow him to perceive more readily both the underlying seriousness of the text and the constant element of half-concealed irony. ACP

Don't bother too much about logic: everything in *Passacaglia* is directed against it. RP

About the Author

Robert Pinget (1919-1997) was the author of numerous plays, essays, and fourteen novels, including *Someone*, *The Inquisitory*, *Baga*, and *Mahu or The Material*. Best known for his association with the Nouveau Roman (New Novel) literary movement, which also included Alain Robbe-Grillet and Nathalie Sarraute, Pinget received a number of awards, including the prestigious Prix Fémina for *Someone* and the Prix des Critiques for *The Inquisitory*.

SELECTED DALKEY ARCHIVE PAPERBACKS